The Hidden
Worlds of Zandra

By William Rotsler

The Hidden Worlds of Zandra

WILLIAM ROTSLER

DOUBLEDAY & COMPANY, INC.

GARDEN CITY, NEW YORK

1983

All of the characters in this book
are fictitious, and any resemblance
to actual persons, living or dead,
is purely coincidental.

Library of Congress Cataloging in Publication Data

Rotsler, William.
The hidden worlds of Zandra.

I. Title.
PS3568.O873H5   1983   813'.54
ISBN 0-385-14614-0
Library of Congress Catalog Card Number 80-2064

For
George Barr

The Hidden
Worlds of Zandra

The mist closed in around the two Zull cloudships as they turned into the dark, narrow mountain passes. Mace Wilde drew his black cloak tighter around him against the chill, his feet spread wide against the gentle swaying and bobbing of the vessel. His eyes never left the spot where he had last seen the pursuing Zurian ship.

"This is a sad way to see my planet, Earthman."

Mace turned away from the curving rail at the sound of the voice. It was Princess Falana, the beautiful dark-haired heiress to the imperial throne of Zandra. She was wrapped in a crimson cloak, her long thick hair beaded with droplets of water.

Mace smiled wearily at her and gestured back toward the Zurian cloudship. "They have long-range weapons which we do not possess, Princess."

She raised her head imperiously. "They would not fire on the firstborn of Morak!"

Mace uttered a short, barking laugh. "Wrong! This is just what they're looking for. They kill us, here in these mountains, and your sister Valora will succeed to the throne—"

Falana made a nasty sound and stepped to the railing to clutch at it with ringed fingers. "My sister—! She has been seduced by the promises of those . . . those beastmen! They arrange her pleasures and keep her satiated with—" She broke off and turned away from Wilde. Her dark brooding eyes swept restlessly around the circular ship. She saw the Kurkan Skylance in the central control tower, peering ahead into the mist, aided by the female warrior Mouthfire.

"We made a peace, Earthman," she said, looking at Mace over her cloaked shoulder. "I would not destroy you and you would show me the planet I shall someday rule."

Mace shook his head. "We made a deal, Your Highness, that I would show you that your Zurians are lying to you, keeping things from you, lying to your father—"

"No one lies to the Emperor!"

Mace smiled sadly. "Uh-huh, that's what they all say. People tell those in power what they want to hear. Morak—"

"*Emperor* Morak, you barbarian!"

"Your father wants to know everything is just fine, no problems, no uprisings, no dissent."

Falana turned away abruptly and moved away along the railing. Firearm, the Kurkan warrior with the laser weapon where his right forearm had been, glanced at her. She drew herself up and looked out at the passing mist.

Mace sighed. Things were happening so incredibly fast and what was happening was so fantastic. Twelve days before he had been a passenger on a jetliner to Spain, en route to train a friendly emir's troops to guard oil fields. Then they had been diverted by a storm to fly through the Bermuda Triangle.

He had to smile. Such fantasies had been built up about that piece of watery real estate! And now it looked as though it were all true! He turned to the rail, watching again to their stern.

Zandra. A planet in another dimension or in some other part of their galaxy. No one knew. Zandra had been an outpost planet of the great Zull Empire. The Zull race was a mighty one, with incredibly long lifelines, aided by a specific drug which was made only upon their home planet. The Zull kept it that way in order to centrally control their immense empire. Then their sun went nova, or so was the belief.

It had happened millennia before. The empire of stars collapsed, became isolated planetary systems. Zandra and the other planets around the star Za were left alone. The Zull masters aged and died. For over a thousand of their years the various lands were hidden away from each other. But under the powerful new king, Morak, the planet was becoming united. Or so the ruling race, called the Kula, believed. Wilde thought the subject races were giving lip service.

Then they had come, a shipload of twentieth-century Earth people. One of Zandra's many sentient races, the Vandorians, who were descendants of hostages kept by the Zull masters, had been repairing and reconstructing ancient Zull devices. For only a few Zandran years they had been hard at work "mining" Earth for sorely needed metals, but on Earth it had been for over five hundred years. The Bermuda Triangle was the first setting the Vandorians had found and their "mining" had produced immediate results: wooden ships laden with gold, silver, and copper. Later there were metal ships filled with strange devices. These had all fallen from the skies, brought in by the mysterious Zull device. But Wilde's airplane had managed to make a crash landing.

The Vandorians had taken them as slaves, immobilizing them with strange weaponry. Divided into groups of six, they had been auctioned off, along with the metallic remnants of the jetliner. Mace and five others were bought by a Kula noble. Mace, who had been a combat veteran, a captain in the Special Forces, found his companions to be varied indeed.

Eve Clayton was a beautiful blonde, a Los Angeles policewoman, and a bow-woman of competition quality. Simon Richter was a distinguished physicist and a scientist interested in many fields. Barney Boone was a wild animal trainer. Liberty Crockett was a famous black movie star. Carole Warren had been one of the airline stewardesses, but she had been killed in an escape attempt.

Mace looked ahead through the gray mist. He could barely make out the form of the other bowl-shaped cloudship. Liberty, Eve, and Barney had escaped, but Mace had been recaptured. The three escaping Earth people had been found by the Kurkans, a race of Viking-like warriors who lived high in the black basalt mountains and raided the Kula strongholds for loot and vengeance.

The Kula were the very human descendants of a subrace that some thought had been stewards or perhaps even slaves of the great Zull. There were several other humanoid races represented on Zandra, but Mace had seen representatives of decidedly nonhuman races. The intelligent dragons, the Saurons; the four-armed, dead-white Vandorians; the Astorix, a "race" of intelligent robots that seemed to have manufactured themselves out of any implanted restrictions; and the black Zurians, a bestial subrace who plotted and schemed against the throne. And there were others he had heard of but not seen, decadent and strange, mysterious and perhaps mythical.

And time was flying. Sixty-two to one was the rate Richter had calculated. One hour on Zandra was sixty-two on Earth; a month was five years. And they had been gone twelve days. Two years since they had been sucked into the Vandorians' beam. The authorities would have written them off, the insurance been paid, the survivors perhaps remarried. Another entry in the odd record of the Devil's Triangle.

So much to assimilate, to understand, to adjust to. He had responded strongly to Eve Clayton, yet he had become physically involved with Falana, who was a sensualist and very used to getting her way. And Eve had seemingly come to care for the tall Kurkan warrior Longtalon. In the ship ahead, piloted by Ironthroat, the actress Liberty Crockett and Redpike seemed attracted to each other. We adjust and make do, Mace thought. We survive . . . or not. If we do not soon find a place to settle Richter and Count Jardek, the one Kula noble who seemed to have any interest in science, so that they can study how we might get back to Earth, it will not matter. Earth will not be a place we know.

Yet it will still be Earth. Earth of a hundred years from now will be less strange than Zandra, he thought. Falana moved from the railing, her cloak flapping. Without a word she went into the base of the control tower that rose like a castle keep in the center of the round ship.

Yet Zandra was not all *that* strange. Humanoid races still seemed to respond to the same stimuli, though tastes differed. In his heart of hearts Mason Wilde knew that if they could not return to Earth he would not be all that unhappy.

But he had a responsibility to those who had elected him their leader. Not only to those fellow Terrans aboard the twin cloudships guided through the barely seen granite cleft by Zull science, but to those who had been sold into slavery and scattered across the face of Zandra. Yes, and even to those who had been captured centuries before and must, due to the time differential, be alive now. The Zull science machines had given them instant common speech. To Mace he seemed to be speaking English, yet he was understood by all.

The Zull race must have had extensive contact with many races to have developed such a device, but it was undeniably useful. Yet the Kula and the other races Mace had seen could not match the wonders of the Zull. The cloudships, the rare ray gun, the antigravity devices—exotic wonders mixed with swords and torches, stone castles and slavery. It was like some medieval world gifted with futuristic weaponry, some mythical kingdom granted technological advances beyond its comprehension.

Mace shook his head wearily. Even Simon Richter was puzzled, and as far as Mace was able to discern Richter was a genius. Not that he was any expert on who was or who wasn't a genius, he thought with a certain sadness. He was army . . . and yet wasn't. He'd always felt just a tad out of phase with the structure. At platoon level, or company level, given a task, a mission, an objective, he'd always been able to come through. At the very least, to give it his best shot.

But here, on this strange world, all bets were off. There was an obvious power struggle between the two heirs to the Zandran throne and if there was anything Mace hated it was the writhings and thrashings of politics. Every time the military got into politics it always ended in woe for somebody—usually a lot of somebodies.

But he felt an indelible obligation to his fellow Terrans. They had elected him leader and had every right to expect him to come through for them. Besides, what were his options? To give up and become a mercenary for Emperor Morak? Join the despicable Zurians? Go hide somewhere?

He shook his head and wiped the mist from his face with an impatient hand. Narrow the focus. Live through today. Then live through tomorrow. Be content to stay alive and keep those in his charge alive and well. And free.

Simple task, sure—in a world where everything was either strangely new or had that haunting familiarity of an old movie. If everything had been *completely* different, he thought he might have coped better. But some things were—almost exact. Falana seemed totally human in her body, in her lovemaking, in her jealousies. A bit imperious and blind to others, but that was nothing new for royalty or people in power. Swords and spears and stone castles were all *too* familiar, as if in some former life he had lived with them naturally. He didn't believe in reincarnation; nature had always been so prolific that it didn't need to recycle any entity. Thousands of sperm cells were produced when only one was needed. A sunflower grew hundreds of seeds. Fish lay millions of eggs. There was no need to keep reusing the same fragile network of electrical impulses that constituted a mind.

Mace shrugged beneath his damp cloak. Keep moving. Keep plugging. Maybe the right combination would appear. As long as you keep moving you were alive. Stay well, keep you and yours well.

He thought of Carole Warren, the image of her impaled body sliding into a fog of blood in the pool came to him.

It could not have been helped. The spearmen had run in from the other direction as Mace kept the guards bottled up in the exit. Carole had taken a lance in the stomach and went into the pool of water in a smoky red blur.

He shook his head and wiped his face free of beads of water. The living must go on. He gripped the railing tensely and peered hard into the mist behind them.

"They will follow?"

Mace nodded at Firearm's question. The burly Kurkan moved closer. "You know this Zurian Durak that pursues us?"

Mace nodded. "Once. I was demonstrating to Falana that she was not all-powerful and Durak tried to intervene."

Firearm's eyebrows went up. "And she did not bring you down with her mindsword?" Mace shook his head. Firearm leaned closer. "Is she . . . perhaps . . . a cripple? All Kula have this power to give pain to others with their thoughts. Perhaps they have lost it?"

"No," Mace said, "they haven't lost it." He thought of Richter writhing in pain shortly after their arrival on Zandra. "But I . . . I put her in a position where using it would undercut her position."

Firearm whistled and rested his metallic arm on the railing. He wiped it dry with a corner of his brown cloak, but it was at once covered with condensed mist. "You Earth people are strange, indeed. The blonde woman, Eve, can pull the bow captured by Dragontooth which no Kurkan could pull."

Mace nodded. The laminated plastic bow was a relic of Earth, a seventy-five-pound hunting bow. "It's the lesser gravity here," he said. "It makes us stronger, though on our own planet we are all just ordinary people."

Firearm shook his head. "Yours must be a strange world, Mace Wilde."

Mace smiled. "You think *ours* is strange—" They laughed together.

"We have a saying," Firearm said. "Another's sword is sharper."

"The grass is greener on the other side of the fence," Mace replied.

"I know you not, Earthman," Firearm said, "but I trust you." He shrugged as if embarrassed. "You are a warrior. We of Kurka understand that. We have fought Zurians—and Kula—and the others who would destroy us, for as long as any can remember. It is our way of life. We take our name from our deeds." He thumped his laser weapon on the railing. "That is why I will not surrender to any Zull medical machines." He snorted derisively. "It would grow back my hand and smooth the scars away, but . . ." He waved the metallic stub. "I would not have a constant weapon, a ruby sword that can reach out for Zurian throats at a great distance."

Mace started to speak but Skylance called out from the control tower. "Mace Wilde! Mace Wilde!"

"What is it?"

"Come up, Captain, there is something ahead."

Mace went into the tower base. Falana was there, holding a hot mug, aloofly alone in the cabin packed with Jardek, Longtalon, Richter, and Eve. Richter called out to Mace as he started up the ladder.

"What is it, Mace?"

"Skylance sees something ahead." He went on up the ladder and Richter followed.

Skylance pointed at the instruments. On a small screen a computer outlined the walls around them. A tiny red dot in the center was their ship, a green dot signaling the leading airship. The canyon seemed to close off ahead. "A dead end," Skylance muttered.

"Rise above it," Mace said. "Find a pass."

Skylance looked unsure. "Captain, I don't know. These are very high mountains. Not even we Kurkans have gone over them." He looked at Mouthfire. For the first time on a Kurkan face Mace saw a flicker of fear.

"What is it?" he demanded.

"Beyond is . . . the land of the Tigron."

Richter came into the crowded bridge, making it even more crowded. "Tigron?"

"They are . . . we hear, we do not know . . . they are suspicious creatures of . . . strange powers . . ." Skylance looked uncomfortable.

Mace gestured to the stern. "We have no choice. Durak is behind us and his weapons can outdistance ours. If he bottles us up in this canyon he can stand back and pick us off."

"But Princess Falana is aboard!" Mouthfire said.

Mace nodded grimly. "I'll explain the politics to you some other time, but they are not going to be happy with anything but total destruction of both ships. The story they take back will be *their* story. Perhaps how they heroically tried to rescue the princess but the renegade Kurkans and the treacherous Earthmen killed her."

"Survivors write history," muttered Richter.

"What do we do?" Skylance asked.

Mace gripped the railing and shouted ahead into the mist. "Redpike!"

"Yes, Earthman?" His voice echoed in the narrowing stone canyon. The cloudships were totally silent, except for the occasional flap of furled fabric or clank of armor and the whisper of wind.

"Rise up! Find a pass! We're being bottled in!"

There was a hesitation before Redpike spoke again. "Did Skylance tell you of the Tigron?"

"Blast the Tigron! Durak is behind us with long-range weapons! Rise up! Get above the mist, get over the mountains!"

"Very well."

"He does not like it," Mouthfire said softly to Skylance.

"Nor do I," he replied, giving Mace a look.

"Give me an alternative," Mace said. No one answered. Skylance touched the controls and the ship lifted silently. The mist did not lessen and the rock cliffs were close.

Liberty Crockett pulled the hood of her dark cape closer around her head, her eyes troubled and searching nervously. The musical score in her mind was somber, full of unresolved chords like some mystery movie. Her little mental trick had always aided her before, setting the scene for a bit of acting, heightening her awareness. But Zandra was not a movie and the mental music was making her nervous and gloomy.

They were never going to get off this crazy planet, she thought. *Never. No more international film queen, no more sex goddess adulation, no more big pay. This was it, this alien circus of totally freaked people.*

Liberty, honey, she thought, *it was time you started thinking of Number One. None of these people are going to help you. They've got their own troubles. Right now you're just another body, not some star. Definitely not a Somebody.*

I liked being a Somebody, she thought. *I was a Nobody for a long time. Being Somebody is a lot better. And you better think about that, girl. Get to be a Somebody in this mad world. Being Somebody is a lot safer. No more alien slave blocks, no more dank Zurian prisons, no more running scared—get yourself together, sister!*

"We're going up."

"Huh?" She started and turned toward the voice. It was Barney, coming through the streamers of wet fog.

"You feeling all right?" he asked. His dark brown hair was glistening wet and he wore one of the cloaks from the cloudship's locker pulled tightly around him.

"Oh, yeah, I'm fine." She turned away, looking ahead.

"We hope to rise above the mists and over a pass."

"Uh-huh, I heard."

"There's got to be some top to these things," he said, gesturing at the half-seen cliffs.

Liberty didn't answer. She gave the animal trainer a sideways look. He was the only one that shared her world at all. He'd trained animals for the movies and they'd worked together once, on *Jungle Queen*. It was a clinker of a film but the poster of her in a scanty leopard loincloth and strings of beads barely covering her ample bosom had sold in the millions. *Barney might understand*, she thought.

"Where we going, Barn?"

He shrugged. "Over the hills and far away. Maybe we can find some place for Richter and that Kula count to work. Then . . ." He shrugged. "Simon thinks it will be some time before they can figure out how to reverse that Vandorian gadget. Zull, rather. It's a Zull machine."

"Uh-huh. No, I mean after. After the mountains. After we settle in Richter. What then?"

"I don't know. Stay alive."

"Oh, rats, Barn, I mean what are we going to *do?*" She turned to him, letting the cloak open up. Never did any harm to advertise. "No, what are we going to do if they can't get us back?"

Barney inhaled and chewed at his lip as he exhaled. The mists left beads of moisture on his face and he wiped them off impatiently. "We'll get by. We'll stick together. We have Falana and—"

Liberty snorted. "From what I've seen of *that* blueblood—or green-blood or whatever they have here—she'll take care of Number One first and there ain't no Number Two!"

Barney looked at her grimly. "Isn't that what we all do? Look out for Number One? She's the heir to the throne, Liberty; she has responsibilities. I don't imagine it's all that much different here than in any other hierarchy. She's going to protect the status quo because that's her reality, her life. Change that and she'll maybe stop being a princess and first in line to power."

Liberty let her hands drop and she pulled the cloak around her, huddling against the chill. Barney put his arm around her. "I don't want to be just a bit player, Barn; I want to *star*. When you're a star you have more control over your life. You pick and choose. You don't have to take the leavings any longer. You can direct your life, your own life."

Barney nodded and patted her shoulder. "Hang in there, star. You'll shine again."

Eve Clayton stuck her head up into the control well. "Any room up here for me? Mouthfire, let me relieve you. There's hot soup downstairs or below decks or whatever you call it."

The Kurkan woman nodded and they squeezed past each other. Eve wedged herself between Skylance and Mace, who was watching to the stern. The Zull airships were round, and the six jets spaced evenly around the circumference could move them in any direction. But in the central tower the controls faced one direction and they thought of that as the "front."

"I think I'll go below," Simon Richter said. "Can I get you anything?"

Mace shook his head but Skylance suggested a bowl of soup. The cloudships did not move very fast. A running horse, if they had one, could keep up on level ground. There were drasks, which were bigger, sturdier animals than Terran horses, but Mace did not know how fast they were. There was so much to learn about Zandra and so little time. Some piece of ignorance might mean their death or defeat.

Eve looked up at Mace. She, too, had felt a strong attraction toward the combat veteran and thought he shared that feeling. Yet circumstances had parted them and she had found Longtalon . . . and Mace had found Falana. But was either relationship permanent? Everything changed so fast!

"What if these things can't lift high enough?" she asked Mace, who shrugged.

"Then we'll try something else," he said. He pulled his gaze from the rearward watch to look at her. "I haven't had time to even ask. Are you all right? What happened after the escape?"

Eve hesitated, then began to speak. "Baron Thelok's mindblast knocked us all out. When we woke up we were drifting down a huge valley. A storm caught us, the ship was wrecked on a cliff. We crashed on a ledge. Barney and Liberty were hurt. Some flying reptiles . . . the Kurkans called them thorgs . . . attacked. I . . . we almost bought the farm but a Kurkan ship arrived just in time. It was Longtalon, returning from a raid." She gave Mace a quick look but his gaze was back through the mists, toward their pursuers.

"Go on," he said.

"They took us to Skyhome. It's a castle on a mountaintop with a sheer drop all around. You can only get there by air. We met King Zur and . . . I guess we impressed him. There was a Zurian raid and we drove them off. Then King Zur decided to raid the Kula. He chose Jardek's keep." She shrugged. The Kurkans had killed Falana's Zurian guards and Falana herself escaped bondage only because Mace Wilde had fought for her. Then Zurian ships came and the Kurkans stayed behind to do battle, not just to allow Mace's two ships to escape, but for the joy of killing Zurians.

"And now we're here," she finished.

"Running," Mace said angrily.

"Nothing else we can do. If we can give them the slip . . ." He shrugged, peering grimly into the gray wall of fog.

"And you?" Eve asked, a shy note in her voice.

"Thelok gave me as a gift to Falana." He gave Eve a sideways look and found her looking straight ahead, her face expressionless. "I managed to convince her she should see her kingdom from the bottom—"

"Like Haroun al Raschid, in *A Thousand and One Nights?*"

"Yeah, something like that. She got permission from her father." He thumped the breastplate of his black Zurian armor. "I got this, which was the only thing they could find in my size. It once belonged to some Zurian hero." He sighed. "Well, you know the rest. We met at Jardek's and damn near killed each other."

Eve inhaled, smelling the wetness of the fog, then let the air out softly. No, she didn't know the rest, any more than he knew the rest, about her and Longtalon. Well, they didn't have any claims on each other and this was not the Victorian Age. It was not even Earth. The old rules didn't matter anymore.

Or did they? Can we really escape our conditioning, even transported by what amounted to magic to another world? She had to smile. What had Arthur C. Clarke said? *Any sufficiently advanced technology will have the appearance of magic.* Something like that. Certainly the old rules were bent or suspended.

"And now we're here," she said, repeating herself. "Look, Mace, I—"

"*Look out!*"

Mace and Eve turned at Skylance's cry. The cliff walls were close, looming out of the fog. They heard a shout from the other ship and both veered away. There was the sound of a rending crash and something banged down the rock cliff, slithering noisily over the stone.

"What happened?" Mace shouted.

"Hit a blasted cliff!" Ironthroat cried. "We're listing a bit. I can't seem to control it—!"

"Get up close," Mace said at once. "We can't lose contact. Maybe we can push against them."

"Push—?"

"Pull alongside!" Skylance obeyed. The first ship became clearer in the mist. There was a nasty rip along the port side and one of the antigravity jets was bent and twisted.

"Look!" Eve shouted. "No more cliffs!"

"We're over the top," Barney cried out.

"Ironthroat! Can you make it?" Skylance yelled.

"I don't know! It's not responding well. I'm tilting down that way . . ."

"Get under and lift," Mace ordered. Skylance shrugged and shouted his intention to the pilot of the other airship. They moved carefully under the ship, then bumped roughly as the railing of Mace's ship came up under the curving bottom of the other vessel.

"What can you see ahead?" Skylance asked. "I've got to watch this."

"Mist," Mace said. He looked at the computer screen. "The cliffs are dropping away. We're over the top." He cupped his hands around his mouth and shouted to Ironthroat and Redpike. "We're going down. Keep against us!"

"We hear, Captain!"

The two ships sank down through the gray mists. The people on board held their breaths.

The mists cleared somewhat, enough for them to see a series of ledges in the sheer basalt walls, then a narrow valley or two, bleak and rocky. "Keep going down," Mace ordered.

Soon a valley appeared that had some vegetation and a stream running through it. The one after that looked better and Mace ordered the ships to land. They pulled back to let Ironthroat have the most room to set down. The Zull vessel went in at an angle but landed not too roughly. Skylance turned his ship gracefully and set down next to it.

Mace let down the ramp and they went to look at the damage. "Dara, Liberty, Firearm, keep watch," Mace ordered. The two Kurkan cloudship pilots joined with Richter and Count Jardek to inspect the damage. They soon reported to Mace.

"We can have it fixed in half a day," Ironthroat said. "We have to straighten the jet and use some of the patching material to seal it up." He shrugged. "These ships are old. Sometimes their guidance controls are faulty. I'm sorry."

Mace slapped his arm. "Don't worry. You and Skylance deserve our thanks for all those hours flying us through the mists."

"Think we lost Durak?" Barney asked. Mace shrugged.

"Well, Terran, how long will it be?"

Mace looked at Princess Falana. She still wore the crimson cloak but it was slightly warmer here and she did not have it wrapped around her. He could see her body in its exotic jewelry-like clothing and he was once again impressed.

"Half a day, Falana."

"*Princess* Falana," she said automatically, a dark look crossing her face. "What do we do then?"

"Watch for your Zurian friends and help the men fixing the rip."

She raised her head. "*You* watch for the Zurians—who are not my friends but my *slaves*—and *I* do not *fix* anything!"

"Snob," Eve muttered.

Liberty said something harsher but Mace stepped between them. "Listen, Falana, you are not in your castle at Kulan. Just remember those Zurians are after you more than they are after any of us."

Falana looked suspiciously around. "Kurkan pirates and runaway slaves?"

Longtalon walked past her and laughed. Falana glared at him and the Kurkan screamed, falling forward, his face contorted in pain.

"*Falana!*" cried Mace.

"He laughed at me!"

"Let him go, Falana!"

"*Princess* Falana, you—!"

Mace cried out as the pain swept over him. Everything hurt. It was like being brushed with a blowtorch. He fell heavily and writhed uncontrollably.

Eve threw herself at Falana but before she could reach the Kula princess she, too, screamed and fell to the ground. Ironthroat whirled from his repairs and threw a tool at her, but Falana's power wrenched his arm as he cried out and the tool bounced across the ground. Then Liberty Crockett leaped into the air, aided by her greater Earthborn muscles and her skill at kung fu. Her kick knocked Falana's head to the side. At once the pain ceased and Mace got to his knees groggily. Falana was still staggering, holding her head, as Liberty closed in with a spade-like hand poised for the kill.

"*Liberty!*"

The crescendo of music stopped as if the tape were cut. In a daze the black actress looked at Mace. She licked her lips and blinked. Falana sank to the ground, still dazed.

"No, wait!" Mace said, stopping the rush of the Kurkans. He stood between them and the Kula princess. "She can't help it. It's their way."

"To blazes with their way!" Eve said, balling her fists. "I'll show her *my* way!"

"No, you won't. The Kula can kill—"

"She can't get us all," Ironthroat said, starting forward again. Mace pushed at him.

"Wait. *Wait!* Let me talk to her." With angry faces the Kurkans waited, naked blades in their hands. Mace glanced up to see Firearm lower his built-in weapon. He was grinning fiercely.

"Almost, Earthman, almost. If I had gotten to the railing a second sooner—!" He shrugged, still grinning.

Mace knelt by Falana, who was looking better. Her golden skin was pale and she twisted her head, still glaring at the semicircle of people. "Falana," Mace began, "you can't fight them all."

She glared at him with a fierceness that astonished him. He thought for a second the mind-fire would explode again, but it did not.

"I am a princess of the royal house, heiress to the throne, a Kula noble. I am *Falana*, you alien slave!"

Mace took a deep breath. "And you are under my command, *Princess* Falana! You will sheath your mindsword or, by god, the next time I won't stop them."

She sneered. "Any Kula can handle as many as you at any time."

Mace grinned suddenly. "So you would have us believe. As many Zurians, perhaps. As many Chuma or any of your other slave races. But Kurkans, *and* five Earth people? Can you be *certain?* We Terrans do not react the same as the others." He leaned down and put his face close to hers and spoke in a voice only she could hear.

"Listen, my fierce little warrior-princess, you do that again, against us, and I will kick your round little bottom."

Her eyes narrowed and she inhaled deeply. A flash of fear went through Mace. He was no stranger to fear but fighting an unpredictable alien noble with the mental power of an armful of lasers was difficult to do. "I mean it, Falana," he said. "In front of everyone."

"You would not dare," she whispered angrily. "You would die for it."

"Perhaps, but it would be done. No dignity, no noble pain, just humiliation . . . and the stories carried to the ends of this world. The would-be Empress, humiliated by a gift slave."

Her dark eyes glittered. "I will not forgive you for these threats, Mace Wilde."

He grinned at her. "Not threats, your royal troubleship, but promises. And I don't want forgiveness, only obedience."

"Obedience—!" Her temper flared again. "I obey no one but my father, the Emperor!"

"Uh-huh, and me. You'll either have to kill me or obey me, Princess. If you kill me, they'll kill you. Or the Zurians will. *They* haven't promised to show you Zandra the way it *really* is."

"But I cannot *obey!* That would be . . . be humiliating!"

"Then will you *cooperate?*"

She straightened her back. "That is different. Rulers must learn the art of cooperation between the forces, even my father. But they must not laugh at me!"

"Then don't be such a pain in the neck." She frowned at him. "Uh, such an uncooperative witch."

"*I* do not have to cooperate! I am Falana, the—"

"Uh-huh, sure, we've heard all that. What if you were locked up in a room with several people and one of them started shooting one of your Zull weapons around at anyone who looked at him?"

She stared at him. "Is he a Kula noble or—"

"It doesn't matter. Say they are all Kula nobles."

"A Kula noble would not do such a—"

"*Falana!* Pay attention. One in that room is acting irresponsibly. What would you do?"

"Stop him, of course. Wait, are you saying *I* am acting irresponsibly?"

"Aren't you?" He waved at the others. "We are trying to get away from the Zurians that would kill us all, even you. I am trying to show you Zandra. And what are you doing?"

She seethed for a long moment, her dark eyes flitting from Mace to the others and back. Then she sighed. "I will not hurt them if they do not offend me. That is all I will promise you, Mace Wilde."

"But you must not take offense so quickly, Falana. These are not your subjects, they—"

"Everyone on Zandra is the subject of Morak, my father!"

Mace sighed wearily. "That is what we are going to make certain about, aren't we?"

"You are speaking to me as a child."

He just looked at her, one eyebrow cocked.

"All right, Mace Wilde, I will try. But they must not take advantage of my goodwill."

"They won't, Falana." He turned to wave at the others, not seeing her form the word *Princess!* "Get back to work. Fun's over."

Liberty walked over and stood over Falana. "Hey, Princess, I'm sorry I had to coldcock you, but you were raising holy—"

"Do not stand over me!" Falana snapped. Liberty shrugged and walked away. Falana glared after her, then grabbed Mace's cloak as he started to rise. "Tell me of this Earthwoman. Why does she have the skin color of a Zurian? Is she, somehow, one of them?"

Mace shook his head. "No, on our world we have several races. Not so diverse as you have here, but we all evolved on the same planet so we are much alike, except for minor differences of skin color or shape of the eyes."

"We have no race that is black except the Zurians. Is she of a slave race on your world?"

Mace sighed and stood up. He offered his hand to Falana, who chose to ignore it and get to her feet by herself. "Some of her race were once slaves, yes. But so were some of almost every race, at one time or another. Humans are not quite perfect yet."

Falana snorted and pursed her lips. "This world of yours, this Earth, seems a chaotic place from what we have learned. Vengeful gods, war after war, torture, intolerance, viciousness, global mismanagement . . ."

"Yup," Mace said. "But we got over the king idea pretty much. We elect our leaders, and where we don't the parliaments have the power, not the kings."

Falana stared at him. "As I said, mismanaged and chaotic. On Zandra we have had peace for—"

A scream cut short the conversation. Mace leaped away from Falana in bounds that no Zandran could match. He drew his sword as he went and it flashed in the weak sunlight. It was Du who had screamed, and now she cowered against the curving hull of the grounded ship, blinking and staring out across the rocky valley and sparse vegetation.

"A . . . a *creature* out there, one of the Kardoon!"

Mace saw nothing. "Kardoon?" he asked. Firearm dropped from the railing and landed next to him.

"Aye, Kardoon." He waved his laser arm. "This whole land is the Kardoon. The land of the Tigron and beyond, the Scarn." He looked at Du with a sad expression. "It's an evil place we are, woman." She nodded fearfully.

Others came closer, all with weapons drawn. "What did you see?" Eve asked, an arrow notched to her bow.

"Something green and scaly and . . . a mouth with fangs . . . bigger than a drask . . ."

Firearm and Redpike stepped out, weapons ready, and Mace followed them. He looked back. "Get that ship fixed," he ordered. "Let's get out of here as soon as we can!"

The mists were thinning somewhat, but the mountain peaks above were lost in grayness and the valleys below were hidden. They were in a pocket of bare rock with the wind stirring the mist into swirls, which blotted and revealed details and textures. Mace looked back again. The ships had become two gray objects and he halted the search team.

"Better stay close to the ship. Firearm, you set up sentries." They turned back toward the ship reluctantly, their body armor glistening wetly. "Redpike, do you think the Zurians would follow us here?"

The Kurkan shrugged and sheathed his sword. "I only know the Zurians in battle, and in stealth, as they try their tricks and illusions. What they might do in this . . ." He left the sentence unfinished. They walked back to the cloudships and orders were given.

"Make a fire, no, two fires. Keep a close watch." He walked over to where the repair crew was working. "How much longer?"

Ironthroat grunted. "Longer than I thought. This metal's hard to bend back." He squinted around him. "Dark soon, but if we have a light . . ."

"Not much to burn up here," Mace said.

"I think I could remove one of the glowpanels from the cabin," Richter said.

"Do it," Mace said. "All right, everyone, get some rest. We'll all take turns on guard. I want someone on each ship and two on the ground." Mace gave further orders to Redpike and they arranged a guard roster.

Darkness came quickly. The patches of moss they had gathered burned smokily but for a long time. The fog did not dissipate and everyone was wet. "Sleep in your armor," Mace ordered.

"We always sleep with a weapon to hand, Earthman," Firearm said. "Even when we are making love."

The cold, wet night went on. The fires sputtered but did not die. Shadows crept in from the rocky cliffs. Most of the party slept wearily. The shadows merged with the night and moved closer.

Liberty was on guard, her wet cloak wrapped around her. *The Dawn Patrol*, she thought. *The Injuns attack at dawn. Fade-out, fade-in: twittering bird, babbling brook, peaceful cabin.* The music in her mind, which had been soft and mostly meaningless background, suddenly changed. It thundered deep organ tones, suspended and unresolved. The adrenaline surge brought her up on her toes, her Zurian sword whispering metallically from its scabbard before she was even aware of any danger.

Her rationalizing backlash embarrassed her. *What the blazes am I doing? Jumping at shadows? I didn't hear or see anything*, she thought. Yet her sword did not return to its sheath. *What am I doing? Am I starting to believe that mental music now?*

She paced impatiently around the ships. Everyone was asleep, including the repair crew, who had surrendered to exhaustion during the night when they had started making mistakes. Firearm was in one ship and Barney in the cloudship which had the drasks below decks. She heard one of the beasts snort and paw at the deck. She rounded the vessel and saw Redpike standing, sword in hand, in the misty early light. He looked at her and put a finger to his lips. He seemed to be listening intently.

She went up to him, raising her eyebrows in a silent question. *Maybe my secret mental music has something after all*, she thought. Redpike motioned for her to go to the other side and she obeyed. *What was up?* The mind music was choppy and switched channels erratically, annoying her. A bit of Korngold, then Morricone; a switch to Alfred Newman, a swatch of Tiomkin . . .

The mists stirred and something came at her.

Something big and vicious and—

Her cloak entangled her arm as she turned and the sword was knocked from her hand. That didn't bother her too much; swords were not her thing. But the dark shape bowled her over. She rolled to her feet, bounding unintentionally high, forgetting the lighter gravity. She ripped at the cape, tearing loose the neck chain without unfastening it. The creature was already past, but another was coming up out of the mists.

It wasn't human and it was big. She caught a glimpse of teeth and eyes, some kind of clawed hand, and then she was falling back, her feet striking out and up, taking the creature in the midsection and propelling it over her head. She rolled to her feet at once, to see it thump against the ship's hull and slide down by one of the landing feet.

She started forward and it snarled and scampered under the cloudship. Liberty then realized men were shouting and there were grunts and snarls all around. Another shape came out of the mist, but at a distance. She saw it gleam in the watch fire, scaly and gray-green, two arms, two legs, reptilian and hunched.

Something flew past her and bounced off the cloudship. She turned just in time to duck a rock. She heard the faint hiss of a laser and the scrape of metal on metal. Dara ran around the ship just as another of the humanoid creatures charged up out of the fog.

Its claws raked at Dara's breastplate and the Kurkan's sword hacked at it. The creature cried out harshly with pain and ran awkwardly back into the fog. Another scampered past, avoiding both Dara and Liberty.

"Report!" It was Mace's voice, shouting above the heavy breathing. The creatures had gone, as suddenly as they had come.

"Redpike! I wounded two, but they ran."

"Firearm here! I swear I hulled one, but I don't see it now. I saw at least seven or eight, though."

"Liberty reporting! Dara wounded one, but they're all gone now."

There was a pause. "Barney?" Mace said loudly. Liberty ran around the ship to see Mace jump up into the drask vessel. He called his name several times, then appeared at the railing. "Barney's missing! Look around!"

They searched in the growing light, apprehensive and cautious, but Barney Boone was not to be found.

At daylight it was still misty. Ironthroat, Richter, and Count Jardek were finishing up the repairs on the damaged cloudship. Mace paced back and forth, then stopped as Redpike came up to him. Firearm and Du trotted up behind and sank to the moss rocks thankfully.

"No sign," the Kurkan reported. "We followed some tracks until the moss gave out," he said, gesturing toward the cliffs. "But that could have been a feint. They might have circled back down."

Mace scratched beneath his black armor and swore. "We can't go off without him."

"Where do we look then, Earthman?" Firearm asked.

Mace struck the pommel of his sheathed sword. "Those blasted Zull! They invent antigravity and DNA rejuvenation and forget simple radios! We could search in both ships except we'd get lost!"

Eve said, "Maybe they didn't need radios. Maybe they had telepathy, or . . . or just didn't *care* to talk to anyone. With their lifespans time was not so important."

"That doesn't help us, though," Mace replied. "How soon?" he asked Ironthroat.

"A few moments, then we test. If all right . . ." He shrugged. "We can go."

"We're going . . . going and leaving Barney," Eve said with determination.

"No, we're not," Mace said, "but we are going to search. The ships are pretty silent, maybe we can hear something."

"How do we keep in touch in these mists?" Redpike asked.

"Tie a rope between the ships," Du suggested and Mace pointed a finger at her.

"Good! Find one." He turned to Redpike. "Let's figure out a series of hand signals or flags or something. Up, down, stop, go, attack, left, right, that sort of thing. I want this to be as silent as possible."

The Kurkan nodded, stepping closer to Mace. "These creatures . . . you know they must have killed him?"

"We *don't* know that. Though I admit it is a strong possibility. But why were they attacking us? What were they?"

Redpike shrugged. "Tigron perhaps."

"Tigron?"

"Perhaps. We do not know. We have only heard the myths. They . . ." He looked around, then spoke softly. "They can change shapes, becoming anything."

Mace snorted in disbelief. "Illusion. Legend."

Redpike shook his head. "No, Earthman. We believe it. There are stories from before the fall of the Zull. The Zull, they . . . when they thought they were dying, after their empire collapsed . . ." He looked around and drew Mace aside. "They experimented with the genetic structure of the Tigron people. We do not know why, but I suspect it was an attempt to forestall their own racial death in some way." He shrugged. "It did not work. The Zull died. The failed experiments lived on."

"The Tigron were native Zandrans?"

Redpike nodded. "So we believe. It was all so long ago. So much has happened, so much has been lost . . ."

"Why would they want Barney? Or any of us?"

Redpike shrugged, then ran his hand over deep scratches in his armor. "Whatever did this could kill. We were lucky. But your friend . . . I think he is dead . . . or worse."

"Worse?" Mace's mouth tightened with dread.

"There are stories . . ." Redpike looked over his shoulder. "They are a suspicious and paranoid race. Perhaps they would cut him open to see if he were different."

"Dissect him? While he's living?"

Redpike nodded. "Perhaps."

"Ready," Ironthroat said. He clambered into the ship and closed the ramp. In a few moments the ship lifted straight up a few feet, then turned this way and that. Then the Kurkan pilot took it around in a tight circle and set it down again.

"Seems all right," he called out. "A little unsteady but I can take care of that. It's like a drask with a mind of its own."

"All right, put the fires out and get aboard," Mace said. "Du, you have the rope?"

"Will this be enough?" she asked, holding up a heavy coil. Mace could see there were three ropes tied together. "It's about four ships' diameters."

Mace nodded. They all boarded and the rope was fastened from one port to the other starboard. Then they lifted. The fog closed in and surrounded them until they were only faint shadows to each other.

The pain came first.

Pain stabbed through the darkness, making him aware of life. Barney felt as though the back of his head had been crushed. He stifled a moan, like an animal trying to hide its injury.

The ground beneath him was cold and rough. Small sharp objects hurt him. Rocks. Faint sounds: voices. A disconnected mosaic of impressions confused him. He opened his eyes.

A blob of light hung in the dimness. A shape moved across it, hulking and hunched. The light was fog, the darkness was a cavern. The shape was . . . one of the things that had brought him here.

A patchy memory returned. A grayish, greenish *thing*, a manlike reptile. A powerful arm, swinging a rock; then pain, darkness. Now this.

Barney tensed his muscles, feeling out his body. Maybe he could dash past the figure, out through the cavern mouth, into the fog. Run. Hide. Carefully he raised himself up, rolling slowly over onto his stomach to rise. His head was splitting. He froze as another figure passed between him and the cave mouth. *Two!* Were there more?

Cautiously he felt the back of his head. A lump, blood-encrusted, his hair matted. *What I'd give for one of those Zull healers*, he thought. He gathered his feet under him, hearing his boots make a slight scrape on the cold rock. *Do I go left, right, or straight ahead?* he wondered.

Maybe we're on a cliff and I'll run right out into a canyon. Better run left or right, along the cliff wall. Go up? Hunted men seem to run downhill; going up might confuse them. But was he able? He still felt dizziness and every movement of his head sent swords of pain into him.

A figure came into the blob of light, swirling the fog, and strode straight toward Barney. A monstrous figure, reptilian and powerful. Barney crouched motionless in the darkness, but as the creature passed it reached down and deftly snagged Barney's arm in a clawed hand.

Barney cried out in pain as he was wrenched erect and half-dragged deeper into the cavern. The darkness split before them; yellow light spilled out, giving Barney his first clear look at the monster that had captured him.

Man and reptile. Grayish-green, huge yellow teeth, powerful muscles beneath a scaled hide. Yet two-armed, two-legged, walking erect. Bulbous eyes, dark and liquid, stared at Barney as he was dragged into the light.

The creature released Barney, who sagged against a smooth wall, gasping in pain.

Smooth wall? The animal trainer from Earth blinked, fighting back the waves of nausea and pain. He was in some kind of man-made, or creature-made, passage. The door through which they had passed slid shut, cutting off the view of the natural cave beyond.

And escape.

The scaly monster loomed over Barney and slapped at his shoulder, grunting. Barney staggered off in the direction of the shove.

Smoothed rock floor. Filled in here and there where the natural hollows had occurred. The same for the walls. Glowpanels were set in the ceiling to make a dim light. Either the panels were old and giving out or the creatures preferred a low light level.

They passed an open arch to a dark room, then a curtained doorway. The passage turned and Barney blinked in surprise. There was an enormous chamber, a crystalline cavern as big as an auditorium. The corridor became a ramp cut through rock and crystal down toward the bottom. Distance and perspective were difficult. Glowballs on rods lit up the cavern fitfully. Some glowed through outcroppings of amber and orchid crystal, others lit narrow paths through massive blocks of broken crystal, fallen ages before from the ceiling.

The huge room was chaotic, jumbled, and faceted. Light glinted off a thousand surfaces, reflecting, re-reflecting. Barney stumbled down the path, trying to look as well as walk, but he kept closing his eyes against the throbs of severe pain from his head wound.

He could see the path twisting through the crystalline blocks, around more prosaic boulders and chunks. It was like the inside of a gigantic geode. Higher up the amber and orchid crystals were lavender and a smoky gray, pinkish and no-color. Then Barney saw a bigger, brighter light reflected from a hundred surfaces.

There was a smaller chamber farther on, one filled with light and life. Barney's heart sank. More of the monsters. Less of a chance to escape. His captor grunted and shoved and Barney staggered on, hoping his head wouldn't split open.

They twisted through the crystal blocks and worked their way up the opposite slope, came around a smoky block as big as a house, and stopped.

The smaller chamber was not so small, and much labor had gone into it. The floor had been filled and leveled, imbedded crystals cut and smoothed. The ceiling curved overhead, rosy-pink and hazy gray. Across the polished floor was a dais and a throne cut from a single block of blood-red crystal. On the throne was a human youth.

The boy was more of a surprise to Barney than anything else. He started forward, words forming in his mouth, but the clawed hand of his massive captor seized his shoulder. Barney winced in pain and he gasped as he was yanked back. The youth sitting erect and expressionless on the crystal throne stared at him without reaction.

"Hey!" Barney said as the pain subsided. "Can you do something about this? Who are these jokers? What am I—"

"Silence." The boy's voice was quiet, but he had an air of command that stopped Barney cold. The Terran thought he had better find out more before he spoke.

The boy looked Barney over carefully. That gave Barney a chance to look around the throne room, or whatever it was. Two scaled creatures much like the one pinching his shoulder stood some distance away to the right. They wore no clothing. The boy-king was dressed in a plain, unadorned tunic of soft gray. Barney looked to the left. To his surprise there were three perfectly normal-looking humans.

Two were elderly, gray and bent, men of age and experience. The third was a matronly woman, erect and hostile. All were dressed in plain, simple tunics, sandal-like shoes, no jewelry or ornament.

"Very well, warrior-leader," the boy said. The clawed hand released Barney's shoulder. He rubbed it, looking from human to green reptile to boy-king. He seemed a king. He also seemed perfectly human. Barney was no longer surprised at the humanness of the races on Zandra. Fanciful explanations had come to him: some humanlike race had seeded the galaxy, parallel evolution, the bipedal shape being the ultimately efficient form, sheer chance, some divine plan. None of these explanations explained, they only opened up more and more questions. He had no answers. He was only concerned with survival.

What had happened to the others back at the grounded ships? Had they been killed? Had they left? Were they searching for him? Was he abandoned? What had been the purpose of his kidnapping?

"You have invaded our land," the youth said. It was not a question. "The ancient laws forbid it."

"Look, uh, Your Highness—"

"Silence." Barney shut up, but not before a quick look at the scaly giant behind him.

"There is no excuse. All Zandra knows the law."

Barney raised his hand, feeling foolish, but not willing to risk another clawed grasp of the creature behind him. His head might fall off next time. The boy-king looked at him for a long moment. Why did he react so slowly at times? Barney wondered.

"Speak."

"Your Highness, uh . . . I am not from Zandra. I am from Earth. It is another planet, far away. So far I cannot even begin to tell you. We do not know your laws here."

The youth stared at him, still without expression. Barney gave a quick look at the three humans at the side. They were all frowning in disapproval. "We were being pursued by Zurians, who wished to kill us, to kill the Princess Falana and—"

He stopped as the humans started. The gray-green creatures stirred and rumbled. The youthful king or prince did not move. "The Princess Falana is in the airships that came?" one of the old men asked.

"Yes, sir," Barney said, not knowing if that was the right thing to say or not. It was the truth, however. But the truth *can* hurt, if it is a truth others do not wish to hear.

For the first time the boy showed an expression. It was only a flicker, but it was fear. Barney suddenly realized the youth was holding himself in tight check, that his expressionless face and motionless body was the result of a taut anxiety. What are they afraid of? he wondered. At most we are a mere handful, not an invading army. Xenophobia was common enough in all human societies. The fear of the stranger motivated many to do strange things.

Barney glanced at the three older humans and then stared in surprise. They had changed!

And continued to change. The two men were trembling, their pale, wrinkled skin darkening and becoming rough. The matronly woman was standing stiffly, but shudders were rippling over her body, making the tunic shimmer. Her eyes were wide with fear, staring sightlessly toward Barney. Blinking, the Earthman looked at the lad on the blood-red throne.

He, too, was changing, his skin darkening and becoming rough, his shoulders hunching, his fingers clutching at the jeweled facets of the throne's arms.

What is going on? Barney looked over his shoulder at the scaly creature behind him. It had moved back, but seemed unchanged, still as reptilian and repulsive as before.

The boy-king made a strangled sound, a squawk. Long fingernails scraped at the red crystal. His bulging eyes stared but he uttered a choked cry.

"No! Do not! Fight it!"

The two old men had slumped back against the crystalline wall, but the woman stood alone, fists clenched, her face distorted with effort. Barney stared; what in blazes was going *on?* It was like some old horror movie when John Carradine or Lon Chaney turned into—

No.

It couldn't be.

Were-creatures? No, that's madness. Fantasy. Horror movie nonsense. Couldn't happen . . .

But . . .

The boy-king sat rigidly, head up, eyes bulging, jaw gripped tightly shut, looking like a trapped animal.

"*No!*" His voice was harsh, guttural, desperate.

His skin lightened, as though a cloud had passed. He shuddered and his hunched shoulders slumped. His hands ceased their whitened grip upon the arms of the crystal throne. His eyelids dropped over his eyes. He fell against the back of the throne, breathing hard.

Barney looked at the other humans. The old men slumped wearily against the wall, clinging to outcroppings of purple amethyst, heads bowed. The woman's head had fallen forward, her hair tangled, hiding her face, her hands hanging limply.

Whatever had been going on, it was over. Barney felt the tension drain from him as well; but it left a bitter taste, an unrealized anxiety. He waited, afraid to speak, his eyes going from one hard-breathing figure to another.

The boy-king raised his head at last. "You should not have seen that," he said in a weak voice. "It is . . . shameful." He looked straight at Barney, his eyes old and tired, startling in a youthful face. "The Zull did it, ages ago. We cannot . . . shake the curse of their genetic sculpturing."

Barney licked at his lip. There were a thousand questions, all dangerous. "The . . . the Zull made you like this?"

"When they knew they were dying. They sought to learn the secret of eternal life." The boy still had trouble getting enough breath and he spoke slowly. "They . . . experimented. With their own sources of prolonged life gone, with the secret knowledge destroyed when their sun went nova, they thought they could . . . restructure themselves. They . . . changed us."

The youth looked around the crystalline chamber with eyes wet and sad. "We were less than animals to them. Servants, slaves, objects. Their own . . . fear . . . fear of death . . . anxiety . . . shadowed their thinking. We are the result. We fight it, some of us." The boy gave a slow look at the scaly creatures around the chamber. "Some cannot. They change. Slowly, swiftly, but . . . they change. They become . . . what they must become."

The monster behind Barney stirred, but said nothing. The youthful leader looked at Barney and sat straighter. "I am Ti-blan, hereditary King of the Clans, Prince of the Crystal World, Lord of Kardoon."

"Your Highness," Barney said, with a slight bow. His head swayed with pain, making him wince.

"You are . . . ?"

"Barney Boone, Your Majesty." He attempted a smile, but it became a grimace. "I am from the planet Earth, which is . . ." *Where?* he thought. *Another dimension? Across the galaxy? Light years distant? Where?* "Which is far away from here. My friends and I were brought here by the Vandorians, using a Zull device."

Ti-blan nodded. "We know of the Vandorian experiments with the ancient Zull artifacts." He did not sound approving. "They have brought metal and . . . other things."

"Majesty."

Barney looked toward the woman. She seemed calmer now. She ran her fingers back through her thick, tawny hair and took a step forward. "Mother," the boy said.

"Majesty, we must inform Ti-mar and the other generals. The presence of the Kula Falana may indicate a probe. They have tried it before."

Barney started to speak, then thought better of it. The youthful king let an expression of concern cross his face. "Perhaps. But it is of overwhelming importance that this information not set off a panic. To change now . . . to . . ." He gave Barney a quick look and became more severe in his manner. "Your name again?"

"Barney Boone . . . sire." *It never hurt to oil them up a bit*, he thought.

"Barney Boone, for ages death has been the fate of all invaders. Death or imprisonment in the crystal mines."

"But why, Your Highness? We mean no harm. We were fleeing from a Zurian ship that—"

"A diversion, Majesty," one of the old men said. "Perhaps even now Zurian ships are coming over the mountains to—"

"No," Barney said quickly. "There was just one, after us, not you!"

"Silence," Ti-blan said.

Ti-blan's mother eyed Barney suspiciously. "I say kill him at once. Or use him to lure the others. The law is the law."

Ti-blan rubbed the smooth surface of the throne's crystal arms, his face betraying an inner nervousness. "That is what we have done since the time of the change. We have always done this. Hid. Killed. Hiding our shameful deformities, destroying all those who know this of us." He gave Barney a pained expression. "We cannot help it," he said, a plea in his voice.

"Of course not," Barney said at once.

"Fear makes us . . . different." Ti-blan glanced again at the scaly monsters, looking as if he hated them and was fearful of them as well. "Stress . . . fear . . . they, they change us. Hormonal imbalances, the wise men say. Our very being changes, becomes . . . like these, like whatever will . . . like whatever will make us survive . . ."

"Ti-blan," his mother said softly, yet urgently, a warning note in her voice.

"Oh, we survive. That was the object when the Zull . . . when they tampered with our genes. But we were . . . failures." The word seemed to haunt him, to drive him into a shame-filled mood. He stared at the crystal floor for a long moment, his young face gaunt and tired. "Failures. We survive like the small creatures of the forest, by running, by hiding, by protective coloration." He raised his head, his pain-filled eyes pleading with Barney for understanding. "We look like the noble Kula. Once we *were* the Kula. But we are no longer like them. We are not people like the others, but . . . but *creatures* controlled by their juices, by their glands, by the altered structure of their being, by . . ." His voice grew harsh and his words came to a halt.

Ti-blan's mother took another step toward the throne, her hand out. Her expression changed from concern to fear and suspicion again. Her eyes stared at Barney. "You did this. You are responsible. Are you some kind of magician? Ti-blan is the king, but you have made him weak! Chor-ti-wok! Take him to the place of death! Let the wise men search his body for answers!"

A clawed hand seized his arm and half-lifted Barney from the floor. A wave of pain nearly blacked him out as his head was wrenched to the side.

"*No!*" Ti-blan was on his feet, his hand pointing at Barney. "Release him, Chor-ti-wok! *Release him!*"

The clawed hand opened and Barney fell to one knee. He fought the blackness and the pain and raised his gaze toward Ti-blan.

"The wise men will find answers, my son! He says he is not of Zandra; then perhaps his cells will give us answers!"

"No, Mother." He looked at her with an expression of sadness. "We must change—within our heads, not our flesh. We cannot go on being eternally suspicious, hiding within the rocks, within the fog and darkness."

"We cannot go out, Ti-blan," one of the old men said.

One of the scaly creatures stepped forward, croaking. "Not *out*, Majesty!"

The boy-king waved an impatient hand at them. "No . . . not . . . not out, but . . ." He looked helplessly at Barney. "I . . . I do not know, I . . ."

"The law, Majesty," the other old man said. "The law of the strangers."

Ti-blan sank back into the throne, his head drooping onto his chest. "I know, I know," he whispered.

"We must stay safe. We will find the answers someday," Ti-blan's mother said soothingly. "Fight the change, my son, but . . . destroy this one. Give him to the wise men, to Ti-hor and the Seekers. They will search his living flesh for the answer."

The young king seemed exhausted. All the strength seemed drained away. Where moments before he had been strong, he was now weak, withdrawn, uninvolved. He said nothing and his mother stepped toward Barney with greater certainty.

"Chor-ti-wok, take him to Ti-hor and the Seekers." The gray-green giant rumbled an answer and once again gripped Barney's shoulder. This time his grip brought blood and Barney staggered with the pain that pounded at his head.

Chor-ti-wok dragged him across the floor and into a side passage. Crystal walls, lavender and gray. More hulking green-scaled creatures. A thin, pallid shape seemed to melt into the crystal facets to let them pass. A wide-shouldered thing, black and furred, stepped aside, its fangs gleaming wetly as its small animal eyes watched Barney. The passage twisted through the crystal, in and out of more dimly lit caverns.

What is going to happen to me? Barney thought fearfully.

Eve Clayton stood at the railing, her dark cloak wrapped around her tightly, the hood up. The fog seemed endless; there seemed to be little difference between day and night. Shadows from the black mountains made patches of darkness. Everything was gray and featureless. Cliffs came out of the fog and disappeared. They were lost.

Eve felt someone near her and turned to see Longtalon. The tall blonde warrior was looking at her with his clear blue eyes, an expression of concern on his face, which he quickly changed to a smile. "Greetings, Eve, daughter of Malcolm and Elizabeth."

She smiled and moved against him. "Greetings, Longtalon, son of Castlekill and Joakka." Her hand crept from beneath her cloak to press against his armored chest. "I'm sorry," she whispered.

"For what?"

"For ignoring you." They had been lovers only days before, high in the Kurkan stronghold on a mountaintop. He had rescued her from the savage thorgs, the vicious flying reptiles. He had been strong when she needed strength; he had been kind when she needed kindness.

The Kurkan warrior shrugged. "We have all been busy. You people of Earth have stirred up events." He laughed softly. "A great adventure this." He waved a gloved hand at the fog. "Even if we cannot see it."

Eve put her cheek against the chill smoothness of his breastplate. Things had happened so swiftly, with such bizarre and dangerous turns, that she had not had much time to think about it. "Still . . . I ignored you." She also knew he had kept away from her to give her time to adjust.

"They are your friends," the Kurkan said into her hair. "You share things with them that I can never know. A whole world, cultures, history, everything." He lifted her chin. "We are new to each other. So much to learn. I find it impossible to believe there are as many Earth people as you say. Millions! Billions! How do you *breathe?*"

"Sometimes, not very well," she admitted.

"Is it not better here? There is land, seas, great adventures. The long darkness is over."

"Long darkness?"

He nodded, his manner sobering. "For centuries we lay hidden from each other, little kingdoms and secret colonies. All afraid of each other, afraid that the Zull might still be—somehow—around. We fought to stay alone. We were afraid to have contact. The Zull, they . . . they changed people. Experimented." He shrugged. "They played at being gods. Maybe they were. They were so powerful, had such knowledge . . ."

Longtalon looked off into the fog, his face hard. "They made us all enemies. The Kula kept it thus, kept us from learning, from cooperating, from organizing against them. They played one against the other, until . . . until they thought they were powerful enough to reconquer the planet. They bred the Zurians like cattle, breeding for vicious fighters, trusting they could control them."

"Can they?" Eve asked.

The Kurkan warrior shrugged again. "They have. The Zurians apparently believe it. Maybe it is true. They have the mindsword. It is a powerful weapon . . . as we have seen."

"As we have seen," Eve repeated. She remembered the strong men the slim Kula princess had sent writhing to the ground. Mace had taken such an incredible chance! But perhaps he knew her better than we know. They were together for days. They must have . . . made love.

Eve shook her head impatiently. *I don't own him,* she thought. *But was it making love or . . . survival? Or—what?*

The *what* became apparent. She kept her face turned away from the big warrior. She felt as if her face were flaming. *No, it wasn't the sex,* she thought; *not just the sex. But sex with the exotic, with the romantic warrior-prince from another planet. But what if Longtalon had been green or had an extra set of arms, like the Vandorians? Would my curiosity have been as great?*

Yet the Kurkans seemed wholly human. Perhaps some grisly autopsy would prove them to have extra spleens or their hearts on the "wrong" side, but so what? They looked, felt, tasted, and made love like humans.

Eve deliberately ignored the odds of such a similarity. Perhaps the "human" type was more common than believed. Perhaps there *had* been starships, maybe even Zull ships, that had seeded the stars. What did that matter? What mattered was the reality of it all—even when the reality was dreamlike and the purest fantasy.

She should not be condemned for being attracted to the handsome Kurkan warrior. Nor Mace to Falana. Back on Earth there had even been a name for it, for the lure of the strange and exotic: "The Tahiti Syndrome." Men and women had crossed color barriers, social restrictions, all the artificial obstructions that societies put up. Some said it was mongrelizing the race; others found it natural, even attractive. Had she not herself, back on Earth, had thoughts about what it would be like with other races, with those from other cultures, especially exotic ones? And Eve knew she was not unique.

She smiled to herself, thinking of her friend Sherry, whose fantasy was sex with an alien who had a sexual appendage for every one of her orifices and breathed out puffs of narcotic air. Or those young girls who had sexual fantasies about the pointy-eared Vulcan television character. The Tahiti Syndrome worked just as vigorously with men, she knew. There were those who had richly embroidered fantasies about harems of dusky beauties, about "native girls" and exotic-eyed creatures in erotic costumes, the Queen of This or the Princess of That.

Perhaps Longtalon had his own fantasy at work, she thought. *The golden-haired amazon who could pull the great bow, the busty beauty from that city of El Dorado, El Pueblo de Nuestra Señora de los Angeles, that street-centurion from the L.A.P.D.*

She turned away from Longtalon and gripped the smooth wet railing. She felt so pulled, so torn, her loyalties and feelings at such odds. Did she love Longtalon? Or Mace? Neither? Both? Why did she have to love *either?* They were both strong, attractive men. Why could she not take her pleasure like a man might? She was neither saint nor sinner, prude nor whore; only human.

"I'm . . . I'm going below," she whispered. Longtalon watched her go without speaking. The mist swirled around her and she was gone.

He heard Skylance and Ironthroat shouting to each other, to keep contact and not strain the rope slung between the ships.

The fog seemed endless, impenetrable. They would never find Barney Boone, not in this. Not alive.

The sight of the gleaming machine made Barney shiver—until he recognized it as one of the Zull healers. It didn't take any persuasion by the reptilian Chor-ti-wok to get Barney up onto the wide, flat platform. He breathed a sigh of relief and watched the lumbering Chor-ti-wok reach out with a clawed finger to push a button. Barney felt only warm and saw a light, then he drifted into unconsciousness.

Vaguely he remembered some story he'd read, or some television show he'd seen as a kid. An alien kept humans alive, kept them warring at each other, feeding off the hatred, never letting them die. Was the Zull healer like that? Never quite dying, always getting back to Square One to start over again . . .

But how good it felt . . .

When he awoke he felt in excellent health. He had climbed into the diagnosis platform like an old and crippled man, but he jumped down with ease. Chor-ti-wok motioned at him, rumbling something deep in his throat. Barney eyed the reptilian giant thoughtfully. Could he take him? Those claws, that obvious strength . . . better search for the weaknesses first. He shrugged and preceded Chor-ti-wok out the door.

Ti-hor was old, with the pale, almost translucent skin that the very old obtain. Yet his flesh was puckered with scars. Not all of them were old. Barney wondered why the old man did not avail himself of the benefits of the Zull healing machine. Superstitious? Some kind of immunity? Fear? Religious reasons?

The Seekers were not at first evident. The room to which he had been taken was circular, with more than a dozen dark niches around the circumference, narrow arches that led to blackness. But with his senses honed by years of contact with animals Barney felt there was *something*, someone beyond the light.

"Come," Ti-hor said, raising a pale, bony hand. Barney looked back at Chor-ti-wok. The reptile-man stood quietly by the exit, watching impassively. Barney walked toward the old man, but his eyes restlessly probed into the darkness of the niches.

"Sit." The old man pointed at a chair in the center. Barney saw that it had no straps or wires and sat down. The old man produced a lump of something from within the dark robes he wore, handing it to Barney. The animal trainer took it suspiciously, feeling it mold itself to his grip as though it were alive. He almost dropped it as it squirmed in his hand; then he almost threw it away in fear; then he held it comfortably. It was slightly warm and had stopped moving. It did, in fact, feel very nice. Comforting, really.

His head came up when he heard a rustling in the niches behind him. He tried to look around . . . and found he couldn't. The grayish lump in his hand squirmed as his fist contracted. The substance blossomed out from between his fingers and turned dark red. The rustling continued—and he couldn't move.

He could move his fingers and his eyes. The old man seemed to be talking, facing away from Barney, but Barney could hear no words. Then there was a scraping sound in front of him and Barney fixed his terrified gaze at the niche before him.

The darkness moved. Something gleamed briefly. He heard sounds; distant, almost echoing sounds, like badly recorded speech. Everything was distorted in a subtle way. Whatever it was in the niche moved again. Into the light inched a portion of clawed foot. But it was different from Chor-ti-wok's reptilian feet. There were six toes, uneven and distorted, with broken yellow toenails. No two toes were alike. It was the foot of a monster, of some kind of Frankensteinian parody, of a genetic mistake.

Barney's skin crawled, then his eyes jerked to the side. Whatever was behind him was moving again. He caught the glimpse of something red —a robe, wrinkled skin, something—then it moved behind him again. The voices—always just a little out of earshot and understanding—continued around him.

The lump grew softer, flowed between his fingers. Around his fingers. Up his wrist. Over his fingers. His hand felt numb, cold. He stared with horror as the lump, now a dull pink, coated his whole hand. He felt pricklings at the wrist. At the arteries. He felt faint and nauseated. His consciousness focused on his encapsulated hand. The circle of focus narrowed . . . and faded out.

"The man is lost," Princess Falana said. "Let us move on, before we, too, come to difficulties."

Mace stared at her as the fog swirled around their slowly moving ship. The other cloudship was barely visible, at the end of the rope. "I'll not leave him, until . . ."

"Until what?" Falana said, irritation making her manner even more imperious. "Until you see his body?" She made a short, nasty laugh. "Not in the Kardoon, Earthman. Those that disappear stay gone."

Mace turned away angrily, trying to find a logical reason. They had wandered over the face of the mountain range, going one way for some distance, then back the other at a lower altitude. They had seen nothing. Barney had to be somewhere, but they could not seem to find any trace at all.

The Earthman gripped the railing and tried to control his frustration and anger, and to stop the rising fear of loss. *Ray guns and antigravity airships*, he thought. *Interstellar overlords, healing devices, machines that permanently changed their speech . . . and none of these marvels could find one lost animal trainer.* He turned to the Kula princess with a sudden thought.

"Your . . . your mindsword or whatever you call it. That's what we call telepathy. Is there any way it can be used in reverse? I mean, can you use it to search for Barney? Read his mind, get some kind of handle on him?"

Falana looked puzzled. "Read his *mind*? What a strange idea! No, no one can do that, no Kula anyway." She shook her head as if amazed at the strange ideas of Earthmen.

"But how do you use that mindsword thing of yours? What's the technique? Perhaps we could use it to hunt for him telepathically."

Falana looked suspiciously at him, hugging her cape close around her. "You cannot do this thing—or you would have struck back. But it is not something you can learn to do—or the Zurians would have learned it long ago." She narrowed her eyes as she studied him closely.

"No, I'm sure it's genetic," Mace said. "But maybe we can . . ." He grinned at her. "Maybe we can rewire you to be a receiver of sorts. How do you focus on one person, to use your mindsword?"

"You just think it. Think pain. It is like . . . reaching out, invisibly . . . to touch someone in a special place in their minds." She shrugged. "But that cannot help you. I was told we tried different things long ago, and some went mad. So we do not try, anymore."

"But think of Barney—not to hurt him, but to locate him. How do you, um, *aim* this mindsword thing? Must you see the . . . the subject?"

She shook her head. "No, or the Zurians would have killed us in our sleep centuries ago." She looked thoughtful. "It is like . . . like knowing your bedroom in the dark, or . . ." She squinted, thoughtfully.

"Reaching for some part of your body. You know exactly where it is."

"But if someone you did not know, had never seen, if he or she were in hiding, waiting for you, would you know?"

"Yes," she replied at once. "You *feel* it. That is, if they intend harm." She looked around quickly. "One of the things we fear is that someday, perhaps, the Zurians would find a way to attack us without *thinking* about us." She shrugged. "We fear an alliance with the Astorix, for the robots have no mind we can touch or sense. If they *did* become allies . . ." She shrugged and hugged herself again, looking stern. "It is one of the things all Emperors—" She gave Mace a quick look. "—and all Empresses try to prevent. The Zurians must not ally with the Astorix."

"But Barney—can you sense him?"

"If he is found, do we go on?"

"Yes, of course."

Falana chewed at her lip for a moment. "I have never done this . . . well . . . almost never. When I was young, I kept watch for my father or my sister, always."

"You had your antennae out."

She frowned at him slightly, then nodded. "Yes, like the insects, I suppose. You want me to try and sense your Barney Boone?"

Mace nodded. "Try. Or would it help if Count Jardek joined you?"

Falana sneered. "He may be a Kula noble, but he is . . . different. His mindsword is a dagger compared to mine. I will try alone."

Her chin came up, but her eyes stared blankly at the deck. Falana stood very still, only moving slightly to maintain her balance on the tilt and roll of the cloudship's movement. Mace looked around. Nothing but mist and dimly seen rock cliffs. Rocky islands in a sea of fog. Limbo. Chill nothingness.

Falana blinked. "I . . ."

"Yes?" Mace said quickly.

"I am not certain. It is very faint. A distant light . . ."

"What direction?" She did not answer and he quickly asked, "Back? Ahead? Down, up?"

"Back . . ." She seemed doubtful. "And . . . and down . . . a bit."

"Skylance!" Mace called. "We're going the wrong way! Turn around! Tell Ironthroat!"

"What is happening?" the pilot called back from the mast.

"The Princess—she senses him with her mind!"

"I . . ." Falana seemed almost apologetic. "It might not be him. He is very distant, very . . . strange . . ."

"Alive? Hurt?"

"Hurt, but . . . strange. No hurt. Different." She looked at Mace oddly. "This is . . . something new. I . . . none of us, perhaps . . . had need to . . . we had been told of the ancients, that they went mad . . . and . . ."

"Taboos," Mace said. Eve, Jardek, and Richter were coming out of the mast-cabin toward them. "Don't worry, just keep focusing on Barney." He made a cautionary gesture at Eve, who was in the lead, and she stopped her companions. Longtalon joined her, coming out of the mist, followed by Firearm.

Falana glanced at them nervously, the first time Mace had seen the imperious woman nervous. Not even during the battle had she acted this way. "Never mind them," Mace said roughly, waving them back. "Concentrate." He heard Skylance shouting to Ironthroat and felt the ships do a careful turn, keeping the rope taut between them. When Mace was fairly certain they had made a 180-degree turn he asked Falana if they were cruising correctly.

She nodded, frowning. "Yes," she said, but there was doubt in her voice. "And down."

"Much down or down a little?"

Falana pointed down at almost forty-five degrees. "That way."

"Take us down," he called out to the pilot. "About forty-five degrees." Mace's eyes never left Falana's face. She put one hand on the railing and closed her eyes.

"Strange," she muttered.

"What is she up to, Earthman?" Firearm rumbled, but Mace waved him silent impatiently. Eve whispered to the Kurkan, who grumbled something and went back to his post on the "prow" of the circular ship.

They flew in silence, except for the wind and Ironthroat or Skylance's shouts to one another about rocks or high barren valleys. The mist thinned, then thickened. The light dimmed; they seemed to be in a steep canyon with sheer walls, going down.

"That way," Falana said, pointing.

"Can't right now," Mace said. "As soon as we get out of this canyon." She nodded, her eyes still closed.

The light grew stronger and they turned in the direction she indicated. The stony cliffs were gray, black, slate, pitted ivory, muddy green, wet with mist, and always sheer. A shelf rose to become a narrow valley and Falana directed them along it. Firearm muttered in the prow and kept his weapon arm resting on the railing, ready for use.

The sudden squawk of a bird made them all jump, and they saw a leathery-winged black thing flop off from a nest in a cup of rock. Longtalon stood near Eve, Mace noted, while the female archer had an arrow notched in her powerful bow.

"Soon . . ." Falana whispered. "He grows stronger, brighter . . ."

"Is he alone?" Longtalon asked.

Falana shook her head, an expression of disgust crossing her face. "No . . . there are Tigron."

Longtalon's face tightened and his sword came from its scabbard in a smooth movement, ready in his hand. He gripped the small fighting shield in his left hand and peered into the mist. Mace heard a low chuckle from Firearm. Mouthfire, in the mast control top, said something that sounded like a slogan or short prayer.

"We . . . we are almost there," Falana said.

Liberty Crockett heard the music clearly. Those unresolved chords again. Stingers, the music editors called them. Tension builders, as if the whole thing wasn't enough. Wandering around in a fog thicker than anything seen in London or San Francisco. Bobbing on the currents of cold air coming out of the canyons and clefts. A person could get seasick. And somewhere out there, beasties that could change shape faster than a Nielsen rating. *I wanna go home,* she thought.

Barney Boone. The only one of these bozos that shares my world. Not that I wouldn't mind sharing a few hours with that Mace Wilde. But that Falana; she's like the producer's mistress who's ticked off because she doesn't have a bigger part and can't act worth peanuts.

Cool it, baby, she told herself. Calm down. Do the number; pay the dues. Use your head. Keep this circus moving down the road until we either get back or find a good gig. The dark beauty looked out into the mist, trying to pick features out of the dimly seen crazy quilt of grays. And it looks like this is becoming a permanent road show, she said to herself.

Her thoughts were broken as Redpike came to the railing and looked ahead and down to the other ship. The drasks in the hold stirred restlessly, their hooves noisy. He turned to gesture to Dara, who went below at once. Everyone seemed to sense the need for quiet; even the cloudship pilots had ceased to call to one another.

They drifted lower and lower, the mists thinning and thickening. Liberty's music was faster now, repetitious and loud.

Shapes blurred and merged, parted and slipped aside before Barney's eyes. Odd shapes, not-quite-human shapes. He felt no fear, only curiosity, a vague desire to know what was going on. Not that it mattered. He was here. *Being here was enough. Why go somewhere else? It wouldn't be here, it would be somewhere else.* The thought was amusing, but not much, and his mind drifted away.

He felt odd. Numb. Uncertain. Shadowy. Like before an operation, that pill they give you. You don't care. Cut off my legs? Sure, go ahead. Whatever you think right. Fine. Right. Sure.

But there was a tingle in the back of his mind, a muffled alarm ringing, an alert being ignored. What was happening, anyway? What were the shapes doing? Were they going to harm him? No, of course not—why would they harm *him?*

He did feel different, though. Oddly, strangely different. Was he changing?

Mace's face was harsh and taut. The mists hid everything now, even the nearby cliffs. His heart jumped when a spire of gray rock came out of the mist almost in front of them, but Skylance dodged it smoothly and Mouthfire called back softly to Ironthroat.

Grayness. Anything could be out there—anything. Mace gripped his sword's handle tightly, ready to draw. But the not knowing was the worst fear.

Fear was man's greatest enemy, he thought. *Subduing fear is always necessary. Nothing discourages a person more than cowardice and a fear of danger, and cowardice is fear of consequences. We fear the unknown and we fear searching for the truth.* Mace Wilde smiled a grim smile. *We fear finding the facts more than the fear itself, so we think whatever it is that frightens us is worse than the reality of it. It is better to know the facts, know the truth,* he thought, *than to go on and on fearing the worst.*

You fear when something important is on the line. But that fear is proof of your humanity. You might even call it your best friend, for your mind, seeing the threshold and below-threshold impressions, always tries to tell you.

But everyone's fear is different. Courage is subduing that fear and going on, despite all. So therefore courage, bravery, heroism are different, too. The difficulty in being ignorant, as they were of Zandra, was that we are frightened of all the wrong things, and maybe brave about the wrong things, too. We think our Terran muscles, much amplified by the lesser Zandra gravity, will save us. But perhaps it marks us, makes us an object to fear to the races of this strange world, he thought. People tend to destroy what they fear.

Mace looked around at his companions. A good lot. The Kurkans, born and bred to war, had learned to conquer their fear. And his Terrans were learning. The Kula, even Count Jardek, seemed above fear in a way, as though nothing could touch them in any case. They were doomed to surprise and disappointment, Mace thought. All overlords, sooner or later, are deposed.

The cloudship swept along through the grayness. Fog streamed over the railings, around the central mast. It was cold and damp, with a bone-chilling feeling that was more than just the chill mountain air.

Mace couldn't help thinking about fear. It was so much a part of him that it was almost odd when it wasn't there. He had fought in so many places for so long—jungles and deserts, mountains and valleys. The action arm. Brush-fire wars. Policing exercises. So far, despite frequent, even constant fear, he had never panicked. Panic was fear on fire. Fear was the feeling you were not capable of handling the situation.

That's why he had taken his men through countless exercises, making them as realistic as possible. Build their confidence with familiarity, remove their anxiety—which is fear unvisualized—by repetition, training, confidence.

But who had Mace Wilde to look to for these things? His grim smile faded. No one. His instincts, perhaps. Some of his training was appropriate, most was inadequate or did not apply.

Then he remembered a line of Kipling's. "Of all the liars in the world, sometimes the worst are your own fears." But fear was not always bad. It sometimes kept you from doing something rash, without thinking, without planning. As long as the fear was not allowed to brush-fire into panic, you were all right. Fear could be your friend, setting you up, putting the whole mind on Red Alert.

He pulled his sword from the scabbard and examined it. The blade was his primary weapon on this weird world and he sought to care for it, just as he had cared for his automatic weapons when he had been a soldier. He grinned and looked out into the mists. Had been a soldier. He was still a soldier, but with a ragtag command of irregulars. What *were* they, he wondered. Guerillas? Partisans? Revolutionaries? One thing they had better be and that was survivors.

He turned his attention to the bare blade. *Zandra may not have much metal*, he thought, *but their metallurgy was fine.* The sword blades he had seen had ranged from very good to superb, tough, strong steel that took and kept an edge. The design varied little, from what he had seen, with double-edged broadswords predominating; well-balanced, unadorned weapons weighing about three pounds.

From his study of ancient weaponry Mace knew that most of the medieval broadswords had been two to five pounds in weight, but many were falchions, or single-edged blades popular for their cutting power. Many of his theories of swordplay and most of his practice had to be abandoned, once he came to Zandra. Here, his somewhat superior strength made the swords seem lighter, for which he was grateful.

But speed, agility and what you might inelegantly call low animal cunning was what was important in a sword fight. Brute strength was of lesser importance, except that one tired less swiftly. And Mace knew —from theory and from life-and-death fights—that wielding a sword for any length of time was one of the more exhausting activities one might try.

Mace had seen only a few shields here, which was rather odd, for without a shield the offensive sword became mainly a defensive weapon. He made a note to see about finding or having made a number of shields for himself and the others. A bare sword made fighting more like the Japanese style, which made the tough swords even more valuable, as the more ordinary steel blades would look like primitive saws with a few exchanges of blows.

Mace knew that the force of a sword blow could be amazingly powerful. When he had first fought the Zurians, in the skirmish that allowed Eve, Barney, and Liberty to escape, he had cut right through the hard Zurian steel armor.

He sheathed his sword and fingered the edges of the black Zurian breastplate he had been given. It was a tight, but adequate fit, nothing more than a cuirass to protect his torso, fore and aft. He had seen nothing more advanced than the plate armor he wore. No mail, composed of interlocking metal rings, either riveted or butted. He wondered if he might somehow get a factory going, to armor those who would follow him.

Mail armor—often erroneously called "chain mail"—was usually composed of four interlocking rings in one. It was one of the oldest forms of armor, known in Europe before 300 B.C. Riveted mail was more resistant to penetration or thrusts than butted mail, where the links are not riveted together. But both could resist a slice or sword cut about the same. Blows that did not strike properly stright on would be deflected, skidding across the surface.

But armor of any sort was heavy. Mail did not absorb the force of a blow, thus giving the wearer considerable bruises, and bones could be shattered. He'd have to consider padded undergarments. Mace grinned again. In moments he had run through the development of armor and was considering becoming the medieval equivalent of a munitions mogul.

But they were so outnumbered, so few hunted by so many. He didn't want to take the armoring process to the ultimate end, encasing warriors in complete suits of armor, but some protection had to be found, or they might not survive until they found a way back to Earth.

Earth.

Once again he wondered about his ambivalence. In the words of the old Jimmy Durante song, he wanted to go and he wanted to stay. His duty was back there, his home, his world. He had a responsibility to his fellow Terrans. His smile was tight and bitter. What had the man said, if you accepted responsibility, there was no way to avoid it?

He sighed. What else could he do? Protect everyone, keep it all together, until a way could be found.

Lamellar. They might investigate that type of armor. Similar to scale, but superior. The Japanese used it, as did the Mongols, the Persians, Vikings, Romans. Lamellar was made of small metal plates with rounded ends laced into horizontal bands, then joined together into a garment that was flexible, fairly light, and better than mail. It was a cast of art affects life, for the armor was not very attractive, as it looked bulky and awkward. Few artists painted it, but it did a very good job of protection against a hostile blade, and that was certainly a consideration; in fact, the main one.

A cottage industry, perhaps, if he could find the metal. Set up Richter and Jardek somewhere, find the craftsmen and armorers to start a factory of sorts, and some warriors for protection. But where? Who could he get? Where would they get the tools and raw materials? And was he making a mistake?

Mace walked along the railing, feeling the ship ride gently on the wind. Was he settling in? Adjusting far too soon? Even to think of starting an arms industry was to accept the inevitability of staying on

Zandra. Was he giving up? Could he, as elected leader of at least the Airworld Nine's passengers, afford the luxury of such thinking? What were all those others doing, the ones he had been separated from? Were they alive? And the ones before them, in the ships and planes and boats that had disappeared in the Bermuda Triangle over the centuries?

Angrily, Mace gripped the railing in frustration. So many questions, so few answers! Why hadn't the Zandrans, with their reliance on primitive swords and other edged weapons, not developed the science of armor? Was it because the Kula lords controlled everything and *they* didn't need any physical weapons and possibly preferred their subjects not to be so efficiently protected? Or were they so beguiled by the remnants of the Zull wonders that they never tried? Was it some sort of taboo? Were they frozen in mind and heart, dooming themselves to a status quo?

Something moved.

A dark shape came up out of the fog below them and gray shapes ran. There was a hoarse shout and a spear came whipping through the mist to clang off the central mast.

"Tigron!" Firearm cried.

Skylance banked the ship and Longtalon severed the rope between the ships with a slash of his sword. Ironthroat sailed by, gaining altitude. A spear was stuck in the underside.

Mace shouted out an order. "Don't land! Eve! Firearm! See what you can do!" As the bow-woman and the laser-equipped Kurkan bent over the railing to loosen their varied fire upon the Tigron, Mace shouted to the other ship. "Cover us!"

Mace turned back to see Falana standing at the railing, looking down. "Falana, get back!"

She did not even look at him. "Don't be a fool, Mace Wilde. I am better than your golden Terran in downing these monsters!"

Mace looked over to see several reptilian shapes lying unmoving on the stony soil. Firearm's laser pulsed and a Tigron sprawled. The twang of Eve's bow was a steady, rhythmic sound.

A gray-green running shape below scampered up the cliff wall, stopped, and right under Mace's startled gaze, changed shape. The arms lengthened and spread, flattening out and growing into long leathery wings. The body shrank, the reptilian tail became thinner, the lower legs shortening and their claws curving even more. Within the space of twenty seconds it had become some kind of leathery-skinned bat or pterodactyl, beaked and clawed. The creature launched itself with a squawk and came right at Falana.

The Kula princess glared at it but nothing happened to the savage new creature. Eve turned and put an arrow into its side just before it could strike at Falana. The black-brown monster cried out and flopped away, squawking loudly. Mace leaped to the side of the princess, sword drawn. She looked shaken and pale.

"It did not die! I thought death at it, but I could not touch it!"

"Don't worry about it, it—"

But the flying Tigron had banked back, its long wings flopping noisily. Mace's sword struck at it but the long-necked creature avoided the blow and bit at Mouthfire and Skylance in the command mast. They ducked below the rim and Mouthfire stabbed up at the pterodactyl-like creature with her sword.

"When it changed I couldn't get to it," Falana said. "Its mind changed, too. It slipped away, I felt it."

"Get below, Falana."

"No, Earthman!" She shook herself free and stood stiffly, glaring at him. "I am a Kula princess and I shall not cower like some Chuma slave!"

"You'll be a *dead* Kula princess if you don't—"

"Look out!" Skylance cried.

Two more of the big flopping creatures came out of the mist. One was much like a gigantic bat, furry and fierce-faced, with black leathery wings. The other was long-beaked and brown, with yellow clawed feet. Its claws raked at Longtalon's shield, its battle cry shrill and ear-piercing.

Simon Richter stood in the hatch of the central mast. "Mace! What the blazes is going on! These creatures—?"

"Get below, Simon! These things are changing shape on us, attacking *us!*"

"Mace!" The tall warrior turned at Eve's scream and saw a nightmarish creature coming low over the railing. It was gray-furred and winged, as big as a car, but lean and fanged, trailing a long ratlike tail.

Wilde struck at it with the sharp edge of his sword, but he was knocked back into Falana and they fell together. He saw one of Eve's arrows thump into its side, but it was futile. The gray dragon-like creature kicked at them with its claws but its momentum carried it on past, across the ship. It sideswiped the central mast, shaking the vessel and sending everyone tumbling to the deck.

The other three flying monsters charged in at another angle, beaks open, claws flexing. Firearm stabbed a fiery pulse right down the cawing mouth of one, ripping it apart. The flopping portions crashed to the deck, spurting blood. The other two slashed at the cloudship's passengers and were gone.

There was a cry of pain, then a shout of triumph from the other airship and a wildly threshing, winged thing fell past Mace's ship. But even as it fell, it changed. Mace stared in astonishment. The wings shrank, the tail diminished, the fur smoothed out. What hit the rocky ground was a very humanlike creature, naked and impaled by a Kurkan spear. Mace whirled to look at the severed parts of the pterodactyl Firearm had killed. His gorge rose as he saw it was a humanoid shape, cleaved in two and very dead.

But there was no time. The biggest of the attackers was coming in, its attack cry deafening. Firearm swung around and stuck his arm straight out, the laser that was part of his right arm flaring with light. The searing sword of light sliced into the screaming creature. Dead, but still traveling at a terrible speed, the corpse struck the side of the cloudship. There was a crunching sound and everything tilted. One of the charging pterodactyls hit the railing and veered away. They both fell in a disorderly fashion to one side of the ship.

Skylance righted the ship and they scrambled to their feet. Princess Falana looked rumpled and angry. She tugged her clothes straight and strode across to the railing with a fierce look. Below, unchanged Tigron cried out in pain and fell writhing.

The last two winged creatures swept in again, wings pumping hard. Longtalon's sword bit into the neck of one while Eve placed a feathered shaft right in its eye. It fell to the deck, threshing wildly and caught the edge of the rail. As it escaped over the side it started changing. The scaly skin smoothed out and the wings began to retract. Then it disappeared over the edge.

The other creature banked sharply and flew off into the mists to be lost at once. Then there was silence and the sound of the wind. "Longtalon!" Mace said hoarsely. They tugged at the bloody remnants of the first-fallen Tigron and dropped it overboard. Mouthfire appeared with a bucket of water and sloshed it across the smear of blood.

They looked at each other, still breathing hard. The tousled Eve, an arrow notched in her Dragontooth bow. Firearm with a bloody wound on his shoulder. Longtalon, grim-faced and pale under his tan.

Mouthfire's set expression. And Falana, still at the railing, holding it with both hands, glaring down in triumph.

Mace went over to her, but she ignored him. He looked down and saw several gray shapes writhing on the rock. One changed from reptilian to humanoid and then into something like a thick legless snake. Another wiggled, grew another set of legs, became almost insect-like, then returned to the screaming reptile.

"Falana!"

"Let them suffer, Earthman! I *want* them to suffer! They attacked *me*, Falana, Princess of Zandra!"

"Falana! Stop it! We've won this round. Kill them or let them go!"

She whipped her head around at him, eyes bright and fierce. "Earthman, you—!" She stopped and a veil dropped over her expression. Below the screams died down. "Someday, Mace Wilde, you will die because of the way you think." Mace shrugged and looked down. The Tigron were motionless, either dead or exhausted.

Falana had regained her former air of imperious authority when he looked up at her again. "Their shape-changing changes their frequency. Next time I will be ready. I shall adapt with more speed. They shall die."

"Uh-huh. Well, you might get a chance pretty soon." He turned toward the mast. "Skylance! Set it down!" He shouted up to Ironthroat. "Stay close, but cover us from the sky!"

"Aye, Earthman," the Kurkan pilot replied. His voice seemed weary and Mace frowned.

"Ironthroat? Is everything all right?"

"Dara is dead."

There seemed little to say, and nothing to do. There was no known Zull healer around, no miracle cure for a Tigron's slashing claws.

The ship descended in silence. The landing pads unfolded and adapted to the uneven rock of the wide ledge before the dark patch which was a cavern mouth.

"Eve, Firearm, Longtalon." They nodded. Eve began to retrieve her precious arrows from the corpses of the pale humanoid shapes that were the Tigron in death. Mace called up to the drask ship. "Du? Liberty? You want to go with us?"

The answer was two armored female shapes coming over the side of the monitor ship, sliding down on the rope that had tethered the two cloudships together. They dropped to the rocky ledge and joined Mace.

"She died well," Du said to Longtalon. "While we are gone they will build a bier." The blonde Kurkan warrior nodded, his face set. He had his naked sword in his hand, cleaning the blood from it. He put it back into its scabbard and looked at Mace.

"We don't *know* this is where Barney is, but Falana feels he is."

"So we're going in," Eve said.

Mace nodded. "The rest of you stay here, get things ready for a fast takeoff. We might be coming out of there in a hurry."

"What can Count Jardek and I do?" asked Simon from the ship.

"Make the ship ready. Put the landing ramp on this side so we can run right up. And . . . help with the burial."

"Let us go, Earthman," Longtalon said. "I saw one of them run into the cavern. They will be waiting."

Mace nodded and started toward the cavern. "Hold, Terran. I will come with you." Falana came down the landing ramp, her cloak billowing behind her.

"Stay, Falana. You are too valuable. We can't risk you."

"Oh, and if you do not return?"

Looking at her but raising his voice so that Redpike could hear in the other ship, Mace said, "Redpike will find a place for Simon and Jardek. He will return you to Kulan. And return with the others to the Kurkan base."

Falana raised her chin and Liberty made a slight giggle. The dark-haired princess looked at the black actress with barely restrained fury. It was obvious that few if anyone had ever found the heiress to the Kula throne humorous. "I can't help it," Liberty said with a shrug and a smile. "I keep thinking of Maria Montez and all those queens of this and that she played."

Falana frowned, distracted by the meaning in Liberty's words. "She was an actress," Mace said. "Played exotic queens and—"

"Played queens—?" Falana was confused but still angry. "And she was not executed?"

Liberty laughed aloud. "She had some bad reviews but no one ever thought she should be shot!"

Falana's dark, level gaze went from Liberty to Mace and back again, her anger building. "You are amusing yourself at my expense, you Terran worms." She took a deep breath, her brows knitted, and Mace quickly spoke.

"Hold it, Falana! On Earth we have actors and actresses who portray all kinds of people—kings, queens, cowboys, gangsters, generals—"

"And they are not executed for their impertinence?"

"No, no, you don't understand," Liberty said. She had realized her error in confusing the Kula noble and in angering her. "It's for amusement, for, uh, educational purposes. Everyone knows they are not the real thing. It's called acting and—"

"It's called treason," Falana said in a deadly voice.

Mace stepped between them. "Look, Falana, we're getting off the track." Falana looked at him questioningly and was still angry. "Uh, sorry. That's an expression. You don't have railroads here." He looked at Eve and Liberty. "That Zull language device, it's got *me* confused! I *think* I'm speaking English, but—"

"Oh, never mind!" Eve said with irritation. She marched over and confronted Falana. For the first time Mace noticed that Falana was slightly taller than Eve.

"Look, Princess dear, we've got a friend in trouble in there. We're not trying to make fun of you, but there are inescapable differences in our backgrounds and language and . . . and philosophies." Falana looked down at her with raised eyebrows, as if a servant had somehow found the madness to tell her the story of her life.

"Believe her," Liberty added. "It's just that—to us, to *me*—this whole thing is like some weird series on ABC." She looked at Mace and grinned suddenly. "Just don't get us canceled in midseason, Captain."

"We're wasting time," Mace said. "Let's go."

Falana swept by the others at once and started toward the cavern mouth, her long crimson cape billowing behind her. She ignored the others as they hurried to catch up, and then pass her.

Longtalon paused just inside the cavern mouth, his sword in his hand, his gray cape thrown back to give his sword arm free rein. Firearm came to the other side, flat against the wall, then cursed.

"As black as a thorg's throat," he muttered.

The rest of the party paused, watching as Mace looked around, just inside. They heard a rattle of sticks and he came out of the gloom carrying a pair of primitive torches.

"Oh, boy," Liberty said in a flat voice, "just like *Pirates of Tortuga*." She watched as they used Firearm's built-in laser to ignite one torch, then they found more torches and most of the little expedition picked up at least one. The notable exception was Falana who waited with obvious impatience.

"Just light two to start," Longtalon suggested. "There is no telling how far we have to go and I don't think many trees grow in here."

With the tall Kurkan warrior in the lead they started off, seven into darkness.

"Tell the Kurkan to keep a torch near me at all times," Falana said to Mace.

"Tell her yourself," Mace answered. He was trying to see ahead into the endless downward darkness.

"Mace Wilde, certain things are done certain ways." Mace turned to look at the beautiful Kula princess, for her voice had dropped to a confidential tone. "I shall not be the one to undermine your position of leadership by bypassing you. Even on your Earth they must know that. I tell you and you tell your subordinates."

Mace's mouth twitched in amusement and he turned away to hide his expression. They were on a fairly flat section of the subterranean passage. A path had been chopped or smoothed throughout the length of it and had obviously been in use for centuries. Small bridges had been constructed over deep gashes. The narrow path had been reinforced by walls of masonry around cold, clear pools of water so still you would not know they were there until you stepped in them. Stalactites hung in frozen drippings from the curved roof and lumpy stalagmites reached toward them from the floor.

Longtalon paused ahead and signaled for a rest. They had been going for an hour. Everyone found a comfortable place to sit or sprawl. Only the tall blonde Kurkan stayed on his feet, moving a little ahead to reconnoiter. Mace turned to the Kula princess.

"Look, Princess, why do you want to come along, anyway? This is dangerous."

"I am the heir to the throne," she said with conviction. "I must find out what every part of my kingdom is like."

"Uh-huh," Mace said, unconvinced.

"Speak to the Kurkan woman," Falana said. Du had been the one carrying the torch just ahead of Falana.

Mace shook his head. "You stay close to *her*, all right?"

Falana narrowed her eyes, then abruptly changed her mood. "This is boring, Earthman." She looked around. The flickering torches cast wavering shadows up the walls. A huge stalactite hung down until it almost touched the swelling of rock beneath it. Everything behind was in darkness. "If there is sand there," she said, pointing, "we could spread our capes and find pleasure." Her hooded eyes returned to Mace.

He sighed and looked at her. The crimson cape was parted and he could see the lush figure with its ornate costume beneath. Her flesh was golden in the torchlight, firm and smooth.

"No," he said with visible effort.

Falana looked amused. "You are shy? Afraid they will hear us? How charming! You look so bold, you *act* so brave, yet . . ." She pursed her lips and challenged him with a look.

"Falana . . ." Mace started and stopped. "You are attractive, we both know that, but there is a time and place . . ."

"Of course, and this is it. I feel the need for diversion, Mace Wilde. You have proven your, shall we say, ability?" She saw Mace look at the others. Her expression faded and was replaced by the deadly no-expression of anger. "You care what they think," she said in an accusing tone.

"Of *course* I care what they think, they are my friends."

"Very well." Mace looked at her. She seemed aloof and withdrawn, as if he did not exist. Falana remained so during the rest, looking around her with a disdainful expression, then returned to the trek without speaking.

Liberty passed Mace and whispered, "A woman spurned, man, a woman spurned." Mace looked at her and made a face. Liberty smiled. "Men ain't the only people who want it when they want it." She walked on ahead, her dark cloak held around her in the even chill of the cave.

Barney sat in a stupor, barely aware of what was going on around him. The lump in his hand had stopped spreading up his arm, but had encased it in a no-temperature sleeve almost to the shoulder, thin and translucent and faintly undulating. He felt weak and didn't care. His thoughts came with excruciating slowness, like dredging lumps of potatoes from a deep pot of stew, and about as shapeless.

Was he changing? Had he already changed? What did they want?

There was a horror here, but it was remote and only faintly hostile, like hearing of an atrocity committed a hundred years before on the other side of the world.

What would they make of him? A scaly monster? A cretinous blob? Was he about to be dissected, skinned alive, disemboweled, pinned across some Zandran examination table?

The strange thing was, he didn't seem to care. It was only curiosity. Idle curiosity. He didn't notice his tears.

Longtalon hissed and the two torches were swung down. Du thrust hers into a pool of water and Liberty, who had been holding aloft the other, crowded back to extinguish hers in the same pool.

Mace slipped past the others and joined the Kurkan at the head of the little column. Firearm and Eve also joined them. As their eyes adjusted they saw a dim glow ahead. The cavern twisted and they could not see the source. Mace tapped Longtalon on the shoulder and the warrior slipped ahead, his booted feet cautious on the worn stone.

After a moment they saw his silhouette against the faint glow. He disappeared and after a time his dark silhouette reappeared and waved them in.

The cave floor smoothed out until it was scattered sand over a terrace of great blocks of stone. A pile of unlit torches was at one side. But it was at the source of light Mace stared.

A wall of immense stones completely walled off the passage. At each side, low down, was a wide slit, well barred, for the drainage of any water. In the center was a deep-set metal door, plain and unadorned, but very sturdy. Above it was a bright Zull glowball, set into a rather crude metal frame.

"Now what?" Eve asked.

They examined the door. There was no handle, keyhole, or lock. "They must have some way of signaling those inside," Du said. "I have never heard of them being telepathic, so—"

Longtalon peered closely at the door and rubbed it with his fingertips. "They strike it. Marks," he said, pointing.

"But what signal?" Liberty asked. "And what's beyond?"

Mace studied the obstacle, wondering how he would have constructed it. "There should be an eyehole or some kind of Joe-sent-me slot, but there isn't. Maybe there's a kind of airlock beyond. They trap you between two doors . . ."

"Maybe we could cut it open," Eve said, gesturing toward Firearm's laser.

But the scarred Kurkan shook his head. "Too thick. It would absorb all of the energy in here and then some. This is a weapon to use on flesh, not steel."

Mace turned to Falana. "I have an idea, if you are willing."

She looked at him archly. "*Now* you ask if I am willing."

Mace made a face and waved his hand. "Look, do you think you could act, well, distressed, in trouble, weak . . . ?"

"Weak?" Her manner grew cold.

The Hidden Worlds of Zandra

"He said *act*, Princess honey," Liberty said. "You don't have to *be* weak, only look it, think it, pretend it."

Falana's gaze was cold as she swung to look at the actress. "We Kula are not—"

"Oh, can it," Liberty responded. "I see what Mace is up to. We hide, you pretend to be alone and bang on the door. When the baddies open up, you go in. They'll want you, all right. Once inside, there's probably some kind of guard, right?" She looked at Mace, who nodded. "You sock 'em with that mind-whatsis of yours and open up the outer door. Am I right, Mace?"

He nodded and looked at Falana. "It's dangerous, but they wouldn't want anyone else as much and we don't carry a concealed weapon like you do."

Falana looked at each of them, her face expressionless. "Why should I risk myself?"

"Because you asked to come along, Princess honey," Liberty said with a grin. "You gotta pay your dues."

"Unless, of course, you are afraid," Eve said, speaking up calmly. "I would be, but then I don't know how you Kula folks look at things." She looked casually at Mace. "The L.A.P.D. procedural manual says to call for backup, but—"

"I will do it," Falana said. Her manner was offhand, as if asked to do a small favor.

Liberty grinned. "I think this calls for a little careful costuming, Princess honey. Take off that cloak for starters."

"Please cease addressing me in that manner," Falana snapped.

"Yes, Your Highness, honey." She tossed the discarded cloak behind a rock as the others moved to find concealment in the darkness. Liberty looked critically at the straight-backed Kula. "First the outside. Pull down that strap. No, break it. Let a little fall out. Dirty up that leg, like you took a fall."

Falana did not respond, so Liberty undertook to do the patchy "makeup" job. "Oh, for a little bit of Max Factor blood," she muttered as she made the haughty princess look disheveled and wounded. Falana stood impassively, letting the actress tousle her hair and rip her clothing.

Liberty stepped back and surveyed the result. The golden body was more naked than ever, but looked as though she had gone through a lot. "Now the inside," Liberty said. "Look, Princess hun—uh, Falana. You've got to be scared. Not act scared. *Be* scared. Something's behind you, something nasty and frightening. Something so terrible that you'd even beg for—"

"I will not beg!"

"Today you will. You are *acting*, Princess baby, acting. But to work, to be real, you must *feel* it. I don't have time to give you a whole course in The Method, just let it be that you've gotta *feel* scared. You ever been frightened, *really* scared?"

Falana just looked at her. Liberty flashed a bright smile. "Don't have to tell me, just tell yourself. It's called sense memory. You remember what it was like. You replay it, amplify it, *use* it—remember it."

"Then what?"

"Don't give them time to react," Mace said from the shadows. "Crowd them. Make them feel it is far enough away to be safe to open the door and close enough to be dangerous. Dangerous enough to tear down the wall. Is there anything like that around here?"

Falana gave her first indication of fear. She made an expression of distaste. "There are threen."

"Threen? What're threen?"

"Terrible creatures," Falana said, the expression still one of distaste mixed with fear.

"Are they around here?" Mace asked.

Falana shrugged. "They could be. They are . . . very swift, very deadly."

"Fine," Mace said. "Use threen. Get ready, everybody."

Liberty melted into the darkness. "Remember—the biggest, fastest threen you've ever seen is right back there. Break a leg, baby."

Falana cast Liberty a look of annoyance. She adjusted a broken strap and looked herself over. Then abruptly she ran toward the metal door and pounded on it with her fists. She looked around and found a rock and smashed away at the metal with it, leaving chalky marks. "Let me in, let me in! This is Falana, Princess of Zandra! There is a threen behind me!"

She kept it up and after a long time they heard the squeal of metal and several clanks. The door opened and a spear point was thrust through. Falana grabbed the shaft and pulled open the door even farther. She was wide-eyed and desperate.

"Let me in, you fool! I am *Falana!*" She brushed past the soldier with the spear and Mace got a glimpse of him. He was humanoid, not one of the scaly monsters they had encountered earlier.

"Just a minute," he began, closing the door and locking it. Mace and the others rose cautiously from hiding and advanced on the doorway. They waited, looking impatiently at one, then the other. They heard the door metal squeak at last and lifted their swords. Firearm had a clear shot at the opening with his laser.

"Be not fearful, it is Falana," she said as the door was opened farther. She stood imperiously, her torn and disheveled appearance gone.

"She let us wait while she fixed herself up," Liberty muttered in annoyance.

"How did it go?" Mace said, moving in past her. There was a small stone room and another metal door standing open. High up around the walls were dark slits.

Falana shrugged. In the guard room beyond six humanoid figures were sprawled. One had a scaly look to him and another had furry hands and chest. One dead, open mouth showed fangs.

Liberty shivered. "Lookit that, will you? A buncha Mister Hydes."

"Something like that, all right," Mace said, examining the dead men. Falana's mindsword had taken care of all of them. He rose up, sword in hand, and motioned toward the only way out.

Falana looked after the departing group without moving. Liberty looked back. "You coming, Princess honey?" When Falana merely ignored her haughtily, Liberty sniffed. "Waiting for a big thank you? Okay, thank you. Now do the rest of your job."

Falana looked grim and Liberty smiled. "Don't you ever get tired of being Miss High-Muckymuck? Must be a big strain on your nose, being up in the stratosphere all the time like that."

"You black—"

"Black *what*, sister?" Liberty took a quick step closer. Her strong muscles, amplified by Zandra's lighter gravity, made her almost leap. In an instant she screamed and went crashing to the floor, gasping, then sliding down a Tigron guard's body to lie unmoving on the floor.

In seconds Mace appeared in the doorway. He looked at Falana but went at once to Liberty. He checked her pulse then glared up at the princess. "You *insane*? She was one of *ours!*"

"She threatened me!"

Mace stood as Eve and Du rushed in with Longtalon right behind. They bent over the black actress and began rubbing her wrists and temples.

"What did you do to her?" Mace demanded.

Falana stood her ground as the Earthman advanced. "I defended myself. I *am* allowed to do that, am I not?"

"She wouldn't have hurt you. *What did you do to her?*"

"I . . . I don't know how to describe it."

"Try."

"I . . . reached in and . . . and made it black." Falana looked away, chin up, eyes down. "You can't describe it, you just do it. I made her stop. I did not kill her. She will live." Her eyes swung again to Mace. "We know how to give pain, how to make everything stop, and . . . how to kill. I did not kill."

"But you could have."

"Yes. I will not be threatened."

"And you, of course, did nothing to start any of this." Mace turned away with a growl. "All right, someone has to take her back. Eve, Du, you—"

"She will awaken soon," Falana said, frowning down at the unconscious actress. "You need not deplete your forces further."

"Oh, thanks," Mace said moodily.

They watched as Liberty blinked her eyes and moved. "Oh, wow, what a *head!*" she said, touching her forehead. She looked around groggily, then found Falana. "That's some handy-dandy thing you got there, Princess honey."

Falana just looked aloof. "We had better hurry," she said.

They helped Liberty to her feet. "You all right?" Eve asked.

"A head like I drank everything in Beverly Hills, but . . . okay, I guess." She took a step, stumbled, but recovered. Over her shoulder she looked at Falana. "Some day, Princess baby, you and I are going one-on-one *without* that brain blaster of yours."

Falana looked momentarily puzzled. "But I am never without it—it is part of my mind."

"Come on, come on," Mace said impatiently. "Get the show on the road. Head 'em up, move 'em out."

Liberty smiled wanly. "You'd do okay in a good gritty western, you know that, fella? Fastest gun in Hollywood, slow to anger, fast on the draw."

"Giddyup," Mace said, slapping her arm.

They moved out into a stone passage and along toward the faint sounds of machinery.

The noises they heard proved to be ventilation machinery. They slipped past the open doorways to the equipment rooms and saw no one. Then Longtalon, in the lead, motioned them to stop as he approached a wide cross corridor. The passages were mostly natural caverns which had been smoothed and floored. Many natural rock formations were visible. The eternally bright Zull glowballs were hung at frequent intervals. Almost unbreakable, these relics of the galactic empire were all over Zandra in the hundreds of thousands, drawing their cold energy from the air, or so the Kula believed.

There was a quiet hiss from the Kurkan and the column moved again, out into a wider passage. They chose a direction at random and went along it. One of the big scaly Tigron warriors came out of a passage just ahead and turned away from them. He stopped, warned by some sixth sense, and started to turn, but Longtalon was already on him, his sword arcing through the air to cut deeply into the creature's neck.

As Mace passed the twitching body he saw a portion of the snake-snout face turn pale and a more human mouth and nose appeared. Then the transformation stopped and the warrior died. Mace wondered about these reputed were-creatures. Some returned to their original humanoid shape, others did not, or only partially so. The guard detail that Falana had killed still bore the scales and fur of some sort of cellular transformation, a distasteful reminder of their slithery genetic structure.

Mace wished Richter were with them, to help discover the reason for their changing. But they were not deep within the Tigron tunnels for scientific research, but to rescue a comrade. But the nagging thought that perhaps their survival depended upon knowing how and why these cousins of the Kula changed kept poking at him. He shrugged it off.

Mace guarded the rear and kept Falana close to him. Her insistence on going with them compromised his situation. He had to guard her and that meant he could not devote all of his time to the rest of his duties, a situation that bothered him. He smiled wryly as they padded almost noiselessly along the tunnels. *She* has a mindsword and *he* had only a metal one. Who guarded whom?

The tunnel descended down some curving steps, past some storage caverns, then into a huge cavern, terraced into gardens under oversize Zull glowballs. A humanoid tending the plants saw them and shouted. An alarm was raised as the invaders heard cries going out along the radiating tunnels.

"Dirty fan time," Liberty said.

"No need for silence now," Firearm growled. A trio of green-scaled

Tigron warriors come out on the highest terrace and a triple red pulse brought them down.

"This way!" Longtalon shouted.

They ran along the path and up another ramp. Two warriors met them with spears but Eve's bow and Firearm's weapon disposed of them before any of the swordsmen could get close. Longtalon jumped over their bodies and stopped in the intersection beyond. Mace joined him and pointed with his blade.

"Look, the walls are different!" Along the passage to the right the rock had been smoothed into a sleek half-cylinder and polished, then banded with strips of stones in a bright mosaic. The colors shifted and changed as they ran along. There were still shouts and echoing hubbub behind them.

A startled humanoid appeared, wearing rich robes. He dropped a platter of food and cowered back, his face changed as they watched. He turned gray and whiskery, then scuttled off, bent over.

Mace followed the running Tigron. Another humanoid, a female, came out of a doorway in the rock, screamed and her scream disintegrated into a horrible cawing as she arched her back and grew black hair along her arms. Her body thickened and her dress ripped and fell away in tatters. Her head became globular, her eyes bulged, her mouth became a fanged beak. That was as far as she got, for Du plunged her sword into the changing body, then pulled it out, dripping pallid juice, and thrust it in again and again. The black-haired arms scrabbled at the blade, seizing the hilt and wrenching the blade from Du's hand.

The Tigron were-thing twitched and screamed shrilly and fell back. With a distaste they all felt Du reached down and grabbed back her sword. The spiderlike creature collapsed, the hair and arms shortening and growing paler. The face changed almost all the way back to a human face. Almost.

Eve shivered, her revulsion almost bringing her to the point of nausea. "What *are* these things?"

"They react to fear," Longtalon said, putting his arm around her. Eve shook free and stumbled away a few steps. Then she straightened her back and ran on after the others.

They crashed through an ornately carved door and found themselves in a large chamber. Tapestries hung from the stone walls. Zull glowballs hung in clusters, but the clusters were dim. The chamber was shadowy and echoed their footsteps. At the end of the room was a dais and on it a throne of sorts, very old and worn stone, with dark blue cushions, different from the one Barney had seen earlier. On one side was a wide shallow dish of hammered metal on a stone base; in it were jewels.

"In the name of Cecil B. DeMille, look at *that!*" Liberty said, stepping up on the dais. She plunged her hand into the pile and brought up a handful. An expression of delight brightened her features as she trickled them through her fingers. Some were cut and faceted, but many were not. They were polished but uncut stones, lumps of red and amber, diamond-blue, deep green, a yellow flecked with gold, tiny stars trapped within deep purple, honey-brown eggs, and blue-green spheres.

"Never mind that!" Mace snapped. He went along the wall, pulling out the tapestries showing battle scenes and pastorals, while Longtalon checked the other walls. They were looking for a way out. Firearm and Eve stayed by the entrance, guarding their back trail. The cloaked invaders hurried along, searching, but Liberty stood entranced.

"I could buy everything in Rodeo Drive with a fistful of these," she said to no one in particular. "Do my own films, get that house in Benedict Canyon, go—"

"Here! This way!" Mace held aside a tapestry and was opening a rather small door. He went through, sword first, and the others followed. Only Falana noticed that the black actress still stood on the dais, staring down at the huge bowlful of jewels. She smiled faintly and went through the door, letting the tapestry fall behind.

The way beyond was through a dimly lit corridor. At the end was another door, which opened at the touch. At once they heard moaning and stopped.

It was dark beyond, but not totally so. There was light to the right and Mace walked carefully along, with Longtalon close behind. They came to an arch and the moans were louder. Mace pulled his black cloak up to cover much of his face and peered carefully around the arch.

In the center, reclining on a padded wooden chair that was almost a table, was Barney Boone. The moans came from him. His right arm was covered with a smooth, featureless translucent shell. But it was what was standing around the captive animal trainer that got Mace's attention.

Four creatures, and *creatures* was the only word that Mace thought fit. The room was dimly lit and the Tigron watchers were caped and hooded. But there were clawed feet, scales, bulging eyes, writhing tentacles, hints of pale spotted flesh and matted fur. The revulsion rose in Mace's throat and he went berserk.

With a cry he charged in, sword swinging. His blade cut into alien flesh, powered by the extraordinary strength of his Terran muscles. He was a killing machine, a primitive savage faced with the terror of the unknown. Thin screams and hoarse bellows filled the room. Blood spurted, but it was not all red. The four creatures fell without offering much resistance and when they had died they did not change back into anything resembling the humanoid base form.

Du released Barney, who sat up groggy and moaning. The blobs of material still covered his arm only now it seemed to be moving, with a shifting of pale colors, rippling and sliding.

Mace stood with one hand against the stone wall, breathing hard, looking at the carnage and feeling both revulsion for what he had seen and revulsion at himself. He had reacted as a savage, from the fear of something different. Xenophobia at its savage worst. Kill the stranger, kill what is different. He felt ashamed, yet within him was a deep satisfaction. The unknown had been conquered—never mind the cost. He would live with his sin.

"Mace Wilde!" Du said. Mace looked at her. From her concerned expression he knew she had been calling him for some time. He looked at Eve, who was looking at him as though she had never seen him before. Mace did not look at the others.

The Kurkan warrior woman pointed at the semiconscious Barney's arm. "What do we do about this? It . . . it is growing, look at it."

Mace blinked, then concentrated on the thick layer of gelatin-like substance. It was moving; tiny flecks and spots were circling, going around the arm slowly, and always up, toward the shoulder. If left alone it would cover Barney's head.

Mace looked around but found no surgical instruments. He pointed at Du's dagger and she pulled it from its sheath and gave it to him. With Du supporting the softly moaning Barney, Mace started to try and scrape the coating from his arm. But at the touch of the blade Barney screamed, arching his back, his eyes bulging with horror and pain.

Mace stepped back. "Let's get him to the ship. Richter or Jardek will know something."

"No, Mace Wilde," Falana said. She stepped closer, her crimson cape swirling around her. "He will die. That is a living thing and it has become part of your friend."

Mace peered into Barney's face. His eyes were dulled and blank, his mouth slack, his skin gray and dead-looking. Whatever the thing was that coated his arm, it was killing him. He looked up at Falana helplessly. This was nothing his rudimentary military medical training had provided for.

Falana smiled thinly. "Only I can save him now, Mace Wilde. You would not get him back in time. Look at him."

"All *right*," snapped Mace. "What's your game?"

She looked very pleased with herself. "Kula do not bargain."

"The hell they don't," Mace growled. "You may call it negotiation, diplomacy, whatever, but that is what it *is*. Now *do* something about it!"

"You have not asked my . . . price."

He glared at her with such ferocity that Falana took a half step back. "*Do* it, Falana."

The Kula princess raised her chin again and an expression of haughty self-confidence came over her like a shield. She looked at Barney's arm and her eyes slitted. Barney moaned and twisted. Mace jumped to seize his friend and hold him as he tried to twist away.

Barney screamed, a long sobbing cry of anguish that made Mace glare at Falana. But the Princess of Zandra ignored him. Her face grew grim and even ferocious. Mace saw the gelatinous coating quiver and ripple, saw the specks and swirls turn pale and thin. The coating shrank away from Barney's shoulder and slithered down his arm. With increasing speed the covering slid down, like peeling away a long glove. It fell from his fingertips in a lump and dropped with a splat onto the smoothed stone. It lay quivering in a shapeless lump, but still Falana glared at it.

Du and Mace pulled Barney to his feet and away. The blob on the floor moved, as if trying to roll away, but then abruptly turned dark. Pustules formed and erupted a tiny spray. A pseudopod of jelly spurted out, quivered, turned dark, and died. The lump quivered and was still.

"What *was* that?" Eve said in a shaky voice.

Falana looked down at the motionless lump as her expression returned to her usual haughty manner. "An enemy."

"Thank you, Falana," Mace said. "Now let's get the blazes out of here!" He looked the princess in the eyes. "I owe you one."

"Yes, you do," Falana said with a slight smile.

"Where's Liberty?" Eve asked. "I thought she was . . ."

"Liberty!" Mace cried out. There was no answer. They went back along the dark passage and into the throne room through the tapestry-covered doorway.

The room was empty. The bowl of jewels had spilled its bright contents down the steps of the dais. Liberty's sword lay on the stone floor.

"They have her," Firearm sighed.

They crossed the room and Mace snatched up her sword. He looked at the blade. There was no blood on it. They began their retreat; they knew it would be a fight all the way. Firearm led the way and Eve brought up the rear, an arrow notched in her powerful bow.

The Tigron struck just as they were about to get to the farming cavern: five scaly warriors, a flying bat that flopped along the top of the passage, a thick-bodied, dark-furred creature as large as a Kodiak bear. Firearm's laser cut into them, but they were swift and fearless. Swords clanged on swords. Falana downed as many with her mental weapons as any of the bladed warriors. Eve put a shaft into a humanoid with a wolfish face who came up behind them.

Then they were free, running out into the terraces and across to the passages beyond. More of the green-scaled warriors appeared, some with swords, but most without, their sharp claws extended. They did not attack, but ranged themselves in a line across the invaders' line of retreat.

"Firearm," Mace said. But the Kurkan stepped close to whisper.

"I am almost without energy, Earthman. I can take a few but not all. This is a time to use the mind, not the sword."

"Falana—?"

The crimson-cloaked princess stepped forward but before she could begin her work a voice cried out.

"No! I, Ti-blan, command it!"

They looked up. On a terrace above stood a boyish figure in a simple tunic. Beside him was an old humanoid, his skin puckered with scars and wrinkled with age. Behind them were a half-dozen of the green-scaled, dragon-headed warriors.

"I am Falana, firstborn daughter of Morak, Emperor of Zandra!"

"Greeting, my cousin, I—"

"I am not of your blood, changeling!" Falana glared up at the boy.

"Ah, but you are," the old man said. "Permit me, I am Ti-hor, the First of the Seekers. Your blood is our blood, royal Kula. The ancient Zull parted us, but we are still cousins."

"You are—"

"Easy, Falana," Mace said softly.

She glanced at him darkly but when she spoke her tone was different. "We came for this Earthman, who is my slave and property. You should not have taken him."

"Perhaps," Ti-blan said. His voice was uneven, as if under great strain. "But you have killed my people."

"They should not have opposed me. I am the future Empress of Zandra."

"We do not acknowledge the dominion of Morak," Ti-blan said with nervous determination.

"You *shall* acknowledge it!" she flared back.

"*Falana!*" Mace growled, touching her arm. She shook free and her eyes narrowed.

"You are rebels, then?" Her voice was dangerously soft.

"No, Princess," the old man said. "We have never been under Kula rule, so we cannot rebel. The great Zull made us . . . as we are . . . long ago . . ." The old man seemed troubled, and his body shook. The young king next to him put his hands on the old man's bent shoulder.

"Ti-hor speaks the truth, Princess Falana." His face twisted and he turned away for a moment, hiding himself behind Ti-hor's shoulder. When he turned back he was pale and his lips quivered. "We . . . we are . . . of the Kula blood, but . . . not like you . . ."

"Changelings," sneered Falana.

"She has all the tolerance of a KKK Grand Dragon," Eve Clayton muttered to Longtalon, but the Kurkan just looked at her in confusion.

"Where is the woman?" Mace said, shouting up at the youthful king in his best command voice.

"The Zurian?" Ti-blan asked.

"She is not a Zurian, she is a person from Earth," Mace said. "We are from another world and . . ." He stopped, seeing they would become involved in explanations that would only confuse. "Give her to us and we will go."

"You have destroyed the Seekers," Ti-hor said, a great sadness in his voice. "They were doing no harm, they—"

"No harm?" It was Longtalon who spoke. "They were monsters who were killing this man!" He gestured with his sword at Barney, who was supported by the strong Du.

"We only sought to learn," Ti-hor said in a weaker voice. "We do not see many who are not . . . who are not like us. We want to find . . ." He looked at the young king, who was looking distressed. They bent their heads and whispered for a moment.

Mace looked around. There were even more of the Tigron warriors now. They came slowly out of passages, watchful and somehow nervous. Only a few had weapons, but there were many of them. Some were shorter and furred, with prominent teeth and stubby claws. One was a bat-like creature, with leathery wings folded around itself. Here and there a humanoid appeared, fearful and wide-eyed. Mace saw one twitch and jerk and turn into a rat-faced thing with teeth and horns. The Earthman's flesh crawled and he gripped his sword anew.

"We will keep the woman, if she is indeed not a Zurian wench," the boy-king declared. "We must study her. The rest of you may go."

"Are you kidding?" Eve snapped. "We aren't going to—"

"Eve!" Mace's voice cracked like a whip. To the Tigron king he said, "We will go. But if the woman is not brought to us we shall return and take her. You will lose many of your people."

To Longtalon Mace said, "Start 'em moving." Then he stood looking up the terraced green slopes at Ti-blan. "Bring the black woman to us."

The Tigron spoke among themselves before Ti-blan spoke to Mace. "We seek only to learn. We do not have much here . . ."

"They *hide*," Falana said. She had stopped near the passage out, disdainful of the large scaly warriors near her.

Ti-blan stepped forward, his features struggling to remain calm. "Yes, we hide. It was you, the Kula, who drove us here, into the mist and the mountains. We could not help what had been done to us but you found us fearful and, and—"

"And disgusting," Falana said. "My grandfather spoke of you. You were sent here as punishment for evil deeds!"

"No!" Ti-blan put out his hands as if to plead, but then covered his face with them and turned away, his shoulders shaking. He drew back, almost out of sight, and was surrounded by the warriors on that highest level. Old Ti-hor spoke, his voice shaky and uneven.

"You have legends, we have legends, Princess. We know we were changed, by the direction of the Zull. Neither of us knows why. But you, too, were changed." Falana's head came up sharply. "Yes, you, too. You are the changelings of the Kulma, who—"

"*No!*" Falana's voice was choked but furious. The old man staggered and one of the warriors caught him. He gasped for air and Mace jumped toward Falana. The Tigron warriors were startled, for the leap was immense.

"Falana, stop it!"

She shook him off and glared up. The boy-king turned and his features changed. His face grew wolfish and hairy, his hands became padded hairy claws. A guttural growl came from his throat.

"Falana! It's only making things worse!"

Abruptly, Falana stood straight, her ferocious expression softening into her habitual haughtiness, which was like a shield against the world. The old Tigron gasped and shook himself. The wolf-headed king turned away and hid in the throng of warriors for several long moments. Mace pulled Falana back toward the mouth of the passage out. He hoped the others were well along.

"Falana, you have got to figure the odds before you do something like that."

She looked at him with hooded eyes. "I shall never understand you, Mace Wilde. Never. You are as much a changeling as these wretched creatures. One moment you are brave, another utterly mad and a slaughterer, and still again, a coward."

"A survivor, Princess, a survivor. A good warrior knows when to fight and when to talk . . . and when to bluff. This is talking and bluffing time."

He took a step away. "The black woman! Bring her at once! We will leave your land. The princess has business elsewhere! Do not anger us further!"

Ti-blan nodded wearily. They carried the old man away, but Mace could see he was alive. "What did you do to them?"

"They are of Kula blood, as they say," Falana said, her voice distant. "At least enough to protect themselves. They do not have the sword of the mind, but they have . . . a shield of sorts." She shrugged as if it were a minor matter.

"Then they are cousins?"

Falana's expression turned dark and cold. "They are further from us than you, Earthman. You saw them change, to become . . ." She made a face, quickly smoothed away. "They are not like us."

"That's no reason to . . ." Mace started to say *kill*, but he remembered his own primitive reaction on seeing the monstrous Seekers. He, too, felt shame.

"Bring the black woman." It was Ti-blan speaking, his voice weary and weak.

In a short time Liberty appeared. She was bound and angry, her clothing torn. They cut her free and she took a leap right off the highest terrace to land in some plants. The green stalks bent and twisted away from her, but she ignored them. Another leap, this one completely over a terrace, brought her to the bottom level. Rubbing her arms she ran along the walk and took her proffered sword from Mace.

"Let's get out of here," she snapped, walking right on past.

"Ti-blan," Falana said and the boy-king appeared. "When the representative from my father appears, you will make him welcome." The youth nodded, looking miserable. Falana turned and followed Liberty out of the cavern.

Mace hesitated. He wanted to say something, to apologize, to make amends, but he could not find the words. Silently, he turned and left.

Halfway to the outside they stopped for a rest in a cavern of smoky quartz crystals. Mace posted Kurkan guards at both ends of their trail, then went to squat beside Barney, who sat on a wedge of crystal holding his head in his hands.

"How you doing?" Mace asked. Eve, sitting next to Barney, gave Mace a sad look and shook her head.

It took a moment, but finally Barney lifted his head and Mace was shocked by the expression of anguish the animal trainer showed. "I'm not doing well at all," he muttered. He rubbed at his red eyes, then looked down at his hands as if seeing them for the first time. They were pink and healthy-looking, but his forearms were hairless. It was as if all the old skin was gone and what remained was the tender soft flesh revealed when a scab was lifted.

"Take it easy," Eve murmured, her arm around his shoulder.

Barney inhaled slowly, his breath shuddering, his eyes tortured. He looked off down the passage toward the hidden subterranean world of the Tigron, his expression haunted. "I should go back," he said in a whisper.

Mace raised his eyebrows at Eve, who looked just as puzzled as he felt. "Why, Barney? We should move on . . ."

"I could help them . . ."

Mace chewed at his lip a moment before responding. "I don't think anyone can. Maybe later . . . if Richter or Jardek . . . someone . . . maybe someone could control or reverse what the Zull did to them."

"No, it's genetic," Barney said. "They have to learn to control it themselves. Make conscious control of their instincts . . ."

"Barney . . ." Eve said soothingly.

The animal trainer shook free from her arm. "I must . . . I really must. They need me."

"We need you," Eve said.

"Eve's right, Barney. We've got to stick together," Mace said.

Barney rubbed at his arms as if they itched, still staring down the curving passage through the rock. "No, I . . . I . . ."

Mace stood up. "Okay, rest over, let's go!" He made rising motions with his hands and the small group of Kurkans and Terrans rose to their feet. Princess Falana rose more slowly, looking around with a haughty expression of weary tolerance. Mace told Firearm to take the lead and for Longtalon to follow up. Mace stayed near Barney as they trudged up the twisting passage toward the misty surface.

Several times Barney hesitated, turning partially back toward the Tigron stronghold, but each time Eve's encircling arm brought him around.

Liberty stopped, letting Mace catch up. She indicated Barney with a tilt of her head and spoke in a soft voice. "He okay? What the blazes did they do to him, anyway?"

"I don't know. Something . . . strange. I don't think he's well."

Liberty shuddered, looking back over her shoulder. "And they might have done it to me, too . . ." She bit at her lip and shivered. "Getting cold. We must be getting close to the outside."

"Not too far. Caverns generally level off around the middle fifties, unless they're ice caverns. On Earth, anyway."

"On Earth," Liberty repeated in a bitter tone. "On good old Earth."

They emerged to the cold and misty mountainside a few minutes later and climbed into the two ships. Mace went around, checking for damage, pulling out the broken spear that had penetrated the tough skin of one ship. He didn't want to meet whatever it had been that had the strength to drive the weapon through the metal hide of the cloudship. They refastened the rope between the ships.

"Where to, Captain?" Skylance called out from the control mast.

"Anyplace," Firearm grunted fervently. "Anyplace but here."

Du was bandaging Firearm's wound and she nodded vigorously as Mace came aboard. "Out of these mists," she said.

The mists were thick. The other cloudship was only a flat gray outline a few yards away, the drasks in the hold thumping nervously.

"Ironthroat!" Mace called out and received an answering cry. "Redpike! Ready to lift?"

"Aye, Captain," Redpike answered.

"Skylance—let's go up!"

The two ships went up slowly, stretching taut the rope to prevent any sudden jerks. Then they hesitated. "Which way?" Redpike called to them.

"East," Mace ordered, and the ships moved into position, with Mace's ship in the lead, and the other, commanded by Redpike and piloted by Ironthroat, trailing behind. The mists quickly covered the mountainside and they were alone in the misty space.

"Hey, Mace!" Liberty called out. "This remind you of anything?" Since her voice had a certain merriment in it, Mace knew it was some whim of the actress.

"The Golden Gate?" he suggested.

"Naw; doesn't it look like one of those movies where Mister Jordan comes along, giving us all a second chance?"

"Oh, thanks," Mace said dryly. But privately he was thankful for even the slightest bit of humor. Anything to lighten the load. Maybe Barney would find it amusing, he thought.

Mace went into the control mast, thinking Barney might be in there, out of the cold, but there was only Firearm, having a hot drink, and bragging to Eve about his triumphs in the past.

"Where's Barney?" Mace asked Eve.

"Isn't he outside?" she answered, but Mace shook his head. "The other ship?"

Mace went back outside and over to the curving rail to call out to Redpike's cloudship. "Redpike! Is Barney in the cabin over there?"

"No, Mace Wilde; is he not with you?"

"Uh-oh," Eve said. "I brought him right to the gangway, then Mouthfire wanted some help splicing the ropes and . . ."

She stopped, staring at Mace and blinking. "Oh, no . . ."

"He went back," Mace said grimly. He turned and shouted a command to the pilots. "Skylance! Ironthroat! Turn back! Barney is back with the Tigron!"

Mace heard several Kurkan curses, but the two ships began to turn, like a dumbbell, swinging around in a dance-like movement.

It was what saved them.

A slashing beam of red flashed through the space Mace's ship had occupied seconds before. Another pulse-beam lanced through the mists, narrowly missing Redpike's turning ship. The pilots didn't have to be told. Redpike's sword parted the binding rope link between the ships and they arced away.

The Zurian pursuers had found them.

Barney could not see the cloudships lift, but he heard their voices fading away. Then he came out from the cleft between the rocks and gave a shuddering sigh. The mouth of the cavern entrance was only an irregular, darker patch on the mountainside. He took a step and stopped.

What am I doing? The feeling of fear was familiar. He'd felt like this the first time he went into the practice ring with two lions. He'd felt something like it *every* time he had gone into the ring, whether at practice or in a performance.

The big cats were scary. You got to know them, not just as animals, but as "people." Sheba had always been the easiest to persuade—one didn't "control" any animal that weighed six to eight hundred pounds— and Solomon the most difficult. Sargon, the big male, had loved sugar, and Cleopatra loved fruit, but was mischievous and got the others into trouble. Xerxes was unpredictable, a kitten one day and a terror the next. He liked attention and was more trouble than any three cats. Mogul and Punjab II, the big Bengal tigers, were difficult, too, but like sulky relatives who resent the attention given other relatives. Tiberius, the largest of the male lions, had ruled his harem with easy authority, but was easily offended and would fight at the slightest opportunity.

My children, Barney thought as he hesitated at the entrance to the cavern. But he had made them all work together, in the same ring, lions and tigers, male and female. The public had never known how difficult that was. Such a delicate balance. They had done their "tricks" because they wanted to, because he had made them want to, not because they were afraid of him. He had never used gun or whip, had never hurt them or frightened them.

Authority, yes. Command, yes. Telepathy . . . perhaps. He had *willed* them to respond, to obey, and they had. Even Dark Cloud, the black leopard, though he had never put the leopard into the same cage with the others.

Crowded together, each smelling the others even if they did not see them, each genetic warning system at full alert, they had toured with the circus. People, elephants, the sounds of laughter and screams of delighted fear, they had all assaulted the animal minds of his cats. The sweet, bitter, smoky, meaty smells, the sudden shouts and the disturbing noise of the crowds, the music and lights. But he had trained his tawny friends to ignore all that, to watch and obey only him.

Perhaps he could do it again.

To the Tigron, to the changelings hiding shamefully in the dark.

Barney Boone took a deep breath and started into the cavern. What, after all, did he have to lose?

Only his life, and what was that? With Solomon and Sheba dead, with the others sold or dead or impossibly far away, what did he have? Certainly no family, and few friends. His family for so many years had been four-footed, communicating not with words but with growls and body language and subvocalizing. He had nothing to lose.

Besides, he was not quite the Good Old Barney Boone that had arrived on Zandra. Not after the Seekers had . . . had done whatever they had done.

He was different. Not Terran, not Zandran, not Tigron, and not . . . quite . . . human.

He went into the cavern and the mists closed in after him.

The cold gray mists seemed to shower down on them as Mace's ship rose swiftly. He could not see Redpike's ship, but that also meant Durak could not see them, either. *Thank god, they don't have radar,* he thought. *I cursed them for not having radio and now I'm glad they don't have radar.*

There was a movement of crimson at his side and Princess Falana stood there, looking haughtily out into the featureless mist, her cape clutched around her.

"I am cold, Captain. Make it warm."

"Go inside then," he said, peering watchfully into the space around them.

"This is undignified," Falana snapped. "I will destroy these Zurians if—*if!*—they attack, if they *dare* attack, then we shall go to where it is warmer and have some time to pleasure ourselves."

Mace gave her a quick glance. "Don't you *ever* think of anything, anyone but yourself?"

"Why should I, Mace Wilde? I am—"

"Yeah, yeah, you are the firstborn of Morak and all that junk. You own the world and everyone bow down."

"At last you understand," she said with a superior smile.

Mace's hands clenched the railing and he glared at her. "Don't you *ever* face the truth? Durak's out there with at least one weapon that can outdistance your mindsword . . . I *think*. It must or he wouldn't get so close. Barney's back there with the Tigron—"

"Where he evidently *wants* to be, Mace Wilde! Though *why*, I could not tell you." She shuddered delicately.

"I'm responsible for him, Falana, Your Royal Painness. I'm responsible for *all* of these people."

"Then get us out of danger," she said imperiously. "This is becoming boring. We could go to the Windsong Islands in the Southern Sea. My father has a palace there, and some slaves who are marvelously trained to—"

"Falana! I *want* to get us out of danger; I'm *trying* to get us out of danger and you are not helping!" His rough words made her face harden and she drew even more erect. But Mace continued to speak. "You know, Princess, you are not a very likable lady. Back on Earth we have a name for people like you and it is something like witch."

"I am Princess Falana. It is for others to accommodate, to fear . . . to obey."

"Princess honey, you have some learning to do. If we live through the next few minutes." He gestured toward the mists around them. "Durak is out there somewhere, with a long-distance laser of some kind. If he finds us, we're dead meat."

Princess Falana looked slowly and imperiously around. "I am not afraid."

Mace sighed. "Well, I am."

The scaly warriors had approached him cautiously, drifting out of their hiding places in the shadows. They looked back up the passage and two of them padded quietly toward the entrance, their long clawed hands at the ready.

The largest of the warriors approached Barney, his reptilian face unreadable, but his manner was guardedly polite. Barney thought of what to say, then his face broke out in a wide grin. "I never thought I'd get to say it . . . but take me to your leader."

The reptilian warrior did not respond for a long moment, then he stepped aside and gestured to Barney to continue. A half dozen of the green-scaled beings closed around Barney, their yellow claws unsheathed, and they started to march down into the bowels of the planet.

To the world of the Tigron.

To the place where they had changed him.

To his fate.

A ship loomed up suddenly in the mists and Mace's sword slithered from his scabbard before he recognized Richter and Count Jardek, the Kula scientist, at the railing.

"Mace! Oh, thank God!"

The two pilots jockeyed their ships until they were floating along close to each other and the crews need not shout. "Are you all right?" Mace asked and was told everything was fine.

"The drasks are restless," Redpike said, appearing in his dew-dropped cape. "Should we tie up again, Mace Wilde? We can easily become lost again."

"No, let's just stay close. And quiet." Liberty sauntered up, wrapped in a brown cape, and gave Mace a sardonic salute.

"When is this charming little adventure due to be wrapped? This mist is murder on my hair." Her grin was ironic.

"I don't want to get too far away from the Tigron caverns," Mace said. "And maybe circling around will confuse the Zurians, who will think we'll run out of here."

Redpike shook his head, his eyes restlessly searching the surrounding mist. "The Zurian dogs are good warriors, tricky and resourceful. They are worthy opponents, Captain. Do not underestimate them. We have fought them for generations."

"I appreciate that, Redpike, but—"

There was a hiss from the control mast and the whispered word that brought fear to all their hearts.

"Zurians!"

The young king was sitting on his blood-red throne of carved crystal, sitting erect and lordly, but Barney detected an air of fear in his barely perceptible twitches.

"Your Majesty," Barney said, making a sweeping bow he had copied from Errol Flynn.

"Outlander, you may speak. What brought you here and what brought you back? Do you imagine you can slaughter more of my subjects?"

"I killed none, Your Majesty. I have returned to help you."

"Help us? *You* help *us?*" The young king made a short, artificial laugh. "The Seekers and the sons of Seekers have thought for generations, have experimented and prayed, and *nothing* can be done!"

"Correction, Your Majesty . . . nothing *has* been done, but something *can* be done."

There was a flicker in the eyes of the youthful monarch and he looked at his mother and the two elders, who stood stiffly to the side. "What can *you* do? You are a stranger to our world, by your own admission. We have used the Zull machines, we have the highest *possible* motivation, we have strived for *centuries* to . . . to erase this shame . . ." His voice choked up and he fought to keep his face unreadable.

"Yes, I'm sure you have, Your Majesty, but perhaps you were looking in the wrong place." The expression of confusion on the young king's face made Barney hurry on. "You have been looking into the cellular structure, have you not? Into what we Earth people call the DNA molecule? Into the physical composition of the hormonal process?"

"Yes, of course. Where else would one look?" Genuine puzzlement was in his voice as the cavern kingdom's ruler leaned forward.

"Your Majesty, on my world we do not have such a wonder as your Zull healer. We are only now learning the tiniest information about the cellular plans, the structural information each living cell contains. Thus, when one of us loses a limb or suffers some kind of debilitating injury, he or she must conform to it. To adjust. To learn to live with that disability."

"How terrible," the young man said. "I once crushed an arm in a fall when I was a child. They severed the limb, seared the stump, and brought me back to the healer." He waved his left arm, which seemed perfectly whole. "I did not have to adjust, as you say, except for the awkward time while it grew again."

"We are not so favored on our world, Your Majesty," Barney said. "We *must* adjust, and it is in that way I can help you."

The king narrowed his eyes in suspicion. "You want us to go without limbs? *Not* to use the healing machine?"

"No, Majesty, you misunderstand me. I think what I can do is make you adjust *mentally* to your . . . to what you think of as your shame."

Ti-blan grew haughty and cold. "It is our shame, outlander, but you need not mock us. You are not so different . . . not now."

Barney gulped softly. "I . . . I suspected that. *You* call your ability to change shape your shame, because you cannot control it. But suppose you *could* control it? Suppose it was something that was a *blessing?*"

The king started. "A *blessing?* How could such a curse ever be a *blessing?*" He looked for help to his mother and the elders.

"One man's meat is another man's poison," Barney said, then regretted it at once, for their expression grew angry.

"Poison?" the queen mother snapped. Several of the green-scaled warriors around the room stirred angrily.

"A saying, Majesty, just a saying. An Earth saying . . . it means what might be a curse to one is a blessing to another."

"How can that be?"

Barney looked around, saw a small table with a tray of food. "Food, for example, Your Highness. You like or dislike certain food, do you not? Yet you know others who like what you dislike, or detest what you love?"

"Yes, of course, but what has that . . . oh." He frowned, exchanging looks with his mother. "You mean that to someone, somewhere, our . . . our ability to . . . to change might be considered something . . . beneficial?"

"Yes. A hunter, for example, could change into that which he hunts and get very close."

The young ruler laughed suddenly. "He might be surprised during the mating season!"

"Warriors, Your Majesty. They could become winged creatures, fly to the highest castle, change into the formidable fighting men I see here. Your people could become whatever they needed for a particular job . . . small to . . . to crawl into secret places, or large, to do heavy work, or into beautiful winged dancers . . ." The startled expression on Ti-blan's face caused him to stop.

"But what would make them do this? We do not change just to dance. In battle, yes, we become what . . . what we become, what is needed. But that is fear. It is always fear . . ."

"But suppose, Majesty, you could do this metamorphosis at will, change when you want, into what you desire." Barney took a half step closer to the blood-red throne. "To *control* this gift . . ."

"Gift?" the queen mother said in surprise. "The Zull gave us no *gift!*"

"Mother," Ti-blan said cautiously. He turned to Barney, his face fighting to remain calm. "You could do this?"

"No."

"Then what—" the young king began angrily, but stopped as Barney raised a hand.

"I cannot do this for you, Majesty . . . but *you* can. All of you," he added, gesturing around.

"We—?"

"Yes, Your Highness, *you* can do it. At least I think you can. What you have to do is to stop thinking of this ability to change as a curse, but to think of it as a positive thing, a wondrous thing."

The expression on Ti-blan's face was suddenly rapturous and one of the elders stepped forward, his voice filled with caution. "Heed me, Ti-blan. This creature is an outlander. Who knows what are his motives, who—"

"Silence!" Ti-blan snapped, glaring at the elder. He looked scornfully around the room. There were other elders standing in the entrances to the passages leading off the room, clustered fearfully together. There were warriors and nobles as well, all holding back.

"Since the time of Ti-clar, the first of this noble line, the Seekers have sought." Ti-blan gave the elders a seering look. "We have made sacrifices. We have given the Seekers all they wanted—precious metals, jewels, slaves, captives, all the Zull machinery we could find. For *generations* they have hunched over their experiments, for *centuries* they have mumbled and chanted, dissected and dissolved, and for *what?*"

The Tigron leader looked angrily about him. None met his eyes except Barney. "None of you has found out *anything!* We fought the War of the Mists to get Kula prisoners that you might test their blood, and we fought the War of the Dagger Peaks so that other captives might be found."

The young king rose to his feet, his face flushed, his voice trembling. "What did we gain from this? The gel that transforms the innocent into ourselves . . . and the *threen!*"

The word "threen" seemed to galvanize the throng. They gasped and looked around warily, as if something powerful and deadly lurked in the branching passages.

"The *threen!*" the king repeated bitterly. "We created our own secret terror from the dark side of ourselves! Yes, the threen!" Ti-blan seemed to enjoy sending waves of fear into the surrounding people. Here and there Barney saw a man or woman suddenly stiffen or hunch, their faces and hands twisting, changing.

"Go on! Shame yourselves! Shame this throne! Shame the ancestors who shared your fate!" Ti-blan was almost shouting now and the queen mother took a step toward him, her own face trembling with fear. "Change!"

Ti-blan's hands stretched out and they seemed to gnarl, and his face

took on a darkened, wolfish look that could have been a trick of light-
ing. "Hide! Rut! Run! *Change!*"

"*Majesty!*" Barney's voice rang through the crystal cavern in a sharp
reprimand of command. The young ruler halted, swaying, then turned
slowly toward Barney. "Your Majesty, do not give in! *You* control the
change, the change does not control you!"

"I . . . I can't . . ."

"You *can!*" Barney took two steps toward the throne, but stopped at
the movement of a green-scaled guard. "You *all* can! *You* control it!"
Barney turned toward the nobles and elders backing away into the passages. "Stop! Stop and think! When you want to raise your hand, you
merely will it, do you not? When you wish to walk, you simply walk,
am I right?" Barney turned toward Ti-blan, who had slumped back on
the smoothed crystal sculpture of the throne.

"Your Majesty, it will not be easy. But on my planet there are those
who have astounding control over their bodies. They can slow their
heartbeat, put themselves into suspended animation, endure fire and
pain without even a welt—and all without the Zull healer. There are
those who can, *with only the power of their mind,* cause objects to
move, blood to flow or not to flow to a portion of their bodies, to do
other things."

Barney gestured at those around him. "Your Highness, what I have
seen here on Zandra—the mindsword of the Kula, your own astonishing ability to alter your cellular structure, the Zull healers, working directly on your DNA in some way—all this convinces me that
Zandrans can do things even greater, even more astonishing than the
people of my planet."

He paused, looking at the king for reaction. But the young monarch
was slumped wearily, staring at nothing, perhaps not even hearing Barney. "Majesty . . . perhaps all your Seekers have been looking in the
wrong place, that's what I mean. Perhaps the cure lies elsewhere, or in
a combination of both. You—all of you—have a duality you must face.
A double nature you *can* learn to control."

"But it is hormonal," one of the elders said. "We can no more control what happens when fear strikes than stop our ears from hearing, or
our eyes from seeing."

Barney said to him, "I saw you fighting the change. I saw your king
fighting it! And you *can* stop your ears, stop your sight. You close your
eyes, you concentrate your thoughts until you *do* not hear the sounds of
work, of rushing water, of traffic . . . no, you don't have traffic . . . uh,

we all learn to ignore certain sounds or smells or even sights. It is a matter of concentration and—"

"What would you have us do, man of Earth?" It was Ti-blan who had spoken in a weary voice. "I tire of the endless frustration. I would do anything, try anything to escape this prison of shame."

Barney smiled for the first time. "Maybe I am wrong, Your Highness, maybe I'm on the wrong track, but I have a few ideas."

"Try them," the young king said.

The cloudships had settled on a rock terrace which slanted into the mists. There could have been a drop of ten feet or ten thousand feet just off the lip of the rock, but no one knew. The cliffs rose, wet and sheer, above them as they huddled together in a group between the landed vessels.

"We'll just sit here a bit," Mace said, "and keep our eyes and ears open. And quiet," he said softly.

Eve squatted near Mace and she touched his arm. "What do you think Barney is doing? Why did he go back?"

"I don't know. Maybe . . ." He looked around and saw Liberty listening to them. "You knew Barney before, right?"

The black actress nodded. "Uh-huh. He was a nice guy, but always kind of distant. Like maybe he was uncomfortable with people, you know? Great with animals, though. Everyone said so. Like telepathy, dig? They did things for him none of the trainers could do. You see *Jungle Queen?*" At their expressions she shrugged. "Never mind. But they had a leopard in that epic, and let me tell you they are *mean* critters. She bit one actor, but when they brought in Barney with his lions, Barney just sat down and had a talk with that beastie."

"A *talk?*" Eve said.

Liberty Crockett nodded. "Uh-huh. Went off into the bushes and just sat and talked for an hour or so. Damndest thing you ever saw. After that the leopard was like some kinda house cat . . . at least when Barney was around. Thing used to lounge all over me—"

"I remember the poster," Mace said suddenly. "Cat all kittenish against your legs."

"That's the one. People think it was stuffed or something, or doped, but it wasn't. The point *is*, Barney kind of had something special going with animals. Cats, anyway, but I saw him with horses, a couple of elephants, and I heard he cooled down a water buffalo, for crying out loud!"

"You think he thinks of the Tigron as animals?" Eve asked.

Liberty shrugged. "Beats me. But he's awfully good at animal training and those Tigron—" She shuddered delicately. "They change *into* animals . . ."

"But what did he hope to *do?*" Mace grumbled quietly. "After what they did to him . . ."

"What *was* that stuff they put on him, anyway?" Eve asked but Mace made a gesture of ignorance.

"It was . . . alive in some way. Like intelligent Jell-O," he said.

"Mace, this is a strange world," Eve said.

This caused both Mace and Liberty to laugh softly. "If I could get a camera crew here for a few weeks I could make something that would line 'em up around the block," Liberty said cheerfully. "Intelligent dinosaurs, antigravity ships, Tigron, these space vikings or whatever the Kurkans are . . . wow, and not one dime for special effects!"

"Holl-lee-wood," Eve sang softly, and Liberty grinned at her.

"And werewolves or whatever," the actress said, jerking a thumb back toward the Tigron caverns.

Ironthroat shushed them, pointing out into the mists. At once swords whispered from their scabbards. To Mace's surprise Falana stepped from between the ships and stood near the edge of the drop-off, a slight wind moving her cape, droplets of water glistening in her thick dark hair.

"Falana!" Mace whispered urgently, "Get back here!"

She ignored the soldier and stood imperiously, head up. Mace looked at Ironthroat questioningly. The Kurkan whispered, "I thought I heard a Zurian curse. The one about rotting in your grave alive."

Mace nodded and put his finger to his lips to warn the others. Then he stood up and on careful feet he went out to where the Kula princess stood.

"What do you think you're doing?" he said softly into her ear, gripping her arm beneath the cape.

She shook free and glared at him, but her voice was not loud as she reprimanded him. "To touch a noble without permission is death, Mace Wilde!"

"To stand out here is death, Princess Falana. Do you really still think they won't kill you?"

She looked at him angrily, then snapped her head back toward the chasm filled with mist. "They will, you know, the second they see you."

"They might *try*," she said through clenched teeth. Mace felt her shiver and then stiffen.

"You're scared, aren't you?"

Falana snapped her head around and glared at him, her voice rising. "Scared? A princess of Zandra *frightened*?"

"Hey!" Mace said soothingly, looking out into the swirling wet mist. "Keep it down." Falana glared at him one more time, then returned to her imperious gaze out over the chasm. Mace looked thoughtfully at her a moment.

"You know, Falana," he said softly, "I gotta hand it to you. You're scared to death and your way of fighting it is to bluff it out, to *dare* the baddies to try. Lady, I don't think I'd like to play poker with you!"

Falana gave him a puzzled look and her lips formed the word "poker" silently, but then she looked back into the misty void. "The heir to the throne of Zandra cannot appear frightened."

"Ahh," Mace said very quietly, close to her ear. She still smelled exotically fragrant, despite all their adventures. "*Appear* frightened . . . ah, yes . . . leaders can never appear frightened, or uncertain, but they can *be* frightened. I have been, many times."

Falana gave him another look, but it was not a glare. "You? But you are a great warrior! You . . . you even defied *me* . . ."

"All warriors are frightened, Princess, if they have the slightest hint of a mind. No one cares to die, at least not any normal person. I get scared all the time. I'm scared now, but—"

"Now? You are frightened *now*?" She pulled away slightly to look him up and down. "You do not appear so." Then she raised her chin again. "Nor does a princess-daughter of Morak, Emperor of Zandra!"

"Falana, would you get off that princess stuff for a while? *You* are the reason the Zurians are after us. They'd probably not bother with just a few escaped prisoners. Not this long, anyway. You're the one they are after. What must I do to convince you?"

"Earthman, you are the most exasperating man I ever met!" Falana's voice snapped sharply and Mace grabbed for her mouth, clamping a hand over her lips before more could be said. She struggled angrily, her eyes glaring and Mace thought she was about to use the mindsword on him.

But she found something else to use her mental weapon on.

A black cloudship drifted up suddenly and silently, parting the mists. Black-armored Zurians cried out in ferocious glee as they brought up strongbows. On the central control mast an armored Zurian fought to swing a snouted weapon mounted on the rim around to bear on the sudden target. A muscular commander on the deck shouted only one word.

"Kill!"

"Just relax, Your Majesty," Barney said. They were in the king's private chambers, a great round room carved from the heart of a crystal lode. Soft lights filtered through the facets of the walls, giving the room a shadowless light. The young ruler sat in a chair of carved wood, depicting feathered serpents entwined with flowers.

Behind Ti-blan was the queen mother, two of the plainly robed elders, and four of the senior warriors, green-scaled giants with permanently suspicious looks. Nearby stood a young Tigron woman named Ti-tang, who, if Barney had taken time to think about it, he would have found quite beautiful. She had been brought in because of all the Tigron she was the only one with any information about what the dead Seekers had been researching. She stood quietly, garbed in gray, her dark eyes watchful.

"On my world we call this hypnotism," Barney said. He lifted a jeweled pendant and set it swinging rhythmically before the eyes of the young king. "Just concentrate on this . . . watch it . . . think of nothing else . . ."

The adolescent ruler stirred slightly, frowning, but Barney's words droned on, soothingly, lulling him into a sense of ease. Barney was not as confident of his abilities as he seemed, for his experience with hypnotism had been confined to reading a few books and some parlor games. However, he knew, in a sense, what he seemed to project to his cats was a kind of hypnotism . . . or maybe extrasensory projection.

Ti-blan seemed to go into a trance with ease and Barney tested him with a simple request that the king raise his arm and hold it out for some time, without becoming tired, which the young man did. Satisfied that Ti-blan was truly in a trance, Barney began to talk to him about the Tigron shape-changing ability.

"Your ability to transform your cellular structure is a power, not a weakness. It is not a shameful curse, but rather a marvelous ability to be nurtured and controlled." Barney repeated this theme over and over, with variations, getting at first a reluctant agreement from Ti-blan, a doubtful acquiescence, then a more enthusiastic response.

Satisfied that he had established a first step, Barney brought Ti-blan from his trance. The young ruler looked around in slight bewilderment, then turned to his mother and the elders. "Am I cured?" he asked.

"Your Majesty," Barney said quickly, before anyone could speak. "It is not a matter of cure, but of acceptance, of discipline, and control. There is no 'cure' as such, there is only a *use* of your genetic structure."

"No cure?" the young monarch frowned. "I will still . . . still change?"

"Yes, Your Majesty, but when *you* want to change, not when your fear overtakes you."

The queen mother touched her son. "Ti-blan, I am not certain what this outlander says and does is true, but . . ." She gave the elders a long look. "But something must be done. The matter of the arm proves that you are capable of extraordinary feats."

"Arm?" the king asked and it was explained to him. But Barney quickly added more information.

"Not just you, Majesty, but *anyone* can do that, if properly trained. The point is that you want a solution for all your people, not just a selected few, is that not correct?"

"Yes, of course." Ti-blan indicated the green-scaled warriors. "What of them? Once they changed, they have remained the same."

Barney shrugged. "I do not know. Perhaps nothing can be done. You tried putting them in a Zull healer?"

"Yes, yes," Ti-blan said impatiently. "They stayed the same."

"Then perhaps their genetic structure has been permanently altered. Are they the only ones in that condition?"

"No, there are others. The Seekers all were, and a few others. Those who changed too often became . . . became what they became in time. Too many fears, too many changes and the bodies they were born with grew inflexible. But they never came to the state of unchangeability in their original forms, only in their . . . their changeling form."

Barney made a face. "I will have to study this."

"Ti-tang will help you," the king said. "Leave me. I wish to think upon this day."

Barney left the crystal room, followed by Ti-tang, but escorted by four of the hulking green-scaled changeling warriors.

"What you did was magic," Ti-tang said as they walked through a snaking passage to the quarters Barney had been assigned.

"No, just low-level technology . . . and pretty much an untested one, too." He sighed. "I wish I knew more, but I *think* the only way is to get in behind the conscious mind, to get through the wall that we all surround ourselves with, even in our mind."

"This is done on your planet?" Ti-tang asked. They reached Barney's rooms, an enlarged cave with smoothed floors and walls hung with tapestries for warmth, and a thick rug of patchy fur.

"To some extent," Barney answered. "There is a lot of discussion and experimentation. There is what we call psi research, as well as ESP, and other explorations of the paranormal." He smiled wryly. "There's also something called the Power of Positive Thinking, and I think that might be the important thing."

Barney dropped into a padded chair and gestured for Ti-tang to do the same. The warriors had remained outside. "What did your Seekers know about the . . . the changing?"

Ti-tang shrugged. "They repeated the same experiments over and over. Using the Questioner . . . the gel that, um, you held in your hands—"

"Ugh," Barney said with a shudder, remembering. "What *was* that stuff?"

"Sentient protoplasm. It is a substance, a creature, a creation of the Zull research. It is very ancient. They keep an egg of it and when they need more they simply activate it in some way I am not permitted to know. And it expands. They slice off what they need and use it. It enters the body, grows and examines and then what it knows appears on a screen of the healer."

"A diagnostic invader," Barney muttered, shivering again. "And that's all they tried?"

Ti-tang nodded. "Usually, yes. They tried severing the limbs of a criminal once—we do not get many of those, as their constant fear gives them away—keeping her alive as they investigated the portions."

"My god," Barney said with disgust.

Ti-tang nodded her head in agreement. "It was not pleasant for anyone, but even the criminal agreed that anything must be tried. She was as ashamed of her fear-change as any of us."

Barney scratched at his face. "This threen which Ti-blan mentioned—" He stopped as an expression of fear crossed Ti-tang's face. "What *is* this thing which causes so much fear just by mentioning it?"

Ti-tang gave a look around, her face tense. Barney thought he saw a brief darkening of her skin, a stirring in her dark hair. "The threen . . . they are very ancient, very ancient . . ." Her voice trailed off and she abruptly got up, hugging herself and striding back and forth nervously. "When the Zull first began their experiments they produced the threen from . . . from their subjects."

"They experimented on humans, I mean on the Kula?"

"There was no Kula then, only Chuma, and the other races. The Kula . . . we Kula . . . are part of the result of that . . . that experimentation. But they . . . we . . . came later. First were the threen."

Ti-tang strode nervously around for a moment before she again spoke. "The threen were . . . are . . . monsters. They . . . they can change shape, too, but they are fearsome things. They escaped the Zull place of experimentation and hid. They lived on, multiplying and growing in their powers. They live in these mountains . . . and elsewhere . . . and . . ."

"Yes?"

"Their food is . . . the children of the Zull." She gave a tremor and abruptly sat down.

"You mean they eat the Tigron?"

"Not just us, but any . . . any Kula, Chuma, even Zurians. They attack and . . . and there is no defense."

"It sounds as if you have a superstitious fear of these threen."

Ti-tang gave him an angry look. "It is not superstition, outlander! My own sister, Ti-ming, was taken and . . . and killed. The son of my brother . . . the brother of my mother . . . our father's cousin . . . the king's own uncle . . . taken and *eaten*, their raw bones found in the deep caverns, smashed and . . ." Ti-tang gave a shuddering grunt and fell silent.

Barney gave her a moment, then spoke. "All right, the threen are not superstitions, but real. On my planet we have numberless legends and myths—the yeti, Frankenstein, werewolves, vampires, pagan gods, and so on. Most of them have no basis in fact—"

"The threen are real!" Ti-tang snapped.

"All right, all right, I believe you. That is not the point. What I must . . . what we must make real is the confidence to control and discipline and *use* your power to change and not have it use you."

"That is not possible."

"Anything is possible, including the impossible and the absurd," he responded with a grin, quoting Mussolini.

"You Earthmen are strange beyond belief," Ti-tang said with a wan smile and a shake of her head.

One of the scaled warriors stuck his head through the entrance to Barney's quarters. "Come! Ti-blan has gone out the Gate of Darkness!"

Ti-tang gasped and stood up, all tense. Barney grabbed her arm. "What does that mean?"

"The Gate of Darkness is through the wall that protects us from the threen in the northern caverns!"

"You mean Ti-blan is going after a *threen?*"

"No—he is testing himself!"

"To see if he changes from the fear of a threen?"

"Yes!" Ti-tang ran out of the room and Barney sprinted after her.

When the Zurian cloudship lifted above the stone terrace Mace grabbed Falana, wrapped his arms around her, and threw them both backward, behind a knob of rock. His Terran muscles, their strength multiplied by Zandra's lesser gravity, propelled them to shelter, but the landing brought a loud grunt from Mace.

Falana cursed and fought free of Mace's arms and started to rise, but Mace pulled her back just as a flight of arrows shot from the bows of Eve, Du, and Mouthfire. Firearm's own laser pulsed twice before it lost its charge.

Mace rolled over and took a quick glance around the rock. The laser operator was gagging on an arrow in his throat, and two of the Zurians had arrows in their writhing bodies. There was a smoking weal across Durak's black armor but he was bellowing commands. The dark ship dropped, then curved out of sight into the mists.

"Into the ships!" Mace shouted, reaching down to lift up Falana.

The Zandran princess wrenched her arm free of his hand, glaring at him. "You fool! If they had seen me they would not have fired!"

"Princess," Mace said, pointing toward the cloudships, "they *did* see you! Now get aboard!"

Falana drew herself up with a sniff. "In any case, I could have killed the disobedient dogs if you had not tumbled me."

"Princess, get aboard! We want to get out of here before they come back." He cast a wary eye at the surrounding monotony of gray mist.

Falana took another long inhalation, then with deliberate slowness she picked her way across the rock and gracefully started up the ramp into Redpike's cloudship. Mace called out to her but she stepped into the bowl-shaped ship without a word.

Mace jumped into his own vessel and cursed as he brought up the ramp. "Up ship! Up ship!" he called. "Redpike—you watch her!"

"Aye, Captain," the Kurkan warrior growled.

They lifted into the mists and kept close together and silent. Mace looked around, checking for faces. They had all scrambled aboard so quickly that the ships now had different passenger lists. Skylance still piloted Mace's ship, and Ironthroat piloted Redpike's, but that ship held Falana, Richter, Count Jardek, and Mouthfire, the Kurkan warrior-woman. Liberty Crockett was now aboard Mace's ship, with Eve and Longtalon, Du and Firearm.

The Kurkan warrior with the laser forearm came grumbling up to Mace. "By the naked talons of the Great Bird, Earthman, what a time to run out of power! I had that cursed Durak in my beam, but it was not strong enough to gut him!"

"We'll get you recharged soon," Mace said, slapping the old warrior on his battered backplate. "I think it was your hit that drove them off, though."

The Kurkan grinned happily. "Generals hate to hear the sound of steel, don't they?"

"I don't think Durak is a coward," Mace said. "But finding us was just as big a surprise to them as to us. Now they know we are around here somewhere and not scampering off through some mountain pass."

"Maybe that is what we should do then?" the warrior said, watching Mace's face.

"No, not yet. I can't . . . I can't leave Barney behind."

"He wanted to be left behind, Captain, it was no accident."

"I know," Mace nodded. "But he's still one of us."

Firearm grinned and gave Mace's back such a resounding clap that they both stopped, looking around in apprehension. The grizzled Kurkan pulled Mace down and whispered fiercely, "That's good, that's good, Earthman. You do not desert a warrior until he is dead and not even then, not if you can bring back the body." He gave Mace another muscular slap and grinned widely. "You might do yet, Mace Wilde, son of Adam and Sara."

Mace's answering smile faded as he turned back to the curving railing. The wet mists seemed endless. Redpike's ship was only a bobbing silhouette, but Mace could make out Falana's cape-wrapped figure at the railing.

So she wanted a little time away from me, he thought. *I hope nothing happens to separate us. She's our ticket to get out of here.* But something troubled the tall warrior. Was his feeling for her solely that of a commander entrusted with the responsibility for her? Reluctantly, he decided that was not completely the case.

But she's not very likable, he thought. *She's haughty and arrogant, likely to get us or herself killed, and she's generally a pain in the neck.* But the appeal of her wanton sexuality was strong, he admitted reluctantly. But it was more than that, he knew. Falana was a challenge . . . as well as an exotic dream.

I'm an incurable romantic in search of a medical miracle, he thought. *I'm a cliché: the young adventurer and the exotic princess.* But he grinned. *And I like it.*

Momentary guilt attacked him. *Am I doing my best to get these people back to Earth? Or do I really want to stay here myself? Richter would probably want to stay, his scientific curiosity being what it is. Liberty's a star back home and that is nothing to give up easily.*

Eve? Mace looked around and saw Eve standing close to the Kurkan Longtalon, her strongbow strung over her shoulder, and his arm around her. *Maybe Eve might want to stay, too.*

And Barney? About Barney he was not at all certain.

But what about all the others? Airworld Nine's survivors, as well as the many who had been sucked into the Vandorian beam over the centuries? Surely some of them would want to return.

He had to keep trying.

Even if he got killed doing it.

The queen mother was at the partially opened gate, looking on helplessly as a platoon of green-scaled Tigron warriors filed back through. The young officer in command spoke in harsh tones.

"Great Mother of Kings, we found no trace. The marks of his sandals stopped after he walked upon the inner rock."

The queen mother looked at the trembling elder behind her. Their eyes were on the heavy wooden door with its bindings of precious metal. It was set into a thick masonry wall but beyond was darkness.

And threen.

The queen mother looked at Barney as he ran up, following the fleet Ti-tang. "You," she said with suppressed fury. "You made him think he could fight a threen. Your skinless body will be a threen feast tonight, your—"

"Majesty!" Ti-tang said quickly. "It was the bravery of Ti-blan which made him seek out the . . . the threen." Her words were punctuated by the clang of the door and the thumping of several stout timbers locked across it.

"Ti-blan cannot fight a *threen,*" one of the elders said, his face tense with fear. "No one can fight a *threen* . . . and live."

The queen mother sent him a withering glance, then turned her hot gaze back to Barney. "Earthman . . . outlander . . . meddler . . . you caused this and for this you shall die!"

Green warriors seized Barney and he winced with the pain from their taloned hands, but his voice rang out in the rock passage. "Then execute me by throwing me after Ti-blan!"

The queen mother gasped, as did the elders. Even the permanently changed Tigron warriors were taken aback. "You . . . you would go *willingly* into . . . into *there?*" an elder asked.

"Well, uh, not willingly, but . . . what have I to lose? If I find Ti-blan before one of these threen do, then maybe I can get him to return. If not . . ." He swallowed noisily. "Then I will be dead, as you seem to wish."

The queen mother stared moodily at him for a long moment, then without removing her gaze from Barney's face, she ordered the heavy gate reopened. The reptilian warriors thrust him through, but before they could close the heavy door Ti-tang slipped through.

One of the warriors shouted hoarsely but the door was slammed shut and the dull, hollow thumps they heard indicated the dead bolts of thick wood. Barney just looked at Ti-tang with exasperation.

"Now why did you do that? Don't I have enough to look after?"

"You don't have to look 'after' me, Earthman; I look 'after' myself!" She looked at him defiantly.

Barney waved at the darkness beyond the dim light of the glowballs hung over the gate. "You know even better than I about what is out there, and still you *volunteer?*"

"Precisely, Barney Boone," she responded primly, using his name for the first time. "I can help. What little is known about the threen, I know. And Ti-blan is my king."

Barney sighed and eyed the closed gate. "They aren't likely to let you back in, at least not until Ti-blan gets back. They were sweating it with the gate open just a bit. Your threen must be something fierce."

"They are," Ti-tang said solemnly. Suddenly all business she looked around until she found two sticks with thongs fastened to the end. Then she lifted down two of the Zull glowballs and Barney saw that the thongs were a kind of net into which she fit a glowball. She handed Barney one and held the other up herself. Her face was tense, but she forced a smile as she said, "Shall we go?"

"Look, I'm the dumb one here, going after something I have no information about, but you must be either the least sane or the most courageous one, because you *do* know what the threen are like."

Ti-tang did not answer, only braced herself, gave him a tight smile, and started along the sandy path between the arching walls of rock.

Barney sighed and nodded and followed her.

"We're off to see the Wizard," he said tonelessly, "the wonderful Wizard of Oz."

The sandy path gave way to rock. Sometimes there was a natural path, a smoothed place that twisted around the pieces fallen from the roof of the cavern in eons past, or went between ancient stalagmites thrusting up from the floor, built up by the droplets of millennia. Other places they had to clamber down dangerous cliffs, cross clefts and ravines that dropped away into nothingness, where the weak light of the glowballs failed to reveal anything.

They passed through huge dark caverns and squeezed through slits in the natural stone. Here and there were the signs of previous passages: a scratching on the rock where armor had scraped, a rotting pack of some sort, discarded in a hurry, some bones, the marks of fire pits. At one of the rest stops some ancient warriors had scratched messages into the stones: *Char-ti-blood hunted threen here. Jukk-ti-wor, in the Year of the Famine, came this far. Lor-ti-throm eats threen for first meal. Prince Ti-Warra died near here in the Year of the Thunder. Threen eat their droppings!*

Defiant words in the darkness of the night cavern. Barney looked at Ti-tang. She was tense and nervous, but still she went on. The scratchings of trained, armed warriors showed their fear, but the young Seeker was controlling hers. Or so it seemed.

And they moved on. Deeper into the darkness. Toward the threen.

The mists were veils of wet gray through which the Zull cloudships passed. They caught brief glimpses of black, bare rock but the automatic ranging devices kept them well out from the cliffs, or centered the ships between opposing masses if there was little room.

Liberty came up to where Mace stood on the forward lip of the circular vessel. She paused a moment, studying the one they had all voted to be their leader.

He looks worried, she thought. *Concerned. Alert. Not bad casting. A little offbeat, but not bad at all.* His black Zurian armor was beaded with cold droplets, his dark curly hair wet. *A curious man,* the actress thought. *When most people avoid responsibility, he takes it. When most wield their power badly, he does not.*

But the circumstances were beyond any one person's ability to fully correct. *He's a survivor, like me,* she thought. *I could do worse than hook up with him. Together, we could—*

She abruptly halted that line of reasoning. She knew that he would never give up that responsibility to his fellow Terrans, that any liaison with him would be marred by his "marriage" to that responsibility. *But there's no harm in having him receptive,* the black actress thought.

She gave a shiver and made a growling sound which brought Mace's attention around to her. She grinned ruefully and moved in close to him. "Cold," she said. Mace nodded and continued his alert checking of the gray world before them. "Hug me, you bum, I'm cold."

"Go inside then," he said, but he let her snuggle close against him. They were silent, companionable rather than erotic in their closeness. The sensual black actress felt his warmth and smelled his unique mansmell and felt a little safer than she had in some time.

"Looks like an old Sherlock Holmes movie," she said, lifting her chin from the wrapping of her cape.

Mace grinned at her. "Still think the Great Director in the sky is going to call 'Cut'?"

"Just as long as it isn't a wrap, nice working with you, goodbye, and your option has been dropped."

They fell silent again. *This is a crazy world,* she thought. *Utterly bizarre. Big-budget weirdness. Like Flash Gordon and Edgar Rice Burroughs rolled into one.* "You know," she said aloud, "when I did some of those pictures, playing the Queen of Lost World or the Queen of Venus or whatever, I never believed it. Oh, I *looked* like I believed it, that's part of my trade. But I never thought any of them had ever—or ever *would*—have adventures like this!"

"Adventure," Mace said softly. "You get into it all too easy, but getting out . . ." He laughed quietly. "Edmondson said adventure is the past participle of disaster. But . . ."

"Yes?"

"Well, you're dead from the time nothing excites you, though it may be years before anyone notices and buries you."

"You, uh, you look for adventure?"

"Oh, no!" Then Mace quickly reversed himself. "Unless being a professional soldier is looking for adventure. Maybe it is." He shrugged. "Mostly it's just survival."

"Where are we, anyway?"

Mace shrugged. "Going back in the general direction of the Tigron caverns," he said wearily. "But I think we've gotten down some other canyon."

"Those . . . those Tigron give me the shivers. It's like a special effects department going berserk. Wolfman time for real."

They were silent a bit, the mists thickening and thinning around them. Mace could hear Skylance in the mast swearing at the blinding fog. Ironthroat, in the trailing ship, called out to Skylance, and on the "starboard" side Firearm muttered a Kurkan curse.

"We gonna get out of this, Mace?" Liberty asked.

Mace grinned at her, taking his attention from the search ahead for a moment. "Tune in next week for the further adventures of Liberty Crockett and her band of Earth people!"

She gave him an elbow, then swore as she banged her arm on his armor. "No, really, you lout—are we?"

"Your guess is as good as mine, Lib."

"Meaning no?"

"Meaning I don't know. I know we won't stop trying, though."

You mean, you won't stop trying, she thought. Well, that does it. Liberty, honey, you better start thinking of setting up a good gig right here. Let your stardom shine on Zandra, baby.

Liberty drifted away, hugging her cape to her, her mind miles away from the present predicament. *Somewhere, she thought, but where? I'm black, the Zurians are black, maybe we can make some kind of deal. But the thought made her squirm. No, they're black in color, but that's all; they're the Bad Guys. Their black is not beautiful.*

But the Good Guys are damned few, she told herself. The only thing we have going for us is a little advantage on strength because of lesser gravity . . . and our alien minds. She smiled to herself. Yes, we are the aliens here. Let's make that work for us. We can be the random factor, the disruptive element. The wild card.

Liberty Crockett knew only two ways to get ahead: get in with the Establishment or turn the Establishment on its ear. Conformity or revolution. Maybe there were other ways, but she might be killed before they came about.

Well, the Establishment doesn't seem to want us—except as slaves—so the only alternative is revolution. Upset their apple cart and grab some apples. Find a weak spot and exploit it. Stake out a turf.

Her mind made up, Liberty Crockett breathed in a lungful of wet Zandran air. *Okay, weird world, watch out! Liberty Crockett declares war!*

Barney helped Ti-tang over a sharp-edged rock, a long-ago fallen fragment of the vaulted ceiling. The glowballs, bobbing at the ends of their sticks, cast shifting shadows, making Barney nervous for they seemed like movement in the dark.

"These threen, what are they like?"

Ti-tang paused, looking around as she spoke, holding high the glowball stick. "Big. Deadly. You'll see."

"Oh, thanks. They are certain, are they?"

"No one has gone this far and returned, I think."

"Where does this cavern go, anyway?"

Ti-tang climbed another rock and Barney followed her. "To the long valley. The threen sometimes feed there."

"They're animals, then?" he said, asking the question again.

The young Tigron female gave him a dark look. "Not exactly."

Her reluctance to talk annoyed Barney. "Come on, tell me. If Tiblan meets one of these threen and he isn't able to . . . to control himself, he might . . ."

"Go on." Ti-tang stopped and looked at him levelly.

"He might not change back, if the scare is big enough. Or he might *not* change, I don't know. Your body chemistry is a mystery to me."

"He is our brave king. His father was Ti-dorn and his mother is Ti-too, daughter of Ti-wari, the Great King. He is—"

"Okay, okay, spare me the genealogy chart. Look, just describe one of these threen."

"Tell me your nightmares."

"Never mind that; the threen—"

"The threen *are* your nightmares. One of them, two of them, maybe all of them. Everything you fear, the threen will become. A threen will appear one way to me, if I am its prey, and another to you, if you are its target."

"Telepathy?"

She frowned and Barney realized the Zull machine that had enabled them to speak the Zandran tongue had its limitations. "Mind power?" he suggested, and she nodded. "They read my mind and become what I fear?"

Ti-tang nodded, taking his arm and urging him on. "If they can. Your nightmare might be too obscure for them."

"Because I'm from Earth?"

She nodded. "Or they might mix them, say becoming a cross between a cavern spider and a fast cat."

"So I'll know one when I see something I fear the most?"

Ti-tang shrugged. "Or something I fear the most."

"Which is—?" But the attractive young Tigron was skipping ahead across a stretch of water-smoothed rock. Barney Boone sighed and hastened to catch up to her.

The cavern eventually lightened and Barney heaved a sigh of relief as they saw light ahead. It was diffused and dim, filtered through a vast mist, but clearer here than where the cloudships flew. Before them was a forest of multicolored fungi, enormous tree-sized lumps of organic growths. The colors were all subtle, pastels and muted golds, pale white and soft blue.

Ti-tang pointed at a footprint in the moist soil. "Ti-blan." She started to follow the direction, but Barney stopped her.

"Listen."

"For what?"

"Just *listen!*"

"I hear nothing . . ." But Barney had put his hand over her mouth. She stared at him indignantly but softened and her shoulders dropped slightly.

There was a soft wind moving the mist through the rounded tops of the fungi forest twenty feet over their heads. Occasional distant tweets caught his ear and he indicated the sound with a stab of his finger.

"Calling-thorms," she whispered. "Feathered lizards."

Sound was very important in a forest or jungle, Barney knew. To man, raised in a city, one grew used to a steady level of sound and blocked most of it out. To one raised in a forest, or upon a desert, sound was also important, but there was less of it and therefore less to block out so you could think. But in a forest, or any wild place, you were advised to listen. To look. To smell.

Satisfied there was nothing threatening he could identify, Barney and Ti-tang started into the columned forest. Within a few feet they were all but lost. The mist blurred the distance or obliterated it and the lumps and hemispheres and thrusting columns blocked their view.

And that was when the threen attacked.

"Ho," Skylance called softly.

"Ho," responded Ironthroat from the other ship.

Mace jumped to the base of the thick control mast. "What is it?" he whispered.

Du looked over the edge and pointed off to one side. "The cavern entrance!"

"Set it down," Mace said softly and then heard Skylance's whistled command to the linked cloudship. The two Zull vessels settled to the ground near the dark entrance. They all agreed it was indeed the same spot.

Mace let down the ramp. "Redpike, take command. I'm going in. Firearm, Mouthfire, come with me."

"Hey!" Eve protested.

Mace looked up at the faces lining the railing of each ship. "Listen, this is not a democracy. We don't take votes on orders, especially battle orders. Now the rest of you stay here. I just want a couple to watch my back. This is not an invasion, but an inquiry. Got that?" he snapped at Eve.

She humphed, but kept silent. "Give me three hours, then take off," he told Redpike.

Princess Falana sauntered down the ramp and stood at the bottom, looking around with idle curiosity. "Get aboard, Princess," Mace said. "If they have to lift in a hurry they won't want to have to look for you."

She stared at him imperiously and did not move. Their eyes met and after a moment she gave a delicate shrug and reboarded Redpike's vessel.

Mace gestured at the two Kurkans and they walked up the slope and into the darkness of the cavern.

What came out of the fungi forest was a charging bull elephant. An African elephant, trumpeting, its broad shoulders knocking chunks out of the smooth-skinned fungi columns. A *Loxodonta africana*, Barney noted. Part of his mind was saying, "Why an African and not an Indian? Why not the smaller-eared *Elephas maximus?*" And part of him was struck dumb with raw fear.

Trapped in the confines of the fungi, attacked by the largest land animal on Earth, Barney knew great fear.

But fear was nothing new. When Sultan had laid back his tigerish ears in the cage in Sacramento, hissing at his biggest lion, Solomon, he knew he was in deep trouble. The delicate balance of tiger and lion was wrecked.

Barney knew he was experiencing that strange phenomenon known as "time-stretch," when even the swiftest of events seems to take a very long time. Barney thought of it as having all the time that was needed to make a decision—and not one nanosecond longer.

But there was time for fear.

Great fear.

He felt suddenly hot. His muscles ached. His head throbbed. The forest seemed to brighten. Scents became sharp, almost intolerable. Every sound seemed sharp and clear: the slight wind rustling the grasses, the brushing of the elephant's shoulders against the thick dry fungi, the distant cawing of some frightened bird.

Barney cried out, a great roar of defiance and anger. The elephant was almost upon him. Ti-tang fell backward, a strangled cry in her throat, tripping over a root.

Barney crouched to spring and as the gray monster loomed over him he leaped. The snakelike trunk lashed at him, the long white tusks slashed through the air where he had been, but he was atop the beast, his claws digging into the tough wrinkled hide, screaming hideously in a shrieking voice.

He clung to the broad skull as the great beast shook violently and attempted to dislodge him by butting into a fungi tree as large as a house. But Barney held on, reaching down with his talons to rip at the left eye of the elephant. The pachyderm trumpeted and rolled his head violently, but Barney felt something soft and thrust his claws into it.

The elephant reared, trumpeting, screaming, shrinking, almost dissolving under Barney's talons. Barney leaped off as the creature became something smaller, something whimpering with pain. Whirling on the moist ground Barney leaped again, sailing over the huddled animal; his powerful back legs slashed down, laying open raw flesh across the head and neck.

He landed on all fours, slid and banked against a fungi pod cluster, crushing some of them, releasing a pungent odor. He snarled, his jaws wide, going for the throat of the creature which was writhing in pain. But one of the creature's legs kicked at him, deflecting him so that he tumbled. Barney rolled to his feet, but the wounded thing was running away, bouncing off fungi trees on its blind side, spraying blood, its voice a wavering wail.

Barney stopped, panting, glaring fiercely after the departing attacker.

He tried to say something but his voice was a growl. The forest seemed to waver and he felt dizzy. He fell to his side, feeling foolish, staring up at the knobbed tops of the great fungi plants.

What's the matter with me?

Barney looked around weakly, his vision blurred, and he saw Ti-tang staring at him. He growled at her, embarrassed of his sudden weakness, but she only shrank back against the pitted surface of a fungus.

"I . . ." He croaked with a dry throat and lifted a hand toward her. "I need . . ." Then he stared at the hand he held out.

It was blunt and hairy, his fingers thick and curved. Even as he watched the aching fingers seemed to shrink, to thin out, the claws painfully becoming fingernails.

Oh, my god . . .

He stared at Ti-tang again, his eyes wide with sickness. *I have become one of them! I changed . . . I changed into . . . into what? A cat, a big cat.* His stomach churned. Up to that moment it had all been intellectual, with only suppressed feelings of fear.

But I've been changed! They changed me! I'm like them! I'm a monster!

He looked again at Ti-tang, but she was looking up, a sick and embarrassed expression on her face. "Ti-tang," he said. She closed her eyes, her mouth slack.

"Ti-tang . . ." She opened her eyes and looked at him with a feeling of sad compassion.

Barney sat up, his whole body aching as if he had taken a severe beating. He rose unsteadily to his feet, head pounding, and stood swaying. "I . . . I changed, didn't I?"

"Yes," she whispered.

"What . . . what was I?"

She gestured ignorance. "Some kind of long, sleek brown, uh, animal. A ferocious face. Hairy, with great . . . with great tusks."

Barney sighed. "A lion, I suppose. A panther. Something . . . something in between." He looked around him. The fungi forest seemed much quieter, much less fragrant, and darker. He kind of missed that.

He pointed down the winding path through the thick towers of fungus. She followed him, walking slowly, fighting her nausea.

The queen mother met Mace in the throne room, standing next to the empty throne. Robed advisers stood behind her and Mace was aware of the green-scaled warriors standing around the perimeter.

She glowered at Mace, his mouth a grim line. "My son went beyond the wall to his death. The line that began with Ti-clar in the time of the Zull dies today."

"Your Majesty, we—"

"Silence." She did not raise her voice, but there was authority in her tone. "It was you, you *Earth* people who made him think he was inadequate! That he could fight a *threen* and not . . . not *change!*" The disgust choked her. "But the one you seek went after him. Beyond the Gate of Darkness. They will die. Your companion, my son, and one of us who would die with them."

"Your Majesty, show us this wall. We are armed, good at fighting, we will find your son, and if we can, bring him back."

The queen mother stared moodily at Mace, her eyes studying the three. Firearm shifted uncomfortably under her dark stare, but Mouthfire looked back, head up and defiant. "Very well. Guards, show them through the wall into . . . into the land of the *threen.*"

The fungi forest became less thick, then great meadows appeared as they climbed higher. The mists were still around them, but it was lighter, yet colder. Barney took the lead, watching for signs: a scruffed patch of small fungus, a broken stalk, an overturned rock. He paused to look at a stem, broken and still oozing a pinkish fluid. "He can't be much farther ahead," he muttered.

Weapons at the ready, Mace and his two companions almost ran along the trail. There were no side caverns and no place for anyone to branch off, so they went as fast as they could, emerging into daylight and the fungi forest at a trot.

Mace pointed to the scraped sections of fungus trees, the crushed underbrush, and claw marks in the dirt. Without a word the trio hurried on. They were not far behind but time was running out.

Barney and Ti-tang heard the screams and cries before they found the young king. He was on a ledge, bloody sword in his hand, his whole left side red and useless. Below were two creatures from the nightmare world.

The sight brought Barney to a halt, with Ti-tang running into him, gasping. There was a rocky ridge. Halfway up was a ledge, where Ti-blan had retreated into a defensive position. But it was the two nightmare creations which had captured Barney's attention.

One was mottled gray, a thick round body on four thick legs, with a ruff of bony protuberances around a thin serpentine neck. The head was a death mask of bone and teeth. The other creature was pink, something like a shaved hog, only huge, larger than a horse, with tusks and horns and cloven hooves. Both of them scrabbled at the rock, snorting and whinnying, screaming out ear-deafening shrieks and thunderous grunts.

Ti-blan caught sight of the two arrivals and shouted at once. "Run! Go before they see you!" He slashed down at the death's head and the creature pulled back. But it was too late, the one like a grotesque boar saw them. It twisted about, snorting, staring at them.

Ti-tang grunted, then whimpered thinly. Barney felt as though a headache had been driven into his skull in the form of a spike. And the boar-creature changed.

It melted and flowed, the pink darkening, the thick neck reshaping itself, the legs curving back. Talons appeared. The piggish eyes slanted. Hair grew in a ruff.

The snake-necked creature paid no attention. It still darted its toothed mouth at Ti-blan's legs. Barney noted that although the young king was white-faced, he had not changed into something nonhuman.

But then Barney was given no time. He heard a choked sob and glanced at Ti-tang to see her cower, her face lengthening, her nose darkening. Her dark hair writhed and flowed. Her eyes hooded over. She moaned with pain, but the metamorphosis continued, reshaping her in radical ways. She dropped to all fours, her voice becoming thin, lapsing into yelps.

Barney felt his own fear surging through his body like liquid fire. He fought it even as he fought an intellectual battle, staring at the still-changing threen.

If I change I can defend myself. But if I change am I not committing myself, giving in to the shame that now runs in my blood? "I am human!" he snarled. His sword came whisperingly from its scabbard, clenched in a tight fist. His head ached so much he could hardly think. His muscles were tense, his stomach tight and sick.

"No!" *I am human!*

Without thinking, Barney launched himself at the threen that was now a fully grown lion, black-maned and angry. *They picked my mind! They chose the greatest of cats! But I have met them before!*

Barney walked boldly toward the snarling animal. *Not too fast, but show no fear. This is not a Terran cat, whose mind I might understand, but an alien animal assuming a form.*

Barney stopped, sword in hand, ignoring Ti-blan's continuing battle, focusing on the sight before him. *They are powerful, but their strength may be their weakness,* he thought. *They assume the protective coloration right out of the minds, of their adversaries. Perhaps if they sensed a rabbit was the most fearsome thing to me it would now be sitting there twitching its nose.*

Behind him, Ti-tang yelped defiance, but he didn't want to look at her, to see what she had changed into. The three-cat still did not attack. It even took a half step backward. *Can they be cowards?* Barney wondered. *Relying too much on whatever is in the minds of their prey?*

Barney laughed and took a step forward. "I've made dozens like you jump through hoops," he said cheerfully. "You've worked for me for years, giving me a good living, but obeying me every single day!" *Forgive me, Solomon, forgive me, Sheba, my friends.*

The three-cat looked bewildered and took another step back. Its shape rippled and it became larger in lumpish swellings. But it was just a larger lion, not some monster. The lion roared, but the sound was all wrong and Barney laughed.

"Back!" he snapped. He waved the sword and his voice cracked like a whip. *"Back!"*

The three hunched down, as if to leap, but its ears were laid back. *Function follows form,* Barney thought. *Look like a cat—act something like a cat.*

The lion roared, twisted around so quickly its back feet lost traction and the creature skidded. It ran off, changing as it ran, but Barney could not see what the new form became.

He turned with confidence toward the three menacing Ti-blan. The snake-headed creature twisted around, its tusks snapping, moving too fast for Barney to avoid. He felt a blow in the side, his sword was wrenched from his hand, and he was sent flying into the underbrush. Purple-flowered plants curled away from him, sending out puffs of pollen in defense, and two small white insects scrabbled out of the thicket, desperately searching for a new hiding place.

Barney felt the pain sweep over him like the blanket of night, and then there was only oblivion.

Ti-blan's arm was barely able to lift his sword when Mace and his companions found them. He was weak from blood loss and the three had pawed some new footholds in the rock, getting his death's head tusks even closer.

"Firearm!" shouted Mace and a ruby-red laser cut into the armored skin of the threen. It screamed and pulled away, the snake neck spasmodically twitching. Mace ran in, plunging his sword into the wound and twisting.

The threen screamed again, its back growing long tentacles in a second, but the tentacles wilted and fell, flowing back into the form as it shifted shape.

It shrank, the back legs growing into powerful limbs even as Mace took another hack at it. The threen keened shrilly and kicked, almost striking Mace, then ran off abruptly.

For a few seconds everyone just stood as they were, weapons at the ready, eyes and ears alert. Then the tension drained away as the sounds of the thrashing threen retreated.

"Captain Wilde, it seems you have saved me," Ti-blan said, his voice weak.

"You saved yourself, Majesty—by staying as you were and fighting." The young king smiled wanly and fainted.

Mace's strong Earth muscles gave him easy access to the ledge and in seconds he was tearing the young king's tunic into bandages. "Make a stretcher," he ordered the Kurkans, gathering the young king into his arms and jumping down. He put down the limp body and went quickly to Barney to examine him.

Much combat in various brush-fire wars had given Mace Wilde a certain minor skill in quick medical aid. He examined Barney, saw a bruised spot on his skull, contusions and scratches, but no serious wounds or broken bones.

"Make that two stretchers," he called out. Then he went to look at the wolfish shape that had been the attractive Ti-tang.

The queen mother almost smiled. "My son tells me he did not change," she said. "Oh, he wanted to, but he fought it." She looked around the crystalline throne room at the other Tigron nobles. "Perhaps . . . perhaps there is hope. I had not thought so, but now . . ."

She left the thought unfinished. She indicated the baskets of pale cavern fruit and slices of fungoid "meat" being brought in by bearers. "They will help you take this to your ship, Captain Wilde."

Mace thanked her graciously. As he turned to go back to the surface, he could not help noticing the look Ti-tang gave Barney. But Barney was still unconscious, lying on a stretcher carried by two of the green-scaled warriors. Mouthfire had already returned to the surface to warn the ships about what had happened.

"We must go," Mace said. "Tell Ti-blan we are proud of him."

The queen mother nodded gravely. "You brought us mixed blessings, man of Earth."

Mace nodded agreement and pointed the way out of the cavern. Firearm started off and the rest followed. Mace walked next to Barney's stretcher, watching him closely.

Something had happened to the lion tamer, something both physical and mental, and Mace felt helpless. *Perhaps Richter or Jardek can help, they know more about this sort of thing,* he thought. *At least, I hope they do.*

Skylance took the cloudship up into the mists. Mouthfire was next to him in the control mast. Eve, Longtalon, and Mace were equidistant around the circular ship, on watch. Falana was in the mast-cabin, ignoring everything and pleasuring herself with music.

They could see Ironthroat in the mast of the other ship in the thick fog, with Redpike next to him. Liberty and Du were seen at the railing, but Firearm, on the other edge, was lost in the swirling mists. Mace hoped that Richter and Jardek, in the cabin, were going to be able to bring the weak and feverish Barney back to health.

The ships were going along the gray mountains, eastward toward the dimly seen rising sun. They were soon at the top of their ability to lift yet there were sharp peaks lifting into the fog above them.

"There must be a pass," Mace muttered. "There *has* to be one." The gloomy prospect of going round and round in the land of Kardoon did not appeal. He longed for sunlight that was not filtered through thick mist and a view that was farther than a spear-throw.

Hours passed. Du called out that Barney was conscious and taking soup. Those on watch clutched their cloaks around their bodies and peered into the mists until they were red-eyed and exhausted. Night was coming when they found a dark slot in the granite walls.

"Try it!" Mace commanded, and the ships turned in.

The pass was dark and a chill wind cut through them. The cloudships bobbed and weaved on the turbulent air. Mace lost sight of the other ship but they kept in contact by repeated shouts. It grew dark before they had transversed the pass and Mace wanted to stop, but there was no place. The walls were slanted, hostile rock, thorned with sharp fingers of stone.

The fog thinned at last and they could see stars above and the faint disk of Arl, the smaller Zandran moon. Mace shouted for them to land and both ships began a descent.

A stab of brilliant red came out of the blackness behind. Mace's ship rocked and there was a nasty smell. Mouthfire cried out and the ship banked as Skylance tilted it away. Mace clung to the railing. Behind them was a third cloudship.

Durak!

Another ruby streak slashed through the night as the powerful Zull laser on the other ship probed for the vitals of the two vessels. Skylance dropped quickly, banked back under the Zurian ship. Mace saw Firearm's reenergized laser stab a series of thin pulses at the Zurian airship, but the distance was too great. The weaponry of Durak's guardship was too powerful. He could cut them to pieces before they could get close enough.

"Run!" Mace shouted. "Separate! We'll meet you at—" He stopped. They had no rendezvous, for they did not know the country that well. Helplessly, Mace saw the faint pale blue of Redpike's airship drift away. Durak turned and shot again at Mace's vessel, but missed as Skylance outthought him and dropped again.

They turned back into the mist, rising swiftly. The fog blanketed the shouts which now seemed to come from every direction. Mace motioned for Skylance to turn eastward, in the direction he had last seen Redpike's ship.

Silence. The faint sound of wind. Longtalon moved along the rail, his eyes searching the gray blankness. He glanced at Mace and they exchanged impassive looks.

After two hours Mace had to admit they were separated from the other ship and he cursed himself. They should have arranged some sort of rendezvous. He kept the ship heading eastward; that was as good a direction as any.

The mountains began to appear, first as darker gray slabs that rose over them for hundreds of meters, then as sheer black granite cliffs. Something of the terrain below began to be seen through the thinning patches of fog. Rolling hills, timbered and steep, then gentler slopes with meadows.

They left the fog behind and ventured out, watchful and alert. The fog-shrouded mountains behind them grew distant as they moved low over the valleys, hoping to make a less obvious target. Ahead, across a rolling plain, they could see another range of mountains, but these were not wreathed in fog.

"The mountains of Scarn," Longtalon said, a certain bitter disgust in his voice.

"Tell me about them," Mace suggested.

The Kurkan warrior shrugged. "A decadent race. We do not know much about them, except . . ." He paused and glanced at Mace. "There are stories brought by travelers. The Scarn are . . . seductive."

"Do you think Redpike might take his ship there?"

Longtalon gestured around at the horizon. "I do not see his ship. But it *is* the next nearest race. We Kurkans have avoided them as much as possible."

"Why? Are they powerful warriors?"

It was a moment before Longtalon answered. "They battle in a . . . different way, Earthman."

"My name is Mace, Longtalon. When you call me Earthman I feel as if I'm in a cheap sci-fi flick."

The Kurkan looked curiously at Mace. "You speak oddly, ur—Mace Wilde. You are here, not elsewhere."

Mace sighed and smiled crookedly. "Yeah, I know. Culture shock, that's all." He smiled again at Longtalon's frown. "Tell me, how did you get your name?"

Longtalon raised his chin and smiled, slapping his sword. "This is my long talon! I took the name after the battle with the Zurians at Grayspire."

"What was your name before that?" Mace asked, then quickly added, "or is that something one does not ask?"

The Kurkan warrior shook his head. "No, just unimportant. You take a name, if it suits you, and you have earned it. Then you take another, if you wish. But we usually take only one. It confuses our friends if we change too often." He looked closely at Mace. "When will you take a name?"

"I have a name."

Longtalon shrugged. "Yes, but an earned name is better than one which is given. May I suggest one? Strangesword." He looked at the mast-cabin and his expression became amused. "Or perhaps Kula-master?"

Mace laughed. "No, I think I shall keep the one I have."

"Eve thinks the same way." Longtalon looked at Mace in a peculiar manner, an expression of curiosity mixed with anxiety. "She is a mighty warrior, Mace Wilde."

"Uh-huh. On Earth she was a peace-keeper. It is a . . . kind of warrior."

"Yours was a strange world, Mace Wilde."

"Was, Longtalon?"

The Kurkan shrugged again and threw back the edges of his cloak. It was much warmer out over the plains. "You cannot return. And why should you?"

"Returning or not returning has yet to be proved," Mace said with some heat. "We'll never fit in here, anyway."

Longtalon laughed softly. "I would say you are doing quite well, Earth-, uh, Mace. Guide to the princess, a mighty warrior, commander of a Zull ship." He gestured out at the world around them. "We are building a new world, Mace Wilde. We are coming out of the Dark Time. The Kula are trying to conquer, but we shall not let them. All the peoples of Zandra are struggling to be free, free of the myths and legends, free of the oppression, free to build as we would."

"Sounds familiar," Mace said with a wry smile. "You can't keep a good man down. Unless you kill him."

"Death is not unknown to us," the Kurkan replied, soberly.

Mace saw Eve approaching and turned toward her. "No sign?" she asked; Mace nodded. She pointed at the mountain range ahead. "Mouthfire says that is the land of Scarn and that we should avoid it."

"Can't," Mace said. "Not if there is a chance Redpike headed that way." He jerked a thumb toward the mast-cabin. "Besides, I promised Her Arrogance there that I'd show her Zandra."

Eve leaned on the railing, her bow unstrung and looped over her shoulder. Her quiver of machine-made arrows was seriously depleted and she had refilled with the somewhat less accurate Kurkan shafts. "Mace . . ."

"Uh-huh?"

"What on earth is going on?"

"Bad choice of words, m'dear," he said with a slight smile. "You mean, what on Zandra is going on?"

"Yeah, yeah." Her chin was on her forearms. The sun was going down behind them and the mountains ahead were becoming purple. "Are we ever going to . . . you know . . . get out of here?"

Mace did not answer for a time and Eve looked around at him. "Are you certain we want to?"

"Hey, what do you mean?" she said, straightening up. "Of course I want to get home."

"Maybe it's different for you," Mace said. "I never really had a home, except the Army. My father was a sergeant, kept moving from post to post, until everywhere looked like every other place. I was at home everywhere . . . and nowhere."

"You feel at home here?" Eve asked, a slight tone of amazement in her voice. She glanced at Longtalon.

"I . . . I don't know. There are resonances . . . familiarities."

"Déjà vu?"

"A little. Kinda. I can't explain it. I'm a stranger, and yet . . . I don't feel all that strange, or rather, it doesn't feel all that strange to me."

"One of the Lost Ones," Longtalon said and the two humans looked at him. "A legend. From when the Zull ruled the stars. People who left their home planet to wander forever, never at home. They are . . . figures of both sadness and attraction."

"I don't feel that, I—"

"Ho, Mace Wilde!" It was Mouthfire in the control mast. "It grows dark. Do we land and make camp or continue in the night?"

"A good fire will do us good," Mace replied. "Pick a good place and set down. I, for one, could use a bath."

The sun was on the horizon when Mace came up out of the stream, shivering. He climbed into his loincloth and went cautiously over the stones to the campfire. "Where's Falana?" he asked Longtalon, who was bringing in an armload of branches.

The Kurkan dropped the wood near the fire and looked around. "Skylance!" The Kurkan looked over the edge of the control mast. "Where is the Kula?"

Skylance pointed upstream. "At her bath. Or so she said."

Mace pulled on his boots and picked up his sword but did not buckle it on. Dried off, he was warmer and he looked for Eve. Skylance said she was downstream, hunting for their supper.

Mace walked back to the stream, then along the bank, looking for Falana. It would do them no good if she tried to get away, or was attacked by some beast. He wondered if her mindsword worked on animals as well as human types.

He did not hear her splashing, nor did he see her until he stepped around some thick-trunked trees. A large flat rock stuck out into the stream, creating a pool downstream from it. Her clothes lay on the bank, but the heir to the Zandra throne was lying naked on the rock, her golden flesh reddened by the last of the sunset.

Mace started to step back, embarrassed at having found her as he did, as if he were a peeping tom. But she had heard him. Without opening her eyes she said, "Come, Earthling."

"The name is Mace Wilde, Zandran," he replied with a little more vigor than he had intended. "How did you know it was me?"

She smiled softly and made no attempt to cover the ripeness of her voluptuous body. "You walk like the forest creatures and only you would dare to spy upon a princess."

"I do not spy, Your Upness; I . . . I was checking you out."

"Checking me out. What does that mean, Earthman?"

"Seeing if you are well . . . protected . . ."

"Oh. Am I?"

"Yeah, you seem to be." He could not keep his eyes off her lush beauty and knew that she intended it to be so. He knew that she had sensed him with her mindsword apparatus, long before he had seen her. She had plenty of time to cover up if she had wanted to.

The reasons were obvious. The royal princess of Kula was in need of diversion. Suddenly Mace felt like a hustler. The thought disgusted him and he turned away, to start back.

"Wait." The single word was a command, yet, within it, there was something else. A plea? Mace looked back at her.

"What is it, Princess Falana?"

"I love sunsets. Do you not like them? They are sad, but beautiful. Better than sunrises. Sunrises mean you have to get to work, do things. Sunsets mean—"

"What do you know of work?" Mace interrupted harshly.

It didn't bother her at all. "I work. All Kula work. We work at leadership, command, planning. That is noble work. We do not labor in the fields, Earthman, if that is what you call work." There was an edge to her voice which she smoothed out in her next words. "But we work at pleasure, too . . . as you may remember."

Mace did remember and he gripped his sword tightly. It had been a silent battle, fought on a linen battlefield, with one side gaining dominance, then the other, back and forth, giving and receiving, until they had reached a kind of truce. But both had fought well, with the tactics of the kind one brought to the bedrooms of queens.

"I remember I was a gift slave who needed an edge," he said.

"Is that all you remember?" Her voice was silken and for the first time she opened her eyes and looked at him. Her expression was predatory, anticipatory, almost eager.

He looked at her for a long, thoughtful moment before he answered and by that time a trace of petulance had crept into her face. "Do you *always* get what you want, Falana?"

Her eyes narrowed in anger. "Yes," she replied shortly. "And why not? I am to be Empress."

"That's an excuse, not a reason."

"Earthman," Falana said with suppressed anger. "I am restraining myself with considerable difficulty. I do not like, nor do I tolerate, insubordination."

Mace Wilde grinned at her with such suddenness that she blinked. "Snap to! Move out! Attention! Double time!"

"Why are you making these rude statements?" She was still angry, but confused as well. "You Earth people are all insane, I think. But at least you are not calling upon some nebulous deity or cursing me with arcane insults."

"You *have* had contact with others before us, haven't you?" Mace said, remembering the "new" Spanish helmet he had seen in her quarters when he first arrived on Zandra.

"This conversation serves no function, Mace Wilde. We insult each other in obscure phrases and receive no pleasure from any of it." Her expression softened. "I forgive you. Now . . . let us pleasure ourselves as we did before."

There was another lull in the conversation as Mace looked her over with such a critical eye that she once again grew angry. "Stop that!" she commanded. "I am not some Chuma wench brought here for your use! I am—"

"Yeah, yeah, Princess of Zandra and all you survey."

"Well, you look at me as . . . well, not as men look at me. More like . . . like the Zurians." She shivered slightly at the thought and crossed her arms briefly over her bare breasts, glancing back toward the camp. "Look at me as . . . as a man."

"Oh, I'm a man now, not just some gift slave?"

"Keep your sarcasm to yourself, Mace Wilde. Come." She opened her arms to him.

He took a deep breath. "Well, no, I don't think so, Princess. It's not that you are not attractive . . ."

Her slitted dark eyes and knotted jaws showed her growing anger. "Go away, Earthman." Her voice rose and she pointed toward the encampment. "Go!"

Mace shrugged and walked away without hurry and did not look back. He stopped short of the camp, staying under a gnarled tree that was folding its crimson flowers for the night. He watched those building a fire near the bowl-shaped cloudship. Eve came into camp carrying the eviscerated carcass of a small deer-like animal and put it down. Longtalon helped her string it up and begin to skin it.

Why did I do that? Mace wondered. *What did I have to gain from it? The illusion of independence? Macho sexuality? I'll pick who I sleep with, woman!*

He sighed and watched Falana reenter the camp area, clothed and haughty. He watched her look from Skylance to Longtalon, a speculative expression on her face. Mace was amused; she could hide much of her feelings beneath her imperial mask, but he didn't think she was aware of how transparent her thoughts were when it came to the pleasures of the flesh. As plain as day he saw her consider the merits of the two Kurkans, then reject them. They had too long been the enemy. She would not give them the satisfaction of satisfaction.

Falana walked without hurry through the camp, disdaining to help at all, and entered the cloudship. Mace took a step forward, then stopped. Would she simply lift the ship and strand them, returning angrily to Kulan? There was no key or security on the cloudships; anyone that knew how could lift them.

No, he thought. *She'll stick. It's her pride. She must prove me wrong and do so in front of me. But she may never forgive me for tonight. It'd be good for her.* Mace felt a childish pride, as though he had refused a favored choice dessert. But the feeling was short-lived.

Why did I do that? I should be keeping the best of relations going with Falana. She was not so different from her sister Valora, whom the Zurians kept supplied with every pleasure, every vice, and every ego-stroking diversion. Was my purpose to declare independence or the traditional one of separating leaders from followers? Mace didn't know. It had been an impulse, a reaction whose origins were buried deep within him and not easily examined.

Mace did not immediately reenter the camp, but stood near the trees, thinking.

Where were the others? Not only Redpike's airship, with Liberty, Barney, Richter, and the others, but all those who crashed in the jetliner. *And all those who had disappeared into the infamous Bermuda Triangle for so many years. Those brought through in ships and boats must have fallen to their deaths,* he thought. *Their own crash landing had left few alive.*

The anger he felt toward the unemotional Vandorians and their "mining" of Earth he kept barely in check. *Someday,* he thought, *we'll return to that damned stone castle and take that Zull gadget away from them and send us back to Earth.*

Someday.

But what about tomorrow?

The island was small and the clearing on it barely large enough for Ironthroat to steer the cloudship to a landing. Redpike ordered everyone out and into a defensive perimeter, except for Du, who was caring for Barney Boone.

Liberty Crockett looked over the large lake from behind the concealment of a broad-leafed plant. Her mental music was muted and distant, much as the sunset appeared.

Baby, she told herself, *you have got to start thinking of Numero Uno. No more Brave New World jazz. No charity benefits for stranded Earthfolks. No hip lawyers to get you out of this gig, sister. You've got to go it alone and make it big.*

But how? Where to go, where to set the lever that will shift the world? Ambition was fine, but you needed an edge, a gimmick, something to set you apart. The Kula have their mind-zappers, plus a lot of tradition and those mean mothers, the Zurians. Ain't no way they are going to accept li'l Liberty as one of them. The bunch in Kardoon was too weird. The Kurkans had promise; they admired physical prowess and courage, but they were pretty well set up with King Zur and that crowd.

No, Liberty m'love, you need some place that doesn't have a rigid setup yet. Some group or country or whatever they call it here that is in turmoil, some folks looking for a leader. Or some outfit she could dominate.

A thought struck her and she explored the idea with eagerness. So far, the people she had seen or heard about were divided up in a racial way. The Vandorians, the dragon-creatures they called the Saurons, the robot Astorix, the shape-changing Tigron and so on. *Could the people of Earth make their own place here? They had the tradition, especially if they were Americans or Australians, Canadians or Spanish. Going to the New World, in this case, was really going to a new world.*

But they were so scattered. They had to be, as she had not yet run across any except those that had come on the jetliner with her. But Zandra was obviously in the throes of change. They were emerging from a kind of Dark Age. Change was always the time for those on the bottom to get to the top.

But what if she got together a kind of consortium? A pirate brotherhood. She had learned a lot from making *The Pirates of Tortuga*. Real pirates had been considerably different from those depicted in films. While during battle a pirate captain was the absolute master and his orders obeyed without question, he was an *elected* official. They could depose him—and did—by electing another.

A pirate community was a kind of guild and totally free from those characteristics that those who chose the outlaw life detested. There was no overbearing authority, no class distinctions, no lack of say in important matters. Privateers were like employees, but pirates shared their ship and worked only for themselves. Major decisions—except in battle—were made by a show of hands. If a sufficiently large number formed a dissident minority they usually left to form their own group.

Privilege was thought to be the first step toward autocracy and was treated with suspicion, anger, and rejection. While a captain might command a large cabin, any crewman might enter at any time and drink his wine or eat his food. Naturally, pirates wanted those who were competent, or, to use their term, "pistol proof." They could not abide, nor did they abide, tyrannical captains, unlucky or incompetent ones. Some captains kept their positions for years, while other ships changed leaders every few weeks or months.

Liberty thought a privateer's life might be more to her liking, but it might not attract the kind of individual she needed. And what would be the reaction of the Kulan nobles? The fact that they had not stopped the Kurkan pirates—who were bound together by racial and ideological ties—but had only gained momentary advantage here and there, wearing down the cloudship brigands by attrition.

Redpike was attracted to her. She knew almost for certain that had been the reason he had embarked on this journey. Firearm was a fighter; offered a chance to kill Kula, one tempered with loot, he would probably go along. Ironthroat she was not so certain about. She would have to sound him out. The female warrior Du was another unknown.

Richter, Jardek, and Barney she did not need. None were warriors and while the two scientists might possibly come up with something she could use, it would not be soon. But she would want to keep them obligated to her, if she could. She *would* find them a safe place to study, but then . . .

Then what? Recruit? How do you recruit pirates? No personal ads here, no television promos. *Join Liberty Crockett and her Merry Band of Madcap Adventurers as they fight the evil of the Zandran Empire!*

It was going to have to be on a one-to-one relationship. Mace Wilde would be perfect—if he'd take orders, but he wouldn't. *At least not from me,* she thought. *He'd—*

"A frangis for your thoughts."

"Uh—!" Liberty was jolted from her reverie and looked around to see Simon Richter nearby. He had one of Redpike's lances, which looked ungainly and awkward in his hands. "A *what?*"

Richter smiled and shrugged. "Don't have pennies here. And I don't know what they call their money. Or even if they have any. I guess they must, though, as we were bought."

"Leased, I think," she replied. "And we just broke the lease, Simon."

They were silent a moment. Something stirred in the shadowed lake and Liberty tensed. A fish. Or something. "That's the trouble with this place," she muttered. "You don't know what's poison ivy and what's cherries."

"I know. It's fascinating."

Liberty gave the scientist a sharp look. "You love it, don't you?"

He smiled and nodded. "I'm afraid so. I . . . I'm not certain I even want to go back. They know so much here . . . or rather, they did. I think I can recover much of that knowledge. If I can just find a place to study. Count Jardek and I have been talking . . ." He paused to laugh. "We each astound the other. Do you know their concept of the arts here is totally different? They have nothing like movies or television, or even stage plays. They do have sculpture and painting, but it is considered somewhat profane. Something like the Mohammedans forbidding any depiction of the human form in their art or architecture. Their metallurgy is quite primitive now, but apparently it was once as good as any we had in the medieval period."

He pointed back at the ship. "Anything advanced is Zull, anything medieval is native. And that includes social organizations as well. Jardek thinks democracy is unworkable and insane. Religions here are . . . well, odd, and minor affectations or hobbies." He shrugged, amused. "But totally fascinating. The Zull were a *magnificent* race who—"

"Who oppressed every race they encountered," Liberty snapped. "They used hostages and the rule of might. They were the ultimate oppressors."

"But nevertheless fascinating. Their scientific achievements were outstanding, almost beyond comprehension. Antigravity, for example. We've long considered that impossible, but they had it uncounted generations ago. If I can just—"

"Simon . . ."

"Yes?" He peered at her with concern.

"Can it. The Zull are dead. We're alive. But we won't be if we don't make ourselves a *force*. We need power, Simon. Can you give us *power?*"

"Well, uh, no; not right away. I see your point, of course, but there is so much I don't understand here. But with time . . ."

"Which is something we have in short supply."

They fell silent and after a few moments Richter cleared his throat, hefted his lance, and walked off down the beach.

The sun was almost gone. The distant mountains were purple, the lake shores dark. Something screeched on the shore beyond. Something else flopped in the water. Night had come.

Somewhere, Liberty thought, *there is a place for me, some starring role in this crazy-quilt world. I'll know it when I see it.*

Lying on a pad on the deck of the Zull cloudship Barney Boone tossed fitfully, moaning from time to time. Du wet his face, then wiped him clean. Firearm came to relieve her and she rose gratefully.

"He dreams," she whispered.

"I'd dream, too," he muttered, thinking of the Tigron hell he had seen.

The thick-bodied warrior sat down and leaned back against the curving railing. Overhead the first stars were appearing. Sundancer and Skullsmasher, with his upraised club. The head of Bassar, the Northking, was rising over the far railing. Soon the Necromancer would appear, with his far-flung ribbons of color.

Firearm twisted his head to look the other way. He could just see Starflower's nebulous glow appearing as the last of the sun glaze faded. Some said that was the home of the Zull, but no one knew. To the south was the Dragonmouth, that blackness in the sea of stars, with the single bright glow of The Hero in the center.

Fire spots without meaning. He rubbed the smooth metal of his forearm and felt the joining to his flesh. Sometimes it hurt there but he would not part with it. He dreaded the day he might be mortally wounded and they might put him into a Zull healer and regrow his arm. He was used to it the way it was. His scars were decorations.

"Uhhh . . ." Barney Boone stirred and tried to sit up.

"Earthman," Firearm said softly, touching his shoulder.

"Uh . . ." Barney looked around, then up at the Kurkan.

"You are safe, Earthman. Sleep."

"What happened? They gave me that stuff to hold . . . then . . . then you rescued me, and . . . and I went back, and followed Ti-blan, and I . . . oh, god, I, I changed, didn't I?"

Firearm shrugged. "They are devils. Your friends, the black woman and the man Simon, they are with us."

"The others . . . dead?"

"Oh, no." Firearm laughed. "Your Mace Wilde is too much a warrior. He is with the Kula witch in the other ship, with the one who can draw the mighty bow. But we are separated . . ."

"Where are we?"

"On an island in a lake," Redpike said, coming over from the control mast. "Are you hungry?"

"No . . . no, I don't think so. No, I'm not."

"Then sleep. Tomorrow we will be into the mountains of Scarn."

Barney lowered himself with a groan. "It's all so . . . so . . ."

"Sleep, Earthman," Firearm said.

Barney nodded and drifted off.

The circular bowl of night over his head dimmed in his mind. A dark circle on a black void. Nothingness on nothingness.

Curling.

Melting.

Changing.

Become gray, becoming shape, becoming gelatinous, shaping itself to him, becoming him, absorbing him, mimicking his cells, then replacing them . . .

He faded. He merged. He—

Barney sat up with a strangled cry, striking out with pinwheeling arms. "Awk! Oh! *Uhhh*—!" He looked wildly around to see Firearm rubbing sleep from his eyes and staring at him. "I was . . . I was melting . . . becoming . . . oh, *god* . . ."

The Kurkan motioned at Redpike, who had come up the ramp from the fire. The cloudship leader stopped, looked at the sweating Earthman, then backed down and disappeared.

"Sleep," Firearm suggested. "But dream of Earth."

Barney fell back. *Dream of Earth?* What was there? Nothing. They had killed his lions, they had made *him* kill his lions. Nothing could replace them. Nothing.

But something might replace me, he thought quietly.

"The land of Scarn," Mouthfire said, pointing. They were past the foothills and the mountains of gray and black rock rose before them.

The breeze caused Falana's long dark hair to stream back over her cloaked shoulders. The colorful awning they had unfurled in a circle rippled in the wind, making a soft flapping noise. The Kulan princess looked as if it were all a minor annoyance.

"What do you know of them?" Mace asked. He wore his Zurian armor but not the helmet.

The blonde Kurkan said, "Not very much. We sometimes trade them booty. They care not the original owners and are useful that way." She slapped the longsword at her side. "I got this at a rendezvous two years ago. It belonged to a Zurian officer, and they have good blades. I traded a Melorian necklace for it."

"And the Melorian necklace you stole," Falana said bitingly, but not deigning to look at the female warrior.

The remark did not bother Mouthfire. "Yes, of course. But unlike you Kula, we do not steal with taxes and deceit. You—"

Mace saw the flash in Falana's eyes and he stopped them both with a gesture. "No!" He looked at Mouthfire warningly, then at Falana. "You know how the Kurkans live. Just accept it and keep your mouth shut."

Falana gave Mace a look of undisguised anger. "You presume entirely too much, Mace Wilde. You do *not* tell the heiress to the throne of Zandra to—"

"At it again, huh?" Eve Clayton said, joining them. She looked at Mace as Falana froze into a statue of haughtiness. "Boy, there is something about your personality that really brings out the best in people. They just clamor to play follow-the-leader, don't they?"

"Thanks a lot," Mace said. "Just when I had royalty eating out of the palm of my hand, you—"

Falana looked disgusted. "What a barbarian idea!" She made a loud expression of distaste and moved along the railing away from them. Eve followed her with her eyes, then smiled at Mace. "I'm glad you were in the Army and not the Diplomatic Corps, luv."

Mace looked disgusted with himself. "I don't think the Kula have any sense of humor."

"And I'm losing mine," Eve replied. She touched shoulders with Mace as Mouthfire excused herself and went to the control mast. "You gotta either laugh or cry."

They watched the mountains coming closer for a while, feeling the cloudship rising and falling on the rougher currents of air in the mountain passes. "What's it like being a cop?" he asked.

She shrugged. "I don't know . . . not anymore. I know it's only been a couple of weeks, but it's like . . . like that all didn't ever happen. It's the dream and this is the reality—instead of it being the other way around."

"They are both realities."

"Uh-huh—only this one is a little bit more real than the other one." She hugged Mace's arm. "You know, I was a cop, but unlike all those cop shows on the tube, I never killed anyone. I shot *at* someone only once, and he was shooting back. But here . . . Mace, I've *killed* people."

"Not people, Zurians, Tigron."

She looked up at him. "Don't let us *ever* start thinking that way. Not *ever*. They were living, breathing *people*, Mace. Not like us, maybe. Cruel and vicious, yes . . . but still intelligent people. I'm not even certain how *many*. It all happened so fast, every time. I just notched and pulled and shot. Like a machine."

"And cool as anything."

"No, just frightened. But don't you think you should at least *know* how many you've killed and . . ." She stopped and leaned out to look up into his face. "What about you? Do you know how many you've killed? Do you *want* to know?"

"No, not particularly. I'm not proud of it, but I'm not ashamed of it, either. If they had left me alone, I would have left them alone."

"What about back on Earth? When you were a soldier?"

Mace took his time answering. "I . . . we . . . had a country; one I think worth defending. There were others who wanted to change it, or to enslave it. I helped to keep that from happening." He was quiet a moment, holding the rail. "In peacetime, soldiers are not much wanted. They are looked down on. Then comes a crisis, or a war, and suddenly you are the Good Guys again."

"Okay, so people are self-serving and greedy," Eve said. "No one likes war and no one stops having them. We all just—"

A cry from Skylance brought Mace's head around. "There!" The Kurkan pilot pointed.

The cloudship was rounding a peak. Ahead was a plateau and it joined a mountain at the far end. Mace could make out what appeared to be cavern mouths, several of them. On the plateau before the caverns were two Zull airships, a few tents, a stone tower, and a number of small figures.

Mace heard a distant horn and the figures began running for cover. Most ran into the caves. By the time their cloudship drifted over the landing area there was no one in sight except a few helmeted figures in the stone tower. A shiny weapon of some sort was aimed at them and Mace called out to Skylance, "What's that they have on us?"

"A Zull weapon, but don't worry—it doesn't work."

"Uh-huh. It didn't work *before,* but maybe they fixed it."

Skylance laughed and Mouthfire joined him. "The Scarn cannot fix anything, that is why they trade."

"Who do those ships belong to?" Eve asked.

"One is from Meloria, I think," Mouthfire said. Their cloudship banked around and Mace was uncomfortable, watching them being tracked by the weapon in the tower. "The other—I do not know."

"A Zurian ship?" Mace asked.

"No," Mouthfire replied slowly. "No, I don't think so. Not Durak, anyway. Shall we land?"

Mace nodded. "Might as well, we've come this far."

Skylance brought the airship closer to the tower and Mace saw that the armored defenders were swarthy and scared-looking, despite a hodgepodge of armor from several different sources, including Zurian. "We wish to land!" Skylance called out.

"What is your purpose?" one called back.

Falana answered before anyone else could. "We need no *purpose,* Scarn scum! I am Falana, daughter of Morak, Emperor of Zandra! I have come to inspect this hidden land of yours!"

There was consternation among the troops in the tower and one hurried down through a thick wooden hatch. The weapon was kept trained on them.

"Land," Falana commanded.

"Princess . . ." Skylance said warningly.

"Land this ship!" she said with authority.

"Princess," Mace said, "it's only polite to—"

"*Land!*" Falana snapped. "I do not ask *permission* to go *anywhere* on this planet!" She glared at Mace, then at Skylance, who brought down his eyebrows and circled for a landing. Falana looked again at Mace. "Must I *continually* remind you I am Falana? These worms are subject to my father. I do not need their *permission* to do *anything!*"

Mace grinned at her, which only made her mouth twitch in further annoyance. "Okay, you've got clout. Let's see if Redpike got here before we did."

"That's not his ship," Longtalon said. He was buckling his armor on and rubbing sleep from his eyes. He'd had the late watch the night before.

Mace felt disappointed, but watched carefully as they landed at a little distance from both the tower and the other ships, keeping them all between them and the cavern mouths.

At this distance Mace realized some of the entrances were quite large. A cloudship could have been flown into them. But what lay beyond?

"Skylance, stay with the ship," Mace commanded. "At the first sign of trouble, lift it. Eve, you stay here with the ship."

"Hey, I want to go, too!"

"No. Your bow won't be as good inside there as it will out here. You can keep any enemy away with it and can float out there like artillery if you have to. Understand?"

She nodded, reluctantly, and watched the ramp go down and the departure of Falana, Mouthfire, and Longtalon after Mace. "Good luck," she called after them.

"What does the blonde one mean?" Falana said as they strode toward the caves.

"Good fortune. Her best wishes. Uh . . . she wishes us well."

"We do not need luck, Earthman. I am Falana."

She said it with such sincerity and certainty that Mace had to hide a smile. It was obvious that Princess Falana had little experience beyond the sheltered world of the Kula capital.

They walked up the broad stone and earth ramps and into the largest of the caves. Eve watched them disappear into the darkness as she bit at her lip. A motion attracted her attention and she saw two helmets appear over the edge of the stone tower. More showed up from around the base. They carried swords and spears, but appeared more cautious and curious than hostile.

But on Zandra, she remembered, you were not always certain of how anything or anyone reacted.

She pulled an arrow from her quiver and notched it, holding it loosely against the bow. She was as ready as she was ever going to be, for whatever was going to happen.

Barney was slithering through the dark passages, melting around knobs of wet rock and across smooth slabs. He held on tightly to the rock bridge across a chasm of vast depth, his scaly gray tentacles scraping as they moved. The dim caverns echoed with distant howls, the anguished cries of imprisoned creatures.

He crept along the ledge, his hairy legs brushing against the stone, his footpads almost silent on the rock. His long tail twitched in fear and he felt a rumbling growl come from his throat. He stopped at sight of the glow, then edged forward, the ruff on his neck rising. He sniffed the air—sweat, blood, sulfur . . .

They were dancing in the glow of a fire, naked humans, erect beasts, things with horrific masks of living flesh. Falana, Eve, dark Liberty, their bodies glistening with sweat, the bloody bones in their hands sending splatters of blood across the torsos of their companions. The voices of the naked humans mixed with the grunts and howls of the beast-creatures.

He started to edge away. His tail brushed against a pebble, and it fell into the chasm, echoing like an avalanche of glass. The figures around the fire froze and looked right at him.

Barney scampered away, backing furiously, paws scrabbling on the wet stone as the figures bounded up from the cavern, leaping over the rocks with superhuman strength, dodging the stalagmites, howling, screaming, bellowing . . .

His foot slipped; the chasm tugged at his weight. He changed, shooting out sticky tentacles, grasping at the rock, but he had no balance. He saw their faces appear over the edge of the cliff—Richter and Liberty, their faces taut and wide-eyed, the beast-creatures with their fanged mouths open. He began to scream as he fell, twisting in the black air, seeing the darkness below, seeing the turgid coils of something wet move . . .

"Barney!"

He fell . . . changing . . . trying to stop it all by evolving a shape . . . trying and failing . . . he—

"*Barney!*"

Richter and Liberty were bending over him as he lay on the rocky ground. His face stung and the black actress was looking at him with a fierce expression.

"You were having a nightmare," Richter said softly.

"No, I . . ." Barney stopped, looking around. His eyes were full of tears, but he could see the others looking, then turning away to their tasks of packing up.

"A nightmare, Barn," Liberty said.

He grabbed her forearm. "Listen, I was . . . I was in a cavern and I kept changing, becoming . . ." He shuddered at the thought, then quickly released her. "All of you were . . . you were different . . . uh . . . I'm not sure if you were . . ." He stopped, his eyes shifting around, unable to meet their gaze.

"Whatever the Tigron did to him might be still affecting him," Richter said, taking Barney's pulse.

"Don't talk as if I weren't here or couldn't understand," Barney protested.

"Sorry. You may not have shaken off that . . . whatever it was that they put on your arm. Look, it's still red and blotched."

"It burns. Like I was sunburned, or a lot of needles . . ."

"I think it penetrated your flesh in some way, perhaps into the bloodstream." Richter shrugged. "The Zull didn't have much in the way of first aid, nor have the Kula developed much. They just pop people into those marvelous healers." He got up, his face serious. "You're running a fever. That arm didn't look like that yesterday, so there may be some infection. That could be causing your nightmares."

"Fix it, Doc," Barney said huskily. "I don't want to have another dream like that."

Liberty patted him and stood up. "Come on," she said, offering him a hand. "Let's get ready. Redpike's about ready to lift."

"Uh-huh," Barney groaned and heaved himself up with her help. "We gotta find Mace and everybody." He walked toward the cloudship, swaying slightly, but shaking off Liberty's assistance.

The actress watched him board, then shivered. The idea of nightmares where you changed *shape*, changed the reality of yourself. She thought if that happened to her—even in the realm of sleep—she might go insane. Not just a nose job or a booby lift, but becoming something like those hideous things that had flown at them out of the fog—!

Liberty Crockett unknotted her fists and strode toward the dead fire, to snatch up a bag of food and her sword. *Nothing was going to change her,* she thought angrily.

The high vault of the cave entrance had been smoothed and once-colorful murals had been painted there. But they were faded now and Mace could barely make out what some of the images were. Kings and queens, with rows of slaves, or possibly subjects, bearing gifts. Trees, flowers, fruit, fanciful birds, geometric designs—their images filled every space. The kings wore high, ornate crowns; the queens were drenched in jewelry and voluptuous.

But Mace gave the murals only an occasional look as they progressed upward, climbing along a wide, well-traveled path, lit by torches stuck in holes drilled in the rock. Falana strode along, her dark head queenly high, ignoring those who stared, gape-mouthed and servile.

Mace walked closely behind her, his hand on the hilt of his long-sword. The two Kurkan warriors, Mouthfire and Longtalon, came along behind, equally as alert and watchful. The path angled down a way, then took a turn and leveled for a way, with a sharp drop-off to the right.

"Wait," Mace said and after a few steps, Falana stopped, looking back impatiently. Mace pointed downward. In the darkness was a line of torches that marked the path downward, and then an entrance to some other chamber. Campfires glowed around it and Mace could see figures in armor guarding the farther chamber.

"The true entrance to Scarn," Falana said, and resumed her stately walk.

Here and there, along the path, they saw still more Zandrans. They seemed befuddled, as if drunk. A few slept in crevices, wrapped in cloaks, hugging their possessions. One hairy-faced male in patched armor stood in Falana's path, seemingly too drunk or mindless to move. He swayed on his wide-spreading feet, watching her approach with goggle-eyed amazement.

"Out of my way!" Falana snapped. Mace hurried to catch up to her, his Earthborn muscles functioning easily under the lighter gravity of Zandra. But the princess angrily slapped the man across his slack-mouthed face. He staggered, then his face changed into one of drunken rage.

No coherent words came from his mouth, but his bellow of anger was enough. He lunged at Falana, but she dodged his clumsy attack easily and chopped at his exposed throat. The man fell with a cry, gagging and clutching at his neck. Falana walked on as if nothing had happened.

Mace looked at the felled man, then caught up to the princess. He grinned at her. "What happened to that mindsword of yours, mighty Princess?"

"Do not mock me, Mace Wilde." She gave him an angry glance. "He was not worth the effort."

"Oh." Mace filed that information away. *Of course,* he thought, *every action requires energy, even mental action.* He had no idea how much energy it took for a Kula to employ the mindsword, but it was probably the limiting factor in how many enemies any one Kula could handle. It might be very exhausting, or it might require no more effort and energy than pushing a button. He was going to have to investigate this more.

They were walking down the last torchlit section of the path when the guards came to life. Already Mace could see that a stone wall had been mortared across the natural entrance. It looked very medieval, with a recessed door set in an arch at the end of a short corridor. Arrow slits vented the side walls. The big door was open and Mace caught a glimpse of more descending caverns beyond and a few more warriors lounging on rocks.

"Halt!"

Falana did not halt, but kept on with her steady pace. "I am Falana, daughter of Morak, Emperor of Zandra!" she said testily, as if she were very tired of repeating herself.

Mace could see that the guards were of a mixed racial stock. Some appeared to be Chuma, others looked like half-breeds between the Chuma and the dark Zurians. They all looked tough and tested, but also a little nervous.

"Halt," the guard repeated, but the authority had gone from his voice.

"Out of my way," Falana said without anger. They obeyed, moving back. Beyond the gate one warrior hefted a spear, his patched armor rusty and ill-fitting. He suddenly screamed and fell to the rocky floor, his spear clattering away. He rolled on the ground with his hands to his head, gasping out small animal-like cries.

"Falana!" Mace said.

The guard went limp, sighing into unconsciousness. "He was going to throw that spear."

"You don't know that. He was young, nervous—"

"I knew it, Earthman. Never contradict me about things like that." They went through the gate without any further trouble and started down a steep path hacked in the rock. Here and there small stone bridges had been built across cracks. They passed an old woman with a bundle of unlit torches, who was replacing a burned-out torch. She stared toothlessly at the four who passed, and Mace examined her as they went by.

They had seen few old people on Zandra, he realized. Mature, yes, but not old and certainly not in the physical condition of the crone. Also, there were few children, and those he had seen were Chuma, the slave race to the Kula. *Their population is stabilized,* he thought. *Is that natural, or what?*

But there was no time for further exploration on that line. They rounded a turn and before them lay the first bright towers of Scarn.

The cavern they were entering was huge. The floor seemed to have been artificially smoothed, then polished. It was not flat, but dipped and rose beneath the fanciful towers. In what Mace assumed were imitations of stalagmites, towers of bright glass rose from the polished stone floor, rising up four, five, and more stories into the air, toward the curving ceiling above.

The roof of the big cavern had also been scraped clean of stalactites, then darkened in some way to give the illusion of a night sky. The towers all glowed in different colors and for a moment Mace stood in surprise, examining them.

One tower was filled in its upper stories with trapped gases that swirled and glowed energetically. Another was a complex of smaller towers through which tiny dots of bright, sparkling light moved in graceful dances. Another edifice was composed of scores of rippling tubes of glowing gases, entwined and complex, in a dozen colors. One tower was an elongated cone, smooth and black, upon which the others reflected their brilliance. Some towers had bridges between them and Mace could see colorfully dressed figures walking along.

At the base of the towers, other figures moved about languidly. Mace saw a young man, looking much like a Kula noble, walk up onto a smooth block of green glass. Immediately one of the naked Chuma slaves crouching along the base of the block rose and bent over. The young man mounted her and she trotted off, carrying him. The other Chuma slaves hopped up one place, then resumed their silent thoughts.

There were only two types of people visible—slaves and masters. Surprisingly, some of the naked slaves were Zurians, but some of the arrogant masters were also Zurians.

"Are you coming?" Falana said, and Mace realized she had walked on ahead and was looking back. The Kurkans followed Mace as he caught up to the princess. Just then they were discovered by the natives of Scarn.

A babble of voices started immediately. The Chuma slaves cringed and a sharp bell-like sound began, as though someone was striking a glass chime. Some of the Scarn ran into hiding, others seemed transfixed, staring with fear as Falana led her companions into the city of glass towers.

The Zandran heiress kept her chin high and her gaze haughty. She walked in as if she knew where she was going, but Mace knew she did not. He kept a wary eye on the inhabitants of this village of glass and was relieved when Mouthfire said, "There, to the left, a kind of square."

Falana turned that way as if it had been her objective anyway and walked out onto it gracefully. The square rose slightly in the center, crowned by a large fountain. The centerpiece in the stone-edged pool was a blossom of glass tubes, lumpy and uneven, through which colorful fluids ran. The Zandran noble turned at the pool edge and surveyed those who peered out at her from around the bases of the towers.

Mace scanned the glass bridges and peered into the translucent bubbles where startled Scarn stared back. Most of the people he saw wore some kinds of weapons, but they were mainly ornate daggers. He saw no Zull hand weapons.

Falana waited calmly, as if ready to wait forever. From time to time she looked here, then there, as if idly curious. There were murmurs from the crowd, which was growing. The chime—evidently an alarm—stopped. Mouthfire, Longtalon, and Mace formed a semicircle before and slightly below Falana. They all waited.

They first heard the trumpets and horns. A drum boomed. There were some cheers and the crowd watching Falana stirred, looking in one direction. Falana and her entourage turned to watch.

The crowd parted and the first seen were beautiful youths, male and female, clad only in ornate jewelry, and blowing on small, brightly colored glass horns. Then six husky Chuma slaves brought in a litter almost smothered in large purple flowers, tiny red twinkling lights, and rich dark furs. On the litter was a short, plump man with shiny black hair, full pursed lips, and alert, speculative eyes that missed nothing. Beside him lay a naked woman, her black hair braided and spurting up from her head to fall back in a spume of dark mist. She wore immense rubies in her ears and another hung from a golden chain low on her flaring hips.

The slaves set down the litter as the clamor from the musicians died away. The plump person in the litter looked first at Falana, then at Mace, then at the Kurkans, but he said nothing. His nude companion looked speculatively at Mace and licked her upper lip.

Falana was angry and Mace took a step toward her as she began to speak. "Worm! Get to your knees! I am Falana, firstborn daughter of Morak, Emperor of all Zandra!"

The man in the litter smiled as he raised his eyebrows. "Old Morak spawned such a morsel?" There were laughs from the crowd, and some stepped closer. Mace put his hand on his sword and the movement stopped. The woman in the litter looked at Mace possessively and licked her upper lip again.

Without warning the plump Scarn noble jerked and fell back, emitting a strangled cry. His arms and legs shot out spasmodically, and his entire body trembled in a terrible fit. Mace looked at Falana, saw her anger, but this time he did not interfere.

The man in the litter gasped and spasmed into a fetal position, but stopped trembling. After a long moment, in which no one spoke or moved, he raised his head. There was venom in his eyes, and saliva dripped from his slack lips.

A handsome young man, wearing a purple loincloth and a thin golden chain with a ruby around his waist, broke through the crowd and bent over the plump man, helping him sit up.

"On your knees," Falana said calmly.

The plump man hesitated, glancing about. But there was no one who seemed willing to do anything else. He forced a weak smile to his lips and awkwardly went to one knee. "Princess Falana," he croaked. He cleared his throat and tried again. "Welcome, Princess Falana, firstborn of Morak, Lord of Kulan."

Falana frowned. "*Emperor* Morak, ruler of Zandra," she corrected. There was a deadly calmness in her voice that no one could miss.

"Of course, Princess. Welcome to the firstborn of Morak, Emperor of Zandra." He bowed slightly and then looked inquiringly at Falana. She pretended not to see him and looked around, raising her voice so that all might hear.

"I have come here as the eyes of Morak, Emperor of Zandra, to accept the vows of allegiance from the people of Scarn!"

A murmur stirred the crowd. Mace saw a frowning man with braided hair whispering angrily into the ear of a plump woman who wore an abundance of gemstones and little else. A burly man in red leather armor half-drew a dagger, then thought better of it as he saw Mace's eyes on him.

"The dark centuries have gone," Falana said, her voice ringing off the colorful glass towers. "A new Zandra is being born. My father rules and all who oppose him shall be dealt with!"

"O, mighty and beauteous Falana, may I speak?" The plump man on his knee was being steadied by the beautiful young man. Falana nodded brusquely. "I am Norg, Lord of the Glittering Towers, Prince of Scarn, Keeper of the Zull Wonders, Baron of—"

A gesture from Falana shut off his self-promotion. "I am spokesman for our mighty king, Naar, First of the Inner Monarchs." The crowd made a uniform gesture, touching forehead, stomach, and loins, and Norg joined them. "Our magnificent king is in temporary seclusion in the Caverns of Meditation, but I am certain he would wish me to convey to you our utmost pleasure at your presence and offer you the bounty and special delights of our noble house." He bowed low and let the handsome young man pull him to his feet.

"I wish to speak to this Naar." An expression of annoyance went across Falana's face as the crowd once again made the gesture.

"I offer you the most humble and gracious apologies of our serene monarch, noble daughter of the imperious Morak, but our king is in only the second unit of a seven-unit vow of seclusion and meditation." At Falana's frown he explained. "We calculate time, brilliant flower of the stars, in units of limestone deposit upon the sacred columns of Scarn." He shrugged eloquently. "It would be the rudest insult, radiance, to disturb our fountain of power."

Falana's eyes slitted and Norg winced, his thick lips puckering. "It would be the rudest insult, Prince Norg, to thwart the wishes of the daughter of Morak."

Norg sighed and bowed his head. "As you wish, brightest of Kula. I shall send a messenger at once." He looked at a man in purple robes, who turned into the crowd and disappeared. Norg smiled up at Falana. "The Caverns of Meditation are at some distance, away from the distractions of all this." He made a gesture around, and under its cover, his big dark eyes inspected Mace and the Kurkans. "May I have the honor, noble eminence, to know your companions?"

Falana dispatched the introductions perfunctorily, in a matter-of-fact voice. "That is Mace Wilde, a man from Earth, who assists me in my voyage of inspection. Those are Kurkans, who assist him. They are called Longtalon and Mouthfire, I believe."

"Great Noble," Norg said, bowing. He fixed Mace with a shrewd look. "From Earth, you say? Ah . . ."

"Why 'ah'?" Mace asked without much formality. "You have heard of Earth?"

"Indeed, my noble warrior. We here in Scarn are, shall we say, at a kind of crossroads? People from all over Zandra . . ." He glanced at Falana, his lips forming a smile. "From all over the kingdom of Morak they come. To trade . . . to, um, purchase the pleasures and delights we offer."

"You mean there are Earth people here?" Mace took a step toward the Scarn prince. "Who? Where are they?"

"In time, tall one, in time. First, I am certain you would wish to rest, to bathe and eat." He smiled at Falana. "We have here ancient artifacts that exist nowhere else, blossom of radiance. We have functioning Zull machines that provide us with all we need—food, pleasure pills, healers, music makers, dream imagers—things you might never have even heard of." He looked expectantly at the princess.

Falana raised her eyebrows. "A bath, yes . . . then food. How long before your king returns?"

"Plenty of time, fountain of might, for you to eat, rest, and pleasure yourselves." He turned toward the crowd. "Prepare the Tower of Fulfillment!"

"What's that?" Liberty said, pointing. They were flying low over the rolling plain, nearing the mountains. Below, trees lined the banks of a meandering stream. Something scaly slid into the water and disappeared in a ripple of bubbles.

Redpike joined her at the railing, his eyes narrowing as he searched the horizon. "There," Liberty said, "see those yellow trees—there!"

A tiny dot cleared the distant grove and moved toward the mountains. It was a cloudship, but the unvoiced question was: is it Mace or Durak, with his band of Zurian assassins?

"Stay low," Redpike called out to Ironthroat in the mast. He quickly toured the perimeter railing of the circular ship, looking out at the horizon. The Zull cloudship dropped lower and flew just above the water of the stream.

"Think they saw us?" Richter said, joining Liberty.

She shrugged. "Hard to say." She turned to look at the control mast and saw Redpike climb into the cockpit. He watched the horizon closely, his face grim. They were no match for Durak and his long-range weapons.

But if it were Mace, she thought, *they might never see each other again.* She felt a kinship with her fellow Earthlings that she knew she could not ever feel for anyone on Zandra. On Earth she had suffered all the prejudice any black, especially any black woman, had suffered. She'd been lucky, born with the kind of beauty that the white world accepted, and she had gotten out of the ghetto. But not so far that she did not remember, nor so far that she was not aware of how she was still restricted. She'd never play the lover of a white man and actually end up with him in the end. She'd never—

Liberty stopped that line of thought. That world was gone, over, through. This was a whole new deal, a different script entirely. *This* script had blank pages past this moment. What would be written there *she* would write.

She lifted her head and looked up at the noonday sky. She'd make, not a ghetto, but a kingdom. Or die trying.

They dipped and curved along the stream bed and Redpike kept a watch for the unidentified airship. The next few minutes might be very crucial.

Eve drew her arm back, pulling the big bow into a taut arc. She aimed carefully and loosened the shaft. The strum of the bowstring was followed by the thunk of the arrow and the startled gasp of the swarthy soldier as his helmet went sailing, pierced by her bolt.

The Scarn guards, who had been jeering at Eve and crowding in closer and closer in an arrogant advance, looked at the metal helmet in dismay. Some of them gaped at the blonde young woman looking over the thick railing of the cloudship. Their laughter died and one by one they found other things to do, glancing at Eve Clayton from time to time and shaking their heads.

Eve exchanged looks with Skylance, who grinned and shook his head in admiration. They settled down again, staying watchful.

Eve went into the mast-cabin and brought out some food. She leaned against the railing and kept an eye on the tower. The fruit was mostly good, tasting a little like mangoes or plums, but one tasted like chicken fat. She spat it over the edge and started chewing on a strip of some unidentified meat-like substance.

What was going on? she wondered. *This was some bizarre stakeout,* she thought. *We need a SWAT team. Or the Marines.*

The bath to which Mace, Longtalon, and the two women were shown was actually a small pool, fringed with fuzzy-leaved plants at one end and a wall-sized aquarium at the other. Mouthfire and Long-talon did not hesitate, but stripped off their armor and weapons and jumped into the steaming water. Mace noted that their swords were kept right at the pool's rim.

The big Earthman looked at Falana. She was looking around, ignoring the bowing Chuma slaves. "Where is my bath?" she asked no one in particular.

"I think they meant us to bathe together, Princess," Mace said.

She looked at him briefly, then walked up to the wall of the aquarium. Fishes so exotic that Mace was not certain they were fish swam leisurely beyond the thick glass, going about their business among gently waving plants and a miniature model of some ruined temple. "I may not always bathe alone, Mace Wilde, but I choose my companions carefully."

"They can fight for you, but not take a bath with you, huh?"

She looked at him with a sudden wide smile. "They fought for themselves, not me. I owe them nothing. I owe no one anything, except for allegiance to the throne I represent."

"And that throne represents the royal house only?" He emphasized the last word gently, then smiled at her frown. "The people are nothing, huh? Where I come from you don't stay in power long without caring something for those you rule."

Falana turned and put her back against the cool glass wall. A bulging-eyed fish with yellow streamers came up to nibble futilely at her back. "No royal house has ruled for centuries on your planet?"

"You got me there, Princess, but as corrupt and aristocratic as they were, they had to give *something* to the people. What do you Kula give?"

"Why should we give anything, you pompous lecturer? We are Kula! We rule. The rest obey."

"Princess, honey, you have a *lot* to learn. Why do you think you have all these rebel states? If it was your divine right to rule, why hasn't everyone we've encountered fallen down on their knees to you?" Her eyes flared and she straightened up. Mouthfire and Longtalon were splashing and laughing. "*That's* the reason I wanted to show you Zandra."

"What do you know of Zandra? You are a stranger. You saw only the Vandorians, and Kulan."

"I saw slavery, Princess Falana, and where there is slavery, there is unrest, rebellion, a desire for freedom. The people of Zandra are just too close to those of Earth for it not to be so."

"Oh, and now you are an expert, Earthman?"

He smiled at her and began unbuckling his sword. He put it on the pool's edge and took off his armor. Already Mouthfire was coming up out of the pool, gleaming wetly, her long blonde hair unbraided and dark with water. Longtalon followed, but he was watching Falana.

"Well, Your Highness honey, I'm taking a bath, whether you feel like one or not." He looked at the two Kurkans, drying off with thick towels, and his eyes moved to the door by which they entered. Longtalon nodded. Mace took off his armor and untied his loincloth, then peeled off the soft boots.

The pool was not big enough to dive in, but he jumped in happily. It was warm, almost too hot, and scented. From his lower position Falana looked like the exotic cover of some fantasy magazine, golden-skinned and decorated with fanciful jewelry. He shook his head with a grin. This entire adventure was so bizarre he sometimes did not believe it was happening. It was all some mass hallucination. Things here were both familiar and bewilderingly strange. A medieval world with Flash Gordon superimposed. Past and future combined, yet . . . yet he was coming to like it. He still felt the tug of responsibility: get those who wanted to return back to Earth.

Those who wanted to return. His unconscious had delivered to him a revelation. Perhaps *he* was one of those who did not want to return. He thought of his career and responsibilities as an officer in the United States Army. He had fought where and how he was told to fight and not every time had he believed what he was doing was totally right. Mostly right, yes. He had the lives and comfort of his men to think about. He was not, had not been, responsible for the world picture.

But here . . . here was different. I feel like a mover and shaker. Here I am affecting the future of a world, he thought. *It is not my world, but then, for an American that was not all so strange. Most Americans were only two or three generations away from some other place . . . not counting Indians, and they, too, were nomads from elsewhere, if you went back far enough. A stranger in a very strange land,* he smiled.

His attention was diverted to Falana. She seemed perfectly absorbed in the activities of the hundreds of tiny fish in the big aquarium, but Mace realized she was only waiting for him to emerge. She might invite him to bathe with her, but she was not about to enter *his* bath. Mace quickly swam to the edge of the pool and pulled himself out.

"All yours, Princess," he said.

"No, thank you, Captain Wilde," she said lightly. "I bathed at the last primitive camp. I would much prefer to get on with my father's business . . . now that you have all pleasured yourself."

Mace pulled up his loincloth and bent over to pick up his boots. Longtalon was close to the door and suddenly hissed at him. Mouthfire's sword whispered from her scabbard and Longtalon's came out with a metallic scrape. Mace picked up his by the hilt and discarded the scabbard with a gesture. It fell against the wall and one of the fuzzy-leaved plants curled away from it, turning dark.

The door opened and Norg stopped short, looking with mild surprise at the trio of drawn blades. "Oh, paragon of beauty, surely you do not fear anything here in the land of Scarn?"

"I fear only my father," she replied haughtily.

"A most productive relationship, I am certain, munificence," Norg replied smoothly, bowing. "If you and your companions would care to dine, we have prepared a modest feast for your pleasure, great star of the heavens."

"Yes, that would be nice," Falana said, walking toward the door. "You have tasters, of course?"

"Naturally, magnificence, but only to make you feel comfortable. There is no need, of course . . . but it is tradition, is it not, truest flower of Kula?"

Falana did not reply and Norg bowed her out, following her closely and ignoring Mace and the Kurkans. Mace picked up his armor and Longtalon helped him into it as they walked along.

Norg hurried ahead, to lead the quartet along a different route. They passed through rooms of ornate luxury, filled with couches and flowering plants, sensuous sculptures and polished stone floors covered with thick carpets in intricate designs. They passed out of the glass structure and across a bridge of cobalt glass. Below was a small park where one old man was entertained by several naked Chuma slaves.

They entered another building, this one a tower of glass bubbles, and went along a vaulted corridor lined with bowing Scarn nobles in ornate costumes. Mace saw a woman with a shaved head, her skin dyed blue, wearing only a pair of high boots and what seemed like two square yards of crimson tattooing. A fat man in red robes bordered in gold embroidery had a horn in the center of his forehead. Mace was not certain whether it was real or some kind of costume.

The walls of the corridor had murals crowded with figures, each of whom seemed to carry, brandish, or display some kind of symbol: swords, writhing snakes, severed heads, flowers, birds, phallic symbols, crowns, glowing dots, flames, and spheres. The murals seemed symbolic, mythic, allegorical, but Mace had no idea of their meaning.

Norg led them into a banquet hall with an ornate roof representing a flight of colorful birds. Murals along the lower wall were of fish, while those painted along the higher wall were of animals: dragons, horned things that could have been horses or possibly deer-like creatures, furry, feathered and glossy-skinned animals of improbable shapes. The Scarn noble led them to a dais of tiers. At the highest tier was a single, throne-like chair. To the sides were places for ten, and here Mace and the Kurkans were directed to sit.

Then the Scarn nobles began to file in, chattering and laughing. Mace waited impatiently, for the procedure was a direct reverse of the usual one on Earth, where the honored guest appears last, after everyone else is seated. He looked at Falana and saw that she did not appear impatient, but then she had a lot of practice at this sort of thing, he mused.

When slaves closed the great doors Norg rose and tinkled a small bell. At once the murmurs stopped and everyone rose. Mace and the two Kurkans were a bit slow in responding, looking at each other, then around at the bowing crowd that filled the large room. Falana made a gesture and everyone sat down.

Hidden musicians began playing. Slaves appeared from behind screened doorways, bearing platters and bowls of food. The scents assaulted Mace's nostrils. He was wary of Zandran food, as some of its most attractive food turned out to have tastes that—to say the least—astonished him.

A Chuma slave appeared at each side of Falana, and Mace examined them with two quick looks. A male and a female, they were obviously the tasters. Tasters did not appear for Mace, nor the Kurkans, and as a result none of them took food from bowls or plates that others did not also eat from.

The banquet progressed smoothly. Wine was brought in flagons. Entire birds, larger than turkeys, were brought in, surrounded by fruit and flowers. Small cooked animals drenched in a scented sauce were produced. Something like pellets of liver pâté was mixed with red peas. Watching Falana, Mace saw that twice she was surprised at the appearance of certain foods.

Mace wanted to talk to her, but the tiered arrangement made that very difficult. One of the pleasures of dining was good conversation, but for the honored guest at the Scarn banquet this was almost impossible. The Scarn noble to his right tried repeatedly to engage Mace in conversation, but he was too busy watching everything and making certain how he acquired his food.

Without preamble the Scarn noble stood up and the beautiful woman on his right slid into his place. The noble sat down in her place and started eating from her plate as if nothing had happened. That drew Mace's attention and the woman smiled, pressing her bosom against his arm.

"Perhaps I could interest you more, mighty warrior?" She was a brunette, with skin like dark gold, with black-rimmed eyes and a mouth that seemed always to be slightly open.

"Did I offend him?" Mace asked.

"Oh, no," she smiled, putting a bit of purple fruit into her mouth and rolling it around before she swallowed. "Count Vorta has only two subjects to talk about, anyway, and one of them I don't think you are interested in. At least not with him."

"And what is the other?"

She stabbed a small round green bulb with her fork, raised it to eye level for inspection, watched the creamy fluid ooze from it, then licked the fluid with the tip of her tongue. "Oh, the old Zull machines."

"What old Zull machines?" She had captured his attention.

"The ones that give us all this, of course," she said, gesturing around. She put the green bulb in her mouth and closed her eyes for a moment, rolling it around before swallowing.

"You have Zull artifacts?"

"Yes, of course. We could not live without them down here."

"Why *do* you live down here?"

She looked surprised. "Because we always have!" She once again gestured around. "Is this so bad? Others in this world do not live so well." She looked up at Falana with an expression of delight. "Not even the Kula, I suspect."

"Well, they don't live in caves, anyway."

She examined him with an expression of wry amusement. "Everyone lives in some sort of cave, Earthman. They live that way on Earth, too."

"What do you know of Earth, uh . . ."

"Oh, I forgot. We have all known each other since birth, and our parents, our parents' parents, all the way back to Before. We sometimes forget to introduce ourselves. I am Nuala, Countess of the Shimmering Crystal, Flame-giver to the Subject Races, Baroness of the Blue Lake, and Hereditary Mistress of the Whip."

Mace looked at her for a bit. "Would you care to explain all that?"

She smiled and picked up a plump bird leg to bite into. She chewed the meat delicately, then took a sip of wine from a glass goblet. "The Shimmering Crystal is a power source. The Blue Lake is a water source here, underground. As Mistress of the Whip and Flame-giver I offer discipline to the Chuma and others."

Mace looked at her with disgust only barely concealed. He drank some wine, relishing the plum-like taste. "What 'others'?"

"Other than the Chuma? Oh, we have some Zurians, or Zurian breeds. Unusual, you know; they usually cannot interbreed. Then there are a few Melorians we have for pleasure. And the Earthman."

"What Earthman?"

Nuala shrugged. "A curious creature, really. Savage person, with the oddest beliefs." She stabbed another green bulb and licked the oozing fluid. Mace put a hand around her wrist and she looked at him in smiling surprise.

"Why, Earthman, you like to do that? Perhaps later we could go to the pens together? We have some beautiful new Chuma from the west, who—"

"The Earthman? Who is he?"

"You mean his name? I haven't the faintest idea. Slaves are given names only for convenience, not as an honor." She winced as he tightened his grip. "Oh." She closed her eyes and licked at her lips. "We must meet later. I have some—"

"*Who is he?*"

"Really, he is only a slave." She looked at him with some annoyance and shook her arm free. Petulantly, she resumed eating. "You care more for that . . . that Earth creature than you do me. Perhaps I should let Count Vorta sit here again, if you prefer that sort of thing."

"His name, Countess." Mace's voice was low, but the undertone in it made her quiver.

She dabbled at her chin with a lacy handkerchief and leaned closer to Mace. She was not wearing much in the way of clothing, and her figure was superb, a fact she used to the greatest advantage. "Would you beat it out of me, if I did not tell?" she murmured.

Mace glanced at the Kurkans, then looked around at Falana. He caught her looking away from him. The banquet hall was noisy with the chatter of the guests. Mace turned back to Countess Nuala. "Can you take me to him?"

"Why would you want to go *there?*" She looked disgusted. "I shall have him bathed and brought to you, if that is your pleasure." She looked at him shrewdly. "What are you planning, Earthman? He does not provide much pleasure. He is an exotic, true, but not to you." She shrugged and raised her eyebrows. "I tried him . . . twice, as a matter of fact . . . but he knows nothing and will not learn. But *you*, ah, that is different." She glanced up at Falana knowingly. "I know of Falana and her tastes. She, too, likes exotics . . ." She looked closely at Mace and smiled softly.

"Have him brought to me, then. Are there others? Others from Earth?"

"There have been. They are new, you know. Some people think they are more trouble than they are worth. Always calling upon some invisible alien creature of vast power—who never answers them. Always complaining, starting trouble. And how they *talk*—the ideas they keep chattering about!" She shook her head and took a sip of wine.

"I suppose you mean such fantastic ideas as freedom, democracy, and nonsense like that?" Mace said.

"Yes—you know them! I do hope you are not possessed with such notions. They are contrary to everything natural. The natural order of things has been long established, is perfectly obvious, and there is no need to change." She bit into her meat and chewed happily.

"Then you think Emperor Morak's rule is, um, unnatural?"

"Oh, no!" She swallowed and smiled. "That is natural enough, I mean, for *him*. We do not have the mindsword ability; they do. It is natural that they should seek to rule us. It is those to whom nature assigned a subject place that should not seek to disturb the natural balance."

"Uh-huh. Then will Scarn fight Morak or what?"

She wiped her lips and hugged his arm, rubbing her breasts against him boldly. "Why speak of that? It is for Naar to decide. He likes to do those things, though I don't know why. Wearisome details, really. I prefer more . . . um . . . *personal* decisions."

"Uh-huh, right. When can you bring this Earthman to me?"

She sat back, an expression of supreme unconcern masking her face. She stabbed a bit of meat and inspected it on her fork. "If that is your wish, I shall have him brought to you tonight." She put the meat in her mouth, chewed it, then put down her fork and rose. She walked calmly down the table and tapped a young man on the shoulder. He rose and came smiling to the seat she had vacated.

"Greetings, Earthman," he said warmly. "I am Baron Maa, cousin to Prince Norg, Controller of the Nightflowers, Custodian of the Black Tower, Viscount Tumla and Commander of the Inner Guard."

"How do you do?" Mace said politely, looking down the table at Countess Nuala, who was engaging an elderly officer in bright conversation.

"I do very well, Mace Wilde, how do you do?" He leaned close to Mace, who looked at him in mild surprise. "This was more than I had hoped!" He leaned back, smiling widely and with great charm. "Scarn is yours tonight, Mace Wilde! Let me show it to you!" He leaned back, closer this time. "We have a *most* unusual world here, as you are only beginning to comprehend, I'm sure. Here, in Scarn, we have pleasures and delights of which you do not know." He put his mouth almost in Mace's ear. "We have Zull devices, you know. Yes! Original Zull machines! *Pleasure* machines that can pluck from your mind your wildest fantasies and make them real!"

"Real?"

"Well, they seem real. You taste, see, feel, smell, everything! What I enjoy is to tap the fantasies as some delicious exotic is using the machines and experience it *with* them!" He seemed very exuberant and outgoing. "Most unusual, I tell you. Something you cannot imagine. Please say you will try one? We have a Blue, a Red . . . though that is beginning to show some defects . . . a Green that must be tried to be believed! We used to have a Gray, when I was young, but it stopped working some time ago. And the Orange we had to stop using entirely as it was giving us nightmares." He shook his head in deep sadness.

"Things *are* changing, that is certain." He touched Mace's arm. "But *some* changes are wonderful!" He looked brightly into Mace's scowl. "Please say you will try the Green with me?" He looked concerned and pulled back. "Unless you prefer a Red?"

"I don't know one from another." He looked at Falana. Norg was whispering to her, bent over and gesturing with beringed fingers.

"I'll show you then! We can try them *all!* It will be wonderful!" He touched Mace again to get his attention. "I hope you don't mind me saying so, Mace Wilde, but I have tried the Green with one of your Earthmen before." He shuddered. "Almost put me off for the longest time! You would not believe the *visions* that one had! Strange vessels of wood and fabric on a blue sea. Golden idols washed with blood. Bearded warriors. Men tortured upon crosses and rising from the dead as though a healer had been there. Flames, oh, how he loved the land of flames. Creatures burning endlessly but never dying. Most extraordinary."

"Hell."

"I beg your pardon?"

"His vision was of Hell."

"Well, I know what the vision *was*, but I didn't like it much. Though I must say his savage bloodletting had a certain cathartic response." He licked his lips and picked up a fork to eat from the plate abandoned by Vorta and Nuala.

"This Earthman you have here, what is his name?"

"Oh, she told you about him, did she? Poor wretch. A great disappointment to us all. We'll trade him soon, I'm sure. I suppose he does have a name, of course, they always do. Long one, too, I imagine. All the first ones seemed to be burdened with very long names."

"His name."

"I'm sure I don't know. I had to have him whipped. He was quite insolent and offensive. All I wanted was to share some pleasure. He wasn't like the *first* ones we had here, though." Baron Maa's eyes slitted in memory and he sighed. "Most extraordinary. Unique, you know. Totally recharged the image bank in the Green and Red, especially. Marvelous new ideas."

"Countess Nuala said she'd have him brought to me."

"Then she shall." He looked disappointed. "Are you planning something together then?"

"I just want to talk to this Earthman."

"Talk." Baron Maa said it flatly, but with some surprise. "That's all? Just talk?"

"Yes."

The Scarn noble sighed and took a drink of wine. Then he sighed again. "Talk," he said. "You'll not find many of these Earthmen very good conversationalists, my dear Mace Wilde. It's like talking to a cavern frog. Your friends from Earth, on the whole, do not hold conversations, they grasp them. They ask endless questions and their answers are . . . no offense . . . often quite mad. You cannot *believe* how they seek to inflate their importance by exaggerating their numbers! Millions, they say. Indeed."

"Billions, actually."

Baron Maa looked at Mace sadly, then sighed. "You, too? Billions, indeed. How could they *live?* They would be crawling all over each other like *worms!*" He made an expression of deep disgust and rinsed his mouth out with wine.

"You may be right there. You control your population then?"

"Of *course*, my dear man. The females only have children when they want children and they only want children when they are told to want children." He looked curiously at Mace. "You mean, on Earth, it is an involuntary act?"

"To a great extent, yes. It has been the source of almost all our troubles, I'll admit that. Too many people, not enough resources."

"Then why do your Earth people all long to go back? Most cannot *wait* to return!" He snorted. "There is no way back, in any case, but they never cease to agitate for it. Disgusting lot, really." He smiled suddenly and touched Mace's arm. "Please, I do not mean to offend. You are obviously one of the nobility there and cannot be responsible for the herd."

Mace looked at him a moment before he spoke. "You would never understand us, I can see that."

Baron Maa looked hurt. "Really, Mace Wilde, I am considered something of an expert on the people of Earth. I am frequently called upon to set a price or to judge the fairness of a trade involving your Earthlings. I understand better than most, I think."

Mace felt a confusing sadness. He did not understand the Zandrans and they certainly did not understand the people of Earth. Poles apart, perhaps even galaxies apart. He felt a sense of great loss and his earlier thoughts about staying seemed futile. He would never fit in. None of them would fit in. They would always be the odd ones, the exotics, pets and slaves, momentarily useful or interesting to the powerful, but no more than that.

He felt an anger growing. Well, he wasn't going to be someone's pet, not even Falana's. If Zandra would not accept the people from Earth after forcing them to come there, then *they* would change Zandra! He felt as the blacks must have felt, after being brought to the New World as slaves, then not assimilated until they made a very big noise. Well, Zandra was going to know that Mace Wilde was there!

"My dear man, what is the matter? You look so—"

"Never mind. I just . . . made a decision."

"Involving me?" Baron Maa said quickly.

"In a way."

"Oh . . . I *did* hope not to have to share you, but if that is your wish."

"Don't get your hopes up, Baron, I—"

The tinkle of Norg's bell stopped the conversation. He stood near Falana's chair, smiling. "O Supreme Flower of Kulan, may I present some entertainment for your pleasure?" Falana nodded, her expression aloof and almost challenging. Norg rang another bell, and things began happening.

Dancers streamed in from the screened doorways, darting between the tables to assemble on the cleared floor. The floor glowed with a soft light beneath them as they danced furiously to music from hidden musicians. The dancers were seminaked, dressed in feathers and ribbons. A beautiful Chuma girl was brought in on a tray, surrounded by fruit and flowers, as though she were a succulent dish. She rose from the tray to leap to the floor and begin an almost frantic dance. Her choreographic symbolism was strong, but not lewd.

A section of the glass ceiling opened and a male dancer appeared to applause. He descended to the floor on a slim line decorated with live birds fluttering wildly and joined the female dancer. Mace looked at Falana and found her looking at him. He raised his eyebrows in a silent, ambiguous question, but she turned to watch the dancers without any response.

The dancers melted away through the tables and the music changed. The floor opened up and a dragon appeared, ridden by a beautiful Scarn woman in a horned helmet. Mace recognized the dragon as a Sauron, wearing some kind of ornate glass helmet through which bits and pieces of what looked like electronic gear was dimly seen. The

Sauron did a kind of dance, raised up on its massive rear legs, with the brightly clad woman riding it. They received enthusiastic applause.

"Countess Nia makes a beautiful Mistress of Dragons, does she not, Mace Wilde?" Mace gave Baron Maa a brief look. "Does she not look like Queen Zador?"

Mace had seen the Kula leader of the Saurons when they had first arrived on Zandra. The redheaded queen was considered something of a rebel and a renegade by the Kula and a possible threat to the throne of Zandra. The Scarn woman looked nothing like Zador, except that she had red hair. There was an air of degeneracy about her, as there was to all the Scarn Mace had seen. Decadent, self-indulgent, egocentric, lazy, corrupt—these were all words that Mace thought applied to the underground nation.

The helmet the massive dragon-like Sauron was wearing was obviously some kind of control. There was no other way an intelligent creature as powerful as a Sauron was going to be so obedient. Mace felt a sudden surge of adrenaline—*free the Sauron!*

The red-haired woman bowed as the Sauron made its obeisance toward Falana and Norg, then they sank into the floor again and were covered over. An explosion of birds erupted from another hidden panel high in the glass ceiling of birds. They swept through the room and out again, chittering, through another opening.

A puff of smoke erupted in the floor and a golden-clad androgynous figure emerged from the mist, carrying brilliant balls of glass in each hand. He smashed the spheres onto the floor, creating explosions of blinding light. Mace's hand was on his sword hilt and he rose in his place. But from the pinpoint brilliance came two more androgynous figures, mirror-bright and totally covered in silver. They danced around each other in a complex, weaving design, with the golden figure making lines of glowing fire in the air with his fingers. The weave of glowing lines floated, gradually fading as the dance progressed.

"Who are they supposed to be or represent?" Mace asked.

"The Zull masters, of course." Baron Maa laughed. "We don't *really* know what they looked like, except in the vaguest of terms, but we like to think of them as something like this."

A Scarn noble broke loose from the excited crowd and threw herself at the feet of the golden figure. Another followed, then two men. The dancers spun and leaped, nimbly avoiding the prostrate nobility. A woman tore off her only clothing—a network of thin golden chains hung with emeralds—and threw it like a net. The golden figure was caught for only a moment, then the links melted and dropped away to much delighted laughter. Mace looked at Falana again.

She was staring at the dancers with a kind of intensity he had not seen before. It was a mixture of fear and attraction and her slim, graceful body was tense.

More and more nobles were debasing themselves beneath the dancers, who could no longer avoid stepping on them. The tempo of the music increased and the supine nobles groaned with delight as the three dancers pranced on their backs. Fire and smoke streamed from the fingertips of the golden figure, spinning in a circle. The floor glowed and unfolded; the center section, with its cargo of writhing bodies, sank out of sight, and the floor closed over them. A faint mist remained, drifting toward the ceiling lazily. Everyone applauded, but many looked toward Falana. She was applauding enthusiastically, her eyes bright and her wet lips parted.

Mace stood up as the others stood up, shaking free from Baron Maa, and went quickly up to the Kulan princess. She looked at him with bright eyes, her lips smiling almost lasciviously. "Was that not marvelous, Mace Wilde? The Zull dancers were the best I've seen."

"Yeah, Princess, they put on quite a show for you. Now tell them to get this Naar here and let's get things settled."

"Why are you in a hurry, Mace Wilde? You are *always* in a hurry. Rushing me from place to place . . ."

"Are you drunk, Falana?"

"Intoxicated, Earthman, not drunk. Princesses are never drunk."

Mace glowered at Norg, standing nearby trying to look innocent. "Look, Your Highness, we—"

"Prince Norg tells me they have a *Green* Zull pleasure machine, Mace Wilde. I have never tried a Green. I, a princess of Zandra, have never had a Green. Shameful." She laughed. It was almost a giggle and Norg looked even more innocent.

Longtalon and Mouthfire joined them, watching the milling throng of colorful Scarn nobles. "Did they give her something, Mace Wilde?" Longtalon asked.

"I drank from the common flagon," Falana said. "We are not fools at Kulan."

Mace looked disgusted. "On Earth it is an ancient assassin's trick to coat the goblet in poison and let it dry. It is the glass, not the wine, that is poisoned."

"They would not poison *me*," Falana said indignantly, putting her arm around Mace and rubbing her other hand across the black breast-plate of his Zurian armor.

"Your father, Princess honey, does not even know where we *are*," Mace whispered angrily. "Maybe they wouldn't kill you, but they might compromise you, subvert you."

"Oh, no, that cannot happen to me," Falana said, laughing. She tried to edge her hand under Mace's armor. "Why do you wear that? Let us go someplace and take it off, Mace Wilde. Let us pleasure ourselves. Then we will try their Green Zull delight and start over!" She laughed and pressed herself to him.

Mace looked at Mouthfire who reached out and put an arm around Falana. "No," the princess said in annoyance. "I do not share him. I do not want you. Go away. Come, my big, tall, angry man of Earth, let us go to my chambers . . ."

"All right," Mace said, looking around. He helped Falana down from the dais but gestured to the Kurkans to follow.

"What did they think might happen?" Mouthfire asked as they left the hall, with Norg ostentatiously leading the way.

"Distraction," Mace answered. "Keeping her busy until they set up something, or . . . I don't know. A stall. Cleopatra kept Marc Antony amused for years by arranging little surprises and delights." He smiled briefly at Mouthfire's questioning expression. "Never mind, a thing from old Earth, from ancient times."

"This way, my noble sirs," Norg said.

"Mace Wilde, Mace Wilde, you are so . . ." Falana's step was uncertain, but she was smiling warmly at him, her eyes bright and fixed.

"I certainly am," he muttered. He glowered at Norg, who pretended suavely not to see.

"Right up here, my supreme delights," Norg murmured, indicating a broad, curving staircase that went up around the inside of a pink glass tower. The room given to Falana was pink and white, pink windows draped in thin rose fabric, thick white carpet, and a gigantic bed of pale soft gray fur with four twisting columns of pink and white glass.

"Come, lie with me," Falana murmured, unfastening her clothes as Mace put her on the bed. Norg bowed as he withdrew, wearing a knowing smile. Longtalon shut the thick translucent doors and joined Mouthfire in a quick survey of the suite.

"A bath and a wardrobe," Mouthfire reported to Mace, a certain envy in her voice.

"One way in, one way out," Longtalon said.

"The windows?" Mace asked.

"They are walls, really, one fused section with clear areas," Longtalon said. "The floor becomes a wall, the wall becomes a ceiling."

"Can we break the window, if we have to?" Mace asked, resisting Falana's graspings.

Longtalon shrugged. "I do not know. They build tall with this glass, it must be very strong."

"We could bring down the whole tower, breaking out," Mouthfire added.

"Tell them to go away," Falana said. "Come, let us pleasure ourselves," she insisted. She was nude now, but Mace was not in the mood.

"Keep watch," he said to the Kurkans. They went to the door and looked out, swords drawn. Mace strode across the white carpet to look at the windows. The floor indeed curved up to become transparent, then shading into translucence, and then opaque as it curved back into the ceiling.

"Earthman, what *are* you doing?" Falana said in annoyance. "Come *here*."

"In a moment, Falana," he said absently. "I'm checking the perimeter."

"That's a good soldier. Leave it to the Kurkans, they do that sort of thing well. Ask my Zurians." She laughed and writhed on the gray fur. "Come *on*, Mace Wilde. Your princess commands you!"

"Hold on, Falana." A big glass cutter, that was what he needed. He didn't like anyplace where the only way out was the way in. Never did, never would. He pulled back the carpet, looked in the luxurious bath, got up on a chair and scratched at the ceiling with his sword point.

"Mace *Wilde*, I shall not wait forever. Prince Norg has told me of a certain Baron Kala . . . but I feel like you, Mace Wilde."

"Hold your horses, I'll be right there."

"Hold my what? I do not do that, Earthman. That is what others do. Now come *here*—I am tired of waiting."

Mace walked across to the Kurkans. "Anything?"

Mouthfire shook her head. They could hear the sounds of revelry below and above, farther up the stairs. Longtalon glanced back at Falana and smiled. "What do you do now, Earthman? You are being called to duty."

"Yeah, yeah. What do you think they are planning?"

"Perhaps nothing. This alone has occupied us and will, um, continue to occupy us for a while," Longtalon replied.

"They need not attack us to keep us busy, Mace Wilde."

"Just call me Mace, will you? But *why*? Why not just get this Naar here and get to the discussions?"

"Maybe there will be no discussions, Mace. Maybe they hope the distractions of Scarn will be . . . irresistible," Longtalon said.

"Mace . . ." There was a petulant quality to Falana's voice. "Earthman . . ."

"You better go," Mouthfire said with a smile. "We'll stay outside."

"Don't go away. Holler if you see *anything* suspicious," Mace said.

"Mace *Wilde—*!"

The Earthman shrugged and turned toward the bed.

Eve Clayton yawned. She was sleepy and leaned on the railing of the control mast, watching the tower through half-lidded eyes. Skylance sat on the floor, his head bowed in sleep. She looked up at the stars beginning to come out. *What was taking them so long?* Should she go in? Should they lift and circle? Probably safer, but if Mace and the others had to come out fast, it might take longer to find them in the dark and get them aboard.

The constellations overhead were all new. None of them were the least familiar. She didn't know how to tell time by them, but then, back in L.A. she seldom saw the stars anyway.

Where were they?

Not just Mace, but Liberty and Barney, all those who crashed with them, all those snatched by the Vandorians over the centuries?

What did it all mean? She was not a religious person, yet she had vague feelings that it *had* to all mean *something*. Not the decidedly odd thing that had happened to Airworld's jet load of people, but the universe, the birth and death of everything, the meaning of life . . .

She inhaled and let her breath out slowly. *There had to be an order,* she thought. *Some kind of order, some governing force, some objective, some reason for it all. That the whole universe had just happened seemed . . . pointless. Even if it was all some giant plaything for the amusement of some celestial child, even if it was an experiment, conducted in the afternoon of a god, even if it was random chance operating at capacity—it meant something. There had to be some reason they were here—wherever here was.*

Eve did not believe in reincarnation and had only vague, half-formed thoughts about heaven and hell. She believed more in reward and punishment in the here and now. *But then,* she thought with a smile, *I'm a cop. Was a cop. Will be a cop again.*

Or will I? This whole thing has to change me, change every one of us. We couldn't go back to just doing what we did before, could we? Back to roll call and routine, to patrol and paperwork. But what would I do, she wondered, *if—or when—I've gotten back to terra firma? The memory of Zandra will be with me. Like soldiers changed forever by war, I will not be the same. I am not the same, already. I've killed men. And they are men, not just phantoms. The Zurians are people, the four-armed Vandorians are people, the weird Tigron are people. And I've killed; that's something I never did in all my time with the L.A.P.D.*

It would be easy to think of them as lesser beings, as nonhumans. You seldom think of a cow when you are eating steak; you kill a Zurian or a shape-changing Tigron and you can easily think of them as animals, insects, things, not people.

Eve shuddered and tried to close her mind to such thoughts.

She jerked her head up. Almost went to sleep there. Watch it, girl. She looked at the tower, fitfully illuminated by a single torch near the entrance.

What were they *doing* down in those caverns?

Liberty walked softly around the grounded cloudship. They had no fire, not wanting to draw attention. They were also short of food. Barney was still feverish. Jardek and Richter were in the cabin with the animal trainer, jabbering away about interspacial vectors and energy stress points, black holes and white holes, and a lot of things she didn't know about. If they wanted to discuss frame lines and special effects, sense memory and Stanislavsky, MOS or a studio's creative accounting, then she could contribute.

What the blazes is going on? she wondered angrily. Was that Durak or not today? Will they be at this Scarn tomorrow? What's there? Maybe I should start thinking about where we should go *next?*

Redpike walked around the ship from the other side and stopped. She stopped, too, and they listened to the night together in silence. But the night was not silent. There were distant yelps, far-off growls, nearby rustlings, the soft flap of night birds, the sound of insects. Nights were never really silent, not if you listened.

"These people, these Scarn—what are they like?" she asked softly.

"Seductive," Redpike said.

"Seductive? In what way? Do they come on to you strong, or . . . sorry. Explain."

"They have no standards but pleasure."

Liberty shrugged. "Nothing against pleasure, myself."

"But as an end in itself?"

"Hmm. No, I suppose not. As a reward, maybe. It's kind of hard to define that." A short silence gave the night a chance to be noisy again. "Redpike . . . how did you get that name?"

"In a battle with the Zurians, as is so often the case. They assaulted the Mountain of Gold. I was but a youth then."

"The Mountain of Gold is—?"

"Was. A fortress. Some metal was once there. A Zull mine, but it is exhausted. The Zurians attacked. I was on guard. They came up without armor, climbing the rocks very silently. I stood in the arch. My sword broke. I took a lance from one of them and held them off. When it was over, my lance was red . . . and I was red."

"Gawd, what a bloody world!" Liberty thought of her own world and its history, of millions killed in purges and racial wars, in religious wars and senseless conflict, by bombs and guns and nerve gas. By ovens and famine and mutated bugs. By neglect and bitterness and overpopulation. "Maybe they're all bloody," she murmured.

"This world of yours," Redpike said, "it seems very strange to me. Crowded, mean, chaotic . . ."

"Yes . . . but beautiful, too. Vast oceans, great forests, cities bigger than anything here, I imagine. Jet planes that can get you halfway around the world in an afternoon. Television and movies." She stopped and smiled. "I still can't get used to the fact you don't seem to have the art of drama. It seems so . . . so natural. Acting out stories, the lives of great people, ordinary people." She shook her head.

Redpike smiled at her in the dark. "That's lying, isn't it? Pretending to be someone you are not? Isn't life enough?"

"But you can learn from other people, what they think and feel, how they act. I mean others than those around you. Sometimes you . . . well, you like to try out different life-styles, be someone else for a bit, try on a different skin."

Redpike shook his head. "It seems so very false."

"It *is*, but everyone knows they are *actors*, not the real people. But life keeps getting mixed up. People believe their own press—that they are special, that they are great lovers or great fighters. They start to act like the images they portray." She smiled as Redpike continued to shake his head. "I guess we'll never make you understand . . ." Her voice trailed off, and then she laughed softly. "One of these days, I'll put on a show for you . . . act something. Maybe a scene from one of my films, or . . . well, something. Maybe you'll get the idea then."

"Perhaps," Redpike admitted and after a moment of silence, he moved on around the perimeter, leaving Liberty with her own thoughts.

No motion picture industry here, she thought with a sigh. *But it's funny; knowing there is none I don't miss it, not really. It was competitive and tough and I fought hard to get where I was. If there was an industry here and I couldn't get in, I'd be really ticked off. But since there isn't, my energy is going toward survival. But it was all survival— getting to the top, staying at the top, making the kind of deal where you get to keep some of it, keeping the publicity mill moving, going on the television shows, getting into the variety shows, keeping those apples and oranges in the air.*

The music in her head was muted, indistinct, a reprise of an old score. She wanted to get back to Earth, she probably would *always* want to get back, but since that didn't seem to be something that was going to happen right away, she had to think about paying the rent.

It all came down to survival. Once it had been simply food and a roof. Then it was getting tht next job, getting the better job. Then it was making the best deal, keeping up the front and keeping that name out where they didn't say, "Liberty *who?*" She'd used her physical assets without hesitation, playing up her spectacular figure, getting the parts that showed her off best. She sought and fought for the best cameramen, the experts who knew just how to make her look beautiful, and she kept in their favor.

In the process she had formulated some rules for herself. *Work hard, learn everything:* be ready to do anything, ride a horse, dance, duel, sing. *Have faith in yourself:* build that confidence that what you are doing is right—for you. *Avoid television series:* because the real stars, the lasting stars, come from the movies. *Control the publicity:* have approval on all photos, on all stories—especially the stories because they always made you look promiscuous and they printed such garbage, anyway. *Go with the power:* don't hang out with the has-beens and never-weres, with the trashy trendy types; don't get that kind of reputation.

Never expose your body completely: scantily dressed, yes; nude, no. Leave some mystery. *Project your sex from the inside, not outside. Ex-*

ercise. Never get tied up romantically with anyone: at least publicly; be seen, be alive and around, but keep those fans' hopes up. *Always be dignified:* even when you are acting crazy; there's a thin line—don't cross it.

Think of yourself as a business: you have only one commodity to sell —yourself. *Never let the power push you around:* pass on the job with the casting couch attachment; pass on the bad roles; pass on the passes from power—they'll end up respecting you for it. *Control your impulses:* be rational and analytical in personal and professional actions. *Never let up:* there's always someone right behind you ready to move in. *Go to bed alone:* at least officially. *Be honest:* but don't be so honest you offend where it is needless.

Liberty sighed. *I obeyed those rules and now look at me,* she thought. *But maybe they are not so archaic a set of rules here as I might think. I must learn to apply them to the world of Zandra.*

Mace walked down the curving stairs slowly, watching the crowd below. He glanced back up at Longtalon and Mouthfire, standing guard at the door where Falana lay asleep. No one would get through without creating quite a noise and he would not stray far from the stairs.

The crowd watched him carefully. Some did it boldly and directly, with challenging, speculative looks, but others were more surreptitious, more guarded in their inspection of this stranger. Norg stood at the bottom of the steps, smiling in his oily fashion, and near him was Countess Nuala, looking aloof and fully as haughty as Falana in a rage.

"My abject apologies for disturbing you, my noble lord," Norg said with a bow, his eyes hard on Mace. "But the good Countess Nuala made a promise, which she now wishes to fulfill."

"Countess," Mace said, turning to her.

She did not answer him, but clapped her hands sharply. Curious bystanders looked around, then parted their peacock ranks to admit a pair of muscular half-breed Zurian guards. Between them was a wild-eyed, black-haired, heavily bearded man in chains. A ragged loincloth was his only garment and he glared about him with a ferocious frown. He fixed his eyes on Mace and did not take them away.

The prisoner was about thirty, lean and muscular, not very tall, almost a foot shorter than Mace, but he met Mace's gaze evenly, even defiantly.

"Kneel," Norg said petulantly. The prisoner did not kneel, but instead spat. The guard on his left raised an armored fist to club him to his knees, but Mace spoke up quickly.

"No!"

Norg was surprised and annoyed. "But, my great and noble sir, this creature must be taught the meaning of obedience!"

The unkempt man glared. "I kneel to no one but Their Gracious Majesties, the King and Queen of Spain, to the Holy Father, Pope Clement VII, and to *God!*" His gaze went to Mace, hard and unyielding. "You may club me to my knees, you may torture and kill me, but I *shall not kneel!*"

Norg sighed. "You see, Mace Wilde? You see what sort of creature we must put up with. This one is nothing but trouble. We have been able to extract no pleasure from him at all." He smiled wryly. "Nor have we been able to trade him . . . so . . ." He looked at Countess Nuala.

"A gift to Princess Falana," she said. Her eyes flicked briefly to Mace. "Perhaps *you* can find pleasure in this abysmal animal, Earthman."

The prisoner thrust his hawkish face at Mace. "You are from Earth?"

"Yes." He held up a hand to stem the tide of words he saw coming. "Release him," he said to the guards. They looked uncomfortable and glanced nervously at Prince Norg.

"He is very strong, Mace Wilde, O Noble Consort to the greatest of divine flowers—perhaps you should leave him as he is?"

Mace looked disgusted and stepped to the prisoner and turned him around. He seized the manacles and, with a strain, popped them open, much to the surprise of the onlookers. The crowd moved back with a gasp. Mace broke the other manacle and tossed the heavy chains to the floor. They were made of black glass, fused around the prisoner's wrists. Then he bent and repeated the process on the shiny foot chains.

"Thank you, in the name of Princess Falana," Mace said with a slight bow to Nuala, then to Norg. "I shall question this man in our chambers."

"Of course," Norg said, returning the bow and smiling knowingly.

"Follow me," Mace ordered and turned back up the stairs.

"My lord—!" the man said, his words an explosion of gratitude. He bounded after Mace, his powerful Terran muscles making great leaps up the staircase. He caught up to Mace and began a barrage of questions, but Mace silenced him.

The bearded man looked sharply at the Kurkans and edged past them into the room behind Mace. He looked startled, then lasciviously eager, when he saw Falana lying on the ornate bed. Mace threw a pink sheet over her and pulled the man into the bath and slid shut the door.

"What's your name?"

"Sir, I am Juan Leopoldo Cristóbal y Tenorio de la Cruz." He bowed, a wolfish grin on his face. "And you, my liberator?"

"Mace Wilde, formerly of the United States Army."

"Ah, a soldier like myself!" He sent a leer in the direction of Falana. "And the woman?"

"Heiress to the throne of Zandra," Mace said dryly and de la Cruz's eyebrows went up. "But tell me—what year was it when you left Earth?"

"Ah, such confusion! Let me tell you, Señor Wilde, I do not understand *any* of this! It must be the work of the Devil! This is somewhere in the New World . . . or a new hell, no? I thought at first—El Dorado! They speak Spanish, but they are not Spanish! I have seen dragons, sir, and creatures you would not believe!"

"They do not speak Spanish, I'm afraid, Juan. May I call you Juan?" The Spaniard bowed, but his eyes slipped around toward the closed door. "They put us all through a machine, a Zull machine, that—"

"The Devil's work, sir."

"Perhaps, but it makes us all *think* in whatever is our language, yet it comes out a common speech. But what were you doing in the Bermuda Triangle . . . excuse me, in that part of the Caribbean?"

"Ah, Liberator, it was my honor to serve the greatest of captains, Hernando Cortez himself! I landed with him in 1519, helped build Veracruz—ahh, what a time! What a commander! We conquered the Aztec, sir, a mighty enemy!" He laughed, his teeth white in the tangled beard. "They thought we were one, our horses and men! Ignorant savages!"

"Yes, I know of the adventures of Cortez. How were you taken? Were you on a ship?"

"A *golden* ship, Liberator! A *treasure* of pagan idols . . . jewelry . . . a great wheel of solid gold, sir! Ai, what a sight! We cast out the ballast and filled the ship with *gold!*" His eyes sparkled as he rubbed his chafed wrists. "The year of Our Lord 1528, sir. We sailed from the port of Veracruz on the *Santa Maria de Trinidad*, for the port of Malaga. We were to stop at Hispaniola, at Port-au-Prince, but a storm swept us north." He shrugged, giving the door another glance. "I do not know how far we went, nor how long. It was a terrible time. The storm passed, but the winds were strong. We furled our sails, but the ship was leaking."

Juan sighed, rubbing at his wrists. "I was asleep. I heard the screams. I ran on deck. It was Satan himself." His eyes grew haunted. "There were colors and the ship tipped and swayed. There was water everywhere, floating in the air in drops, Liberator. I seized a bit of rope and pulled myself to the mast. I . . . you will not believe this, sir, but I swear on my mother's grave it is true—I *floated!* I heard the gold crashing about and men were screaming with fear. I did not cry out, of course, for I am a de la Cruz." He blinked at Mace, then continued.

"The colors, they swept us on, then . . . by St. Francis, we were *falling!* Falling, sir—falling out of the sky! It was as though the sea had opened and we had fallen through the bottom—right to this Hades!" He seemed overcome with emotion and Mace waited. To a man of the early sixteenth century such an experience must have been beyond comprehension—it certainly was to a man of the twentieth!

"I seized a fold of sail. It billowed and tore loose as the ship crashed down. It was terrible, sir, terrible! My compatriots, Miguel, the Dominican, Captain Hernandez, Aurelio Gomez, all were lost! The ship crashed into the mountain, leagues from the sea, sir. There was no sea in *sight,* sir!" He grabbed Mace's arm to make his point and the army officer nodded.

"We arrived ourselves as you did, but we were . . . in . . . ah . . . a machine that flies . . . er, flew."

Juan de la Cruz stopped to stare at Mace for a moment. "A devil ship, such as those I have seen, the bowl-vessels?"

"No, but . . . well, something like that. I come from a time more than four hundred years after you, Juan. Almost five hundred."

"Five *hundred*, Liberator?" Juan looked skeptical. "I knew much time had passed. I heard from one wretch that my beloved Captain Cortez died poor and in obscurity in 1547, but he was a fool. He said he traveled in ships that used no sail, great ships of *metal*. Bah! They think Juan Leopoldo Cristóbal y Tenorio de la Cruz is a fool!" He peered closely at Mace. "I am not a fool, sir. Five hundred *years?* This man, he said that Spain did not rule the world, he said he was a sailor in a war that consumed the world, on a ship called the . . ." He paused to think. "The *Cyclops,* a ship full of coal, he said. Not even a man of war!"

"Nineteen eighteen," Mace said, remembering what the jetliner navigator Stokes had said about the vessels that had disappeared.

"But he would have been long dead, sir! A man does not live so long! From 1528 to this 1918? No, impossible!" He shook his head angrily.

"Look, Juan, time is different here. That is, there is some kind of time differential. A year here is sixty-two back on Earth."

"No, Liberator, a year is a year. They all think to trick me, but I do not fall for their magic. A year is a *year!* How can it be anything else?"

Mace sighed. "We'll have to try and explain it later. But how did you survive, falling like that? Did the sail act as a parachute?"

"Sir? No, the sail, she billowed out and the ship had already struck and split open like a melon when I fell to earth. I was in great pain, Liberator, great pain. Creatures from hell came. I tried to fight them off, but I had lost my sword." He struck his thigh with a fist. "The bone, sir, it was sticking out. I was near death. These imps of Satan— very big imps they were, and white with *four* arms, sir—they made a light and I could not move."

"Vandorians, Juan. They were Vandorians. They operate the Zull device that . . . never mind, go on."

"They put me in a device, sir. I thought they were to put me to the question, but instead, I . . . I passed out from the pain. When I recovered, I . . . Liberator, you will not believe what I will now tell you."

"Your wounds were healed. Your scars were gone. You never felt better in your life."

De la Cruz blinked. "You have seen this device of the Devil?"

"It's not a device of the Devil," Mace said wearily. "It's a healing machine. It works on your DNA and . . ." He looked at Juan's puzzled expression and stopped. "It's like a doctor. Go on, what happened then?"

The Spaniard shrugged. "It is a story of shame, sir. I was sold on a slave block. They had brought the idols, swords, armor, even the iron gear of the ship, the fittings and smallest bolt and ring. And the iron brought a higher price than the gold! These are strange people indeed. But I, the youngest son of Fernando Baldomero Carlos y Serrano de la Cruz, was sold on a bidding block!" His head came up and he glared at Mace.

"We were, too, Juan. Who bought you?"

"A woman of unsurpassed beauty—" A leer crossed his face to be replaced quickly by a brooding frown. "And of unsurpassed evil."

"People who are different from you are not always evil, Juan."

"Liberator, I know evil. She was evil. Her name was Countess Nudia and she was of this clan of a cursed mother goddess. They worshiped a pagan idol, sir, a female with many breasts. Their men were capons, sir!" He shuddered at the thought. "I have seen many things, sir. I have let the blood of many warriors, and not just the Aztec. My father fought the Moors at Granada. His father and *his* father fought the Moors. I have seen the pagan city of Cholula, sir, and the volcanos of New Spain. I was with Cortez when we fought across the causeways to Mexico, the city the pagans called Tenochtitlán. I have not always lived in chains, sir. I have seen things that would chill the blood of most men."

"Yes, you conquistadores carved quite a place for yourselves . . . in blood."

"Thank you, sir. I am pleased you know of us. We were few, they were many, but we fought them tooth and claw! Gold, Glory, and God! That was what Captain Cortez proclaimed. The cross and the sword, sir."

"But this countess . . . ?"

"Ah, she was a wench!" De la Cruz smiled wickedly. "We had a time. She was quite taken with me." He stroked his moustache. "Not that such a thing is so unusual, of course. I gave a good account of myself, but . . ." He shrugged. "It was not to be. She took me to this pagan ritual. They are a godless lot here, from what I have seen, but this mother clan is the worst, Liberator! Imagine—the *woman* rules? Impossible! Against nature! Not even our Lord thought that possible!" He rolled his eyes upward. "What a time! When I denounced them they tried to stop me. I was grievously wounded, but they revived me in their hell's spawn machine, and I fought again. Ah . . ." He shook his head. "A godless lot, worse, idol-worshiping devils!"

"And they sold you?"

"No, I was given away. It is my shame. I was given to another religious zealot, a Lord Kaa, who worshiped the sun like the Aztec, he and his band of decorated madmen! When I refused to bow, when I would not acknowledge their heretical rites, they put me in prison! Prison! Me, a de la Cruz! I was presented at court, you know, my friend. To King Carlos the First, in 1518. He was but a lad, as young as I, but fully a king, sir. I well recall the day. I—"

"Juan, how did you get here?"

"Oh. Well, I broke away from their jail. I am very strong, you know.

Much stronger than these devils. I can jump a great distance, fight like a man possessed. It took a year, but I fought my way out with a bar from my cell window, which took weeks to loosen."

He shrugged. "They set the priests upon me, with their spells and incantations. I was made motionless. The work of the Devil, sir. They returned me to my cell and there I languished for many months. Sometimes I was questioned and they made me sleep. Then I was brought here." He shrugged. "Another machine, but what a device!" He smiled broadly, leering around. "Such visions, sir—so real! The women here . . . godless, but at least they do not attempt to make me bow to their idols, for they have none. I was the two-backed beast with some, then . . ." He made a gesture of resignation. "Back to my cell. They sometimes bring me out, put me to sleep in their machines, but I know not what they do. Then you came, Liberator."

He grinned broadly at Mace and slapped him on the arm. "A warrior like myself, no? Together we shall conquer and—"

"Mace Wilde . . . ?" They left the bath at the sound of Falana's voice. Falana was sitting up in bed. The Spaniard turned quickly at the sound of her voice, his eyes burning at her revealed beauty. She gave him a cursory glance. "Who is this? Get rid of him," she said, lying back and stretching. "Come to me, Mace Wilde."

Juan de la Cruz started toward the bed but Mace stopped him. The Spaniard snarled at him, then controlled himself. "Many pardons, sir. She is perhaps your woman?"

"There's a bath in there, Juan, why don't you use it?"

"That's all right. I'll just use some perfume and be right back." He went toward the indicated door but his eyes were still feasting on Falana.

"No, Juan. Take a bath." There was that hard edge of command to Mace's voice and the Spaniard gave him a sullen look. "I will sicken and die. Everyone knows to expose the skin is wrong. Even the good Fathers bathe only a time or two a year." Mace made an abrupt gesture and the Spaniard smiled thinly, shrugged his shoulders expressively, and bowed gracefully, first to Mace, then in a deeper bow to Falana, his eyes raked over her body boldly. "Your pardon, Excellencies . . ."

Mace went over to the bed as Juan shut the bathroom door. "Well, Princess, have you seen what kind of people they are here?"

"Oh, Earthman, forget them." She patted the silken sheets. "Come."

"Eve and Skylance will be worried, and we have yet to find the other ship. You know we must find a safe place for Richter and Jardek. I sent a messenger to our cloudship, but we should get back."

She frowned at him in annoyance. "But *why?* Let us linger here, enjoy a rest. Let us stop this nonsense of running around risking our lives. We will rest here, eat, pleasure ourselves, and enjoy some of the rather special activities that only Scarn can provide."

"What of Naar? What of the rest of your kingdom, Falana? What of loyalty to our companions?"

"Loyalty to—? No, no, Mace Wilde, it is they who must have loyalty to me . . . as a representative of my father, the Emperor, of course."

"Of course." He stood over her, becoming more and more exasperated. "But what of your responsibilities to them? Leadership is a two-way street, *Princess* Falana."

She crossed her arms across her chest as she sat half-submerged in a mountain of silken pillows. Looking straight ahead, she said, "I am truly wondering why I came on this journey. It has been nothing but either dangerous or boring. One chance to rest and pleasure ourselves and you want to spoil it." She looked up at Mace, her dark brows in a straight line. "I am beginning to wonder what I see in you, Earthman. Who was that filthy creature? He looks like one of those chattering bores that first came here years ago."

"He is. One of the first, I mean. A conquistador under Cortez . . . almost five hundred years before my time."

She looked at him in mild disbelief. "Your Earth is a very strange place, Captain Wilde."

"We're wasting time, Your Highness. Get off your duff and let's collar this Naar and get his loyalty oath, then get on with finding a haven for the scientists."

She looked at him in puzzlement. "There are more men on this planet than I could count who would give their lives to be invited into my bed, yet *you* . . . a nameless, honorless *gift slave* . . . are trying to get me *out* of it."

Mace smiled at her. "That's right. There's a time and place for everything, Princess. Didn't they teach you that at Queenship School? Or are you going to let Valora take over?"

At the mention of her younger sister Falana's eyes opened wide in sudden anger. "She will never be Empress!"

"Are you so certain? She has the backing of the Zurians, that's certain . . . for as long as she serves as a pliable puppet." He stemmed her protests with a raised hand. "The best thing *you* can do is find out more about Zandra than your sister . . . *or* your father . . . can ever know. How can you rule anyone you have never seen?"

"You are a brute, Mace Wilde. Do you treat all queens this way?"

"I only met one queen, Falana. Her name was Maryann Love, and she was the Citrus Queen of Ventura County, California. For one year, that is."

"Such a short reign. Was she assassinated?"

"No, they elected another one, I imagine."

"Elected a queen?" She looked again with great skepticism. "You people from Earth are such liars. You boast of billions, of great machines of war, of incomprehensible heroes, of prophets and miracles . . ." She shook her head and sat up to put her feet over the side. "I am no longer in the mood. Send me my maid and . . ." She looked toward the bath. "Get that *savage* out of there! I wish to bathe."

Mace grinned and went over to extract Juan, singing and drinking perfume, from the tub. He wrapped a large towel around the protesting man and hustled him out.

"First you say bathe, then you take me from it," the Spaniard said, his breath reeking. He broke off as he saw Falana walk naked and unembarrassed across the room. "Aiii, such a world!" Mace shoved him out the door and followed. Several Chuma women were waiting patiently, some bearing trays with bottles and jars. Mace motioned them in and then spoke to the two Kurkan guards.

"Did the messenger return?"

Mouthfire nodded. "He said that the one who can draw the great bow almost spitted him, but she said everything was hunky-dory. Is this some code, Mace Wilde?"

"Just slang, and it translated very well."

"I am getting cold, Liberator."

"Can you find Juan here some place to finish his bath? I'll stand guard." Longtalon nodded and pointed with his naked blade.

"There. They said we could use that." The Kurkan took the elbow of the suspicious Spaniard and led him away.

"*Another* bath? Jesus and Mary, you people are possessed! When do I get my armor? I want my weapons, not those great heavy swords such as that. Do I get a maid, too, to join me in the bath? Who is that golden-skinned one? Is she the woman of my liberator? When do we—"

The door closed behind them and Mace sighed. The Spaniard was going to be a handful.

When Longtalon returned, Mace sent him and Mouthfire to find where the Sauron was kept. They returned flushed and slightly drunk and grinned under Mace's frown. "We had to blend in, Mace Wilde," Longtalon laughed. "A bit to drink, a bit of laughter. These Scarn, they think of nothing but pleasure! We saw a woman who—"

"Where's the Sauron?"

Mouthfire sighed. "The tower of black glass, we think. I saw the woman, Nia, enter there, bearing a bar of glass with wires and little things imbedded in it."

"A control rod of some sort," Mace muttered. "Mouthfire, will you see if Her Arrogance is ready? Tell her we are going to conduct a tour of inspection."

"And what is that?" Princess Falana said.

"The Tower of Fulfillment, O Great Star of the night," Prince Norg answered. He kept at her side, watching every expression closely. "It is where we are headed, my princess. There the Zull machines await and—"

"Very pretty," she said languidly. "We shall get there in time. What is that great spire of ebony?"

"It is called the Black Tower, beauteous one, but it is the red tower that should—"

"Such a prosaic name," Falana said, stopping to study it. "All the others have such fanciful names: the Tower of Fulfillment . . . imagine! the Spire of Flame and Ice, the Tower of Crystalline Dreams, the Spear of Zull, the Temple of Ultimate Temptation . . . but the *Black Tower?* Most interesting." She started walking toward it, but Norg danced around in front of her.

"Generous fountain of wisdom, that is . . . a place of government, sadly necessary, but hardly of interest to one such as you. Now the red tower, over there, it—"

"Incorrect, my dear prince. I, as future Empress of Zandra, am *most* concerned with government. There are those who say I cannot be *too* concerned with such matters." She gave Mace a level look, one significantly without expression. "I will inspect it."

"I . . . uh . . ." The usually glib Norg seemed at an impasse. He twitched and looked at the other nobles for help. Baron Maa stepped forward, bowed, and started to speak, but Falana walked right past him.

"Princess Falana," Maa said. "I am Custodian of the Black Tower and—"

"Then open the door for us," she said without slackening her pace.

Mace caught up with her and in an undertone said, "Attagirl, just what we wanted."

She looked at him with raised eyebrows. "Attagirl? Is that a Terran term of endearment?"

"Yes, in a way. Get them to show us everything."

"I said I would gain us entry, Mace Wilde, but I do think it will prove very boring."

Baron Maa opened the thick glass door, which moved silently and easily. The interior was very quiet; they could see the nobles, whom Norg was holding back, crowding around outside. Some of them started drifting away almost at once, bored.

The ground floor was a series of black glass knobs extruded from the glossy floor. Each knob had a computer terminal and a small screen. Norg came bustling in as Baron Maa explained this part was a library. Norg tried to get them out as soon as the brief explanation was finished, but Falana was having none of it.

"This is your seat of government? From where do you govern? Where is the throne of King Naar?"

"We . . . uh, His Highness sets policy and, um, there are devices which see they are carried out," Norg said.

"Computers," Mace explained. "Electronic brains? Electrical life programmed to work on certain principles?" The Scarn nobles looked at him in bewilderment.

Baron Maa cleared his throat and said, "His Magnificence speaks into the, um, controlling aperture and . . ." He shrugged. "It is done."

"You don't know how it works, do you?" Mace asked.

The two Scarn nobles looked at Mace with barely concealed antagonism. "Such things are beneath me," Norg said haughtily. "It has worked since our distant ancestors came here in the time of the Great Death. It has worked ever since, all of it." He gestured at the surrounding small city. "Is it not magnificent?"

"The princess would like to see the rest of the tower," Mace said and Falana gave him an annoyed look, then sighed in resignation.

With great reluctance Norg and Maa escorted their inquisitive guests up a curving staircase. "No one goes here," Maa said with faint disgust. "Except the Chuma who clean."

There were rows upon rows of spheres enclosed in dark glass, lifted from the floor at the end of a cone. Some of the spheres glowed, others did not, and one was blinking fitfully. Mace examined several but they were all sealed off. He didn't know if the dark spheres were burned out, inactive, or redundant.

There were two more floors that were much the same—spheres, cubes, amorphous shapes enclosed in glass and raised like exhibits.

"There, you've seen everything," Prince Norg said with an oily smile. "There are refreshments waiting, my dear, *dear* princess, and Countess Nuala herself has agreed to be your instructor in the use of the fabulous Green pleasure machine, which—"

"We haven't seen the basement," Mace said.

"Basement?" Baron Maa blinked.

"The floor under the ground. Surely you have one?" Mace grinned. "Or are you hiding something from the princess?"

"Oh, no, not at all," Norg hurried to say. "But . . . well, it is a trivial thing, nothing that might interest a Kula noble."

"I shall decide that," Falana said. "What bores me and what doesn't has been somewhat redefined lately." Mace looked at her but she was ignoring him.

Norg nervously lead the way down, then around under the central staircase to another door and more steps down.

They found no empty silences here. Countess Nia, in a costume of glossy black straps, was sitting before a huge console with a murky glass helmet that almost covered her head. In a cage of thick, crisscrossing glass bars, was the Sauron. The huge scaly creature sat without moving, its vestigial wings drooping, its yellow eyes dulled. Juan crossed himself, staring. The helmet of glass was still on the Sauron's head and within shone tiny lights. Mace noticed that the blinks and colors corresponded to blips of light on the console.

"Countess Nia is, um, training this beast," Norg said smoothly. "You see, it is nothing of much interest."

"The Saurons are intelligent beings," Mace said and Norg gave him a quick venomous look, swiftly masked.

"That is one theory, yes, but we have seen no evidence of that. They are . . . aliens, you know. Savage creatures brought here as hostages by the great Zull."

"You don't use hostages with animals," Longtalon growled, and the two Scarn nobles shifted uneasily.

"It is of no importance," Baron Maa said, turning toward them as if to herd them out. "The countess, she has her . . . um . . . pastimes. It is harmless."

"Except to the Sauron," Mace said. He allowed Maa to move them out and then followed a much more energetic Norg across the square to the red glass Tower of Fulfillment.

Juan de la Cruz moved up nervously next to Mace. "That was a demon, Liberator, a thing from Hades." He was nervous and kept looking back. "Are there no priests to rid us of that, that thing?"

Mace looked down at the former conquistador, dressed only in a clean loincloth. In his day, the Spaniard had been probably a man of average or above-average size, but next to a twentieth-century Earthman or the tall Kurkans, he was almost a youth in size. But nothing seemed to daunt his spirit—except the machinations of Satan.

"He . . . or she . . . is not a devil, Juan. Saurons are aliens, from another world, another star."

As they entered the red tower Juan looked up at Mace with suspicion. "We know that the world is not flat, Liberator, as some once believed, but no one lives on the stars." He acted as though Mace were somewhat mad and therefore dangerous.

"Remember the sun you saw when you arrived here, Juan? That's another star than the sun that shines on New Spain. This is another world than Earth. There are millions of stars . . . billions . . . and billions of worlds other than Earth. It is *not* the center of the universe. It is not even the center of our galaxy."

The Spaniard did not speak for a moment, but his face was closed and harsh when he did. "As you say, sir."

"Not as I say, Juan, as it *is*. It . . . oh, never mind." Mace stepped on, to catch up to Falana, who was being offered a drink. Mace took two glasses from the tray and deftly switched them by handing them to Baron Maa and Countess Nuala, then getting another for Falana and himself. *Better safe than sorry,* he thought, *even if this place gives me the galloping paranoia.*

"This is a Green, Your Royal Highness," Countess Nuala said. "You merely sit here . . . recline . . . and think about something you should like to see happen."

"Anything?"

"Anything, Magnificence. The mystery of the ancient Zull is such that whatever you think of . . . *whatever* you think of . . . will be translated into a most marvelous and heightened reality. You might have difficulty at first. Scenes will merge and shift and it will not seem to be controllable, but I assure you, Your Highness, that it is, once you are used to it."

Falana gave Nuala a look of penetrating severity, but sat down in the couch gracefully, handing her untouched wine to a Chuma slave. "I will monitor from here, supreme delight," Nuala murmured. Mace saw Maa and Norg exchange sly looks. He watched very carefully what Nuala was doing and once Falana's expression slipped from one of imperious arrogance to serene happiness, he reached down and lifted Nuala from her seat.

"Wha—?" She appeared slack-mouthed from beneath the glass helmet as Mace took it from her.

"The princess likes her privacy," Mace said with a smile. Then he put it on.

Almost at once he took it off and Nuala laughed at his red face. "The throne of Kulan breeds lusty wenches, does it not?" she said, reaching for the helmet. Mace gave it to her in a daze, his mind a blur.

What he had seen was a fantasy, but one of startling reality, in which he, Mace Wilde, starred. But it was a version of him he did not think he could possibly equal—nor could any man. The Kurkans and Juan looked at him in concern, disturbed by his sudden embarrassment, but the Scarn nobles smirked knowingly.

"Let her dream," Mace muttered, pulling the Kurkans aside, but not excluding the Spaniard, who crowded in.

"What is her dream, Liberator?" the follower of Cortez asked. "Is it lascivious and carnal? She looks as one who might dream such things, the pagan." His words were spoken harshly, but he looked back at the golden-skinned woman with raw lechery in his eyes.

"Never mind," Mace said with still some embarrassment. "We must liberate the Sauron. But not until this Naar appears."

"If he appears," Mouthfire said, looking over her shoulder. "They keep her busy, feed her pleasure and distraction, just as you said. The Kula witch has no discipline." Mouthfire growled in annoyance.

Juan de la Cruz looked at them curiously. "Naar? The old king? But isn't he dead?"

"Dead? Where did you hear that?" Longtalon asked.

The Spaniard shrugged. "In the prison. It is said that Norg keeps him alive, but that he is dead. I do not know what that means, but it is only until the Celebration of the Discovery. Some kind of feast day; when they found this accursed place, I believe."

Mace exchanged looks with the Kurkans. "But why not just let the king die and take over? Isn't Norg the next in line? Or is he?" They all looked at Juan de la Cruz.

The Spaniard shrugged. "I do not know—they are all mad here. They do not acknowledge our Holy Mother the Church; they have never heard of Jesus or Moses, never heard of King Carlos, or even the English dog, Henry. Nor Francis, of France, Balboa, de Córdoba, even the heretic Luther." The Spaniard shrugged. "They are an ignorant lot, my friends. They have no sane order of succession. They struggle for power like the cursed Turks. It is decided here by some hidden means, I heard."

"The computers," Mace said. "In some way that is the deciding factor. But how—and why?"

They had no answers and for a time they stood around and watched Falana lying on the couch of the Zull machine. Mace saw her body twitch and move, almost sinuously at times and in a kind of lascivious rhythm at other times. Maa and Norg seemed quite content to stare, and Nuala was transfixed beneath her helmet, but Mace and his companions grew bored.

"Perhaps I should send Eve another message," Mace said and the Kurkans agreed. He went outside and looked around until he found a Chuma slave and beckoned the woman closer. She cringed but sidled up to him. He explained what he wanted but the woman grew big-eyed and fearful, bursting suddenly into tears.

A Scarn noble strolling nearby introduced himself as Viscount Nika and silenced the Chuma with a word. "These are simple creatures, my lord, and we do not permit them to go beyond the walls. If you wish to send a message to the surface you must use one of the soldiers. I shall get you one, if you will permit me?"

"Yes, thank you. But I sent a message last night or . . ." He squinted around at the glowing towers that provided Scarn with light. "Or some hours ago."

Viscount Nika smiled. "A Chuma? One of the tower Chuma would have passed your message to a soldier, who would have received permission from his officer. But, no, we do not permit these animals to leave. They would become lost in the mountains."

Mace contained his anger and gave a message to a soldier—a half-breed Zurian he guessed—who saluted the Scarn noble and left quickly. Mace went back to the Tower of Fulfillment to watch Falana create a fantasy which he knew he could never fulfill in real life.

Redpike ordered the cloudship lifted at dawn. They flew low, with the three landing legs left extended, in case they had to drop to the ground suddenly. The mountains were quite close, and the green rolling hills were rising, with less and less vegetation.

Liberty kept watch, her eyes making a complete circular check of the horizon in a steady, repetitive pattern. The flowing rhythm of the ship, riding on antigravity power, was much like a ship at sea, under sail. She heard the snort of the drasks in the hold. Apparently the pills given them by the drask master back at Jardek's keep were wearing off and they were becoming restive. They reminded her of Percherons, the massive beer-truck pullers.

Beer.

She had drunk much wine on this odd world and the Kurkans had a kind of beer, but it was bitter and weak at the same time. She longed for a big cold mug of steam beer. Even a Michelob or some of that Mexican stuff. Bad for her figure, but oh, so *nice!*

A brief menu of delicious dishes went through her head, and she smiled. Food, drink, and attention, that was what she missed. Oh, the attention. Coming out in that flowing snow-white dress at the Academy Awards, the one that looked like wet paint on her figure. The *lust* and pleasure that had come up at her had been like adrenaline! Looking at a videotape of it later, at home, she had seen how she blossomed.

Being wanted. Being sought after. Being courted—sexually, socially, professionally, artistically—oh, that was very, very nice. The salesgirls dropping their prosaic customers to come right over. The headwaiters finding a "good" table. The look in the eyes of strangers. The bull spread by the producers and studio executives who wanted her to work for them. The presents. She smiled softly. The new Rolls, the old but beautifully restored Jaguar, the personalized plates that only said oo, to indicate her "Zero-Zero" series of high-action, high-grossing films. The flowers and jewelry. The brassiere and necklace of sterling silver, made by the lost wax method by Dale Enzenbacher, of dragons and damsels, given her by an imaginative television producer. The "Liberty Crockett" rose, the street in Watts renamed in her honor, the special little parties. The paid vacations in Hawaii and Tahiti, in Rome and Athens. The smitten astronaut who gave her a smuggled moonstone pendant. The crafty producer who saw that the best dress designer in Beverly Hills did her important gowns.

Liberty sighed. She did miss it. She didn't miss the insults, the callous remarks, the "Do this for me and I'll do that for you" propositions.

She hated the racial insults and snubs, the critical reviews on her acting ability, the columnists' innuendos that she was sleeping here or there, with this one or that, of either or both sexes.

She cherished critic William Warren's comment that she was "The only actress on the screen that acts as if she knew, approved of, and practiced all known sexual perversions." She was sorry that the Zero-Zero doll deal had fallen through with Mattel, on the heels of a temporary antisensuality tide.

"Helen Hayes, I'm not," she muttered to herself. "I'm not even the 'black Raquel Welch.' But I'm no flat-back dumb starlet, either." Then she laughed quietly to herself. *Don't give up, huh?* Still think you're going back to Hollywood, land of the fee and home of the rave. Back to the Rodeo Drive charge accounts, the private screenings, the Lear jets, and "A" party invitations. Uh-huh. Forget it, girl. At least until this Richter and that Kula fella say we can confirm our return tickets. This is a one-take scene. No covering cameras, no retakes, all in tight close-ups, Panavision, Dolby sound, and *live.*

The morning sunlight was bright and hot. Eve could see the far mountains, shrouded in fog, where the Tigron lurked in their paranoid world. The soldiers seemed to ignore her now, stumping about sullenly, with the drawn, haggard look of men trying to sober up. A troop came out of the cave, not marching in ranks, but lumbering along in patchwork armor. Some even dragged their spears in the dust. The officer in charge, wearing a Zurian breastplate and a spiked helmet, squinted up at Eve as they relieved the tower guard.

"Ho, you! Bowman!"

"Bow-*person,*" Eve retorted, putting more liveliness into the response than she felt. She was sore from sleeping on the deck.

The officer snorted. "The lackey of the Kula witch sends a message."

"He's not a lackey, he's . . ." Eve stopped. What *was* he? Lover, guide, adversary, prisoner, warden, what? Maybe all of them.

"The tall one, the man from Earth," the officer said. His soldiers walked by, ill-tempered and red-eyed. Several of them were females, broad-faced, dark-skinned women who seemed to be both Zurian and Chuma. Few of them paid Eve much attention. "He says they will not be much longer." The officer grinned and shook his head. "They all say that, but the pleasures of Scarn are many!" He laughed as he followed his men into the tower.

After a few moments the other guards came out, scratching and squinting. A few called up obscene suggestions to Eve, how she might enjoy the rest of the day. She ignored them, but her eyes kept going to the cavern entrance.

"He'll be back," Skylance said from the mast. "They'll all be back."

"Yes," Eve said, absentmindedly. But she was not so certain. *What was it like in there?*

There was no natural day or night within the caverns, but ages underground had given the inhabitants of Scarn a kind of cycle, approximating the day and night of the surface. But with no work but pleasure-making and pleasure-giving, no one was in much of a hurry to get up. Mace stood outside the red tower, waiting impatiently for Falana, who had been very slow to rise.

Longtalon strode up, tall and blonde among the slow-moving, rather subdued few who were on the curving streets. "She ready?"

Mace shook his head, and the Kurkan made a face. "And she thinks someday to rule Zandra."

"Early risers are not necessarily great leaders," Mace said with a smile.

"They are if there is work to be done." They turned as Mouthfire hailed them from the tower's entrance.

"She comes," the Kurkan warrior-woman said. She stopped between her friends and looked annoyed. "She would comb her hair and apply lotion while the alarm bells were sounding."

Mace said nothing. Mouthfire wore her hair simply tied back, or braided, and no makeup or artifice. And she all but slept in her armor. But then, the Kula princess did not *look* as if she wore makeup either. Such feminine activities were foreign to the army officer, whose morning toilet was confined to brushing his teeth, shaving, running his fingers through his hair, and utilizing a toilet.

Princess Falana emerged from the ornate entrance of the red glass tower looking radiant. She smiled at everyone, even the two Kurkans. "I'm famished," she announced and took Mace's arm.

Surprised at the friendliness, Mace pointed toward the complex of green glass bubbles seen through the towers. "Baron Maa said that was an excellent place. Original Zull food machines and everything."

"Very well," Falana said, starting off. The Kurkans walked just behind, acting as none-too-hidden bodyguards. "Ah, is this not a marvelous place, Mace Wilde?"

"Will you just please call me Mace? When you use my whole name like that I feel I ought to recite my serial number."

"Your what?"

"Never mind," Mace said, realizing that once again he had stumbled over a cultural difference.

"Ah," said Longtalon and Mace looked back at him. "You have billions on your Earth world, so you give everyone a number to keep it all simple. Ingenious."

"No, uh . . . never mind. Warriors have numbers."

"Instead of names?" Mouthfire asked.

"No . . . uh . . . some of the great soldiers earn their names, as you do. 'Black Jack' Pershing, 'Blood and Guts' Patton, 'Dugout Doug,' 'Ike,' 'Stonewall' Jackson, 'Bull' Halsey, Rommel the Fox, and . . ." He stopped as he realized the expression on his three companions.

"Those are the names they chose?" Longtalon said in amazement.

"No, uh, they were given their names by their followers."

"Blood and Guts?" Mouthfire said with some revulsion.

"You had to be there," Mace said. He'd done it again.

The Zull machines were white metal, all different sizes, and very organic-looking. At the back, Chuma slaves were dumping garbage, refuse, ordinary rock, and debris into hoppers. Glass pipes brought in water and sent it spurting into the big hoppers. The machines each stood two or three times taller than a man and were arranged in a long row. Geometric symbols were embossed on the front and below was a simple white button and a slot with a door that slid up and down.

Mace saw a red-eyed Scarn press the button on a machine with nine circles, squares, and triangles in different colors. Then the man lifted the door and took out a goblet of some blue liquid and drained it. He tossed the goblet, which was of exquisite workmanship, into a refuse container and walked to the next machine. Before he got there his step was firmer, his eyes less red, and a smile came to his face.

"A line of those on Third Avenue would make a fortune," Mace muttered. They went down the line, with Falana pointing out what the different symbols meant.

"I've never seen so many machines before," she said with delight. She thumbed the button of one machine and impatiently tried to lift the door, but it was a few seconds before it came up. When it did it revealed a glass tray with a steaming bowl of something brown and fragrant, silverware—or rather, glassware—a glass of chilled wine and a dark flagon, a curious purple fruit, halved and cold, and a small bowl of something green.

"Oh, lovely," Falana said and passed on without removing the tray.

"Aren't you going to eat it?" Mace asked.

"Oh, no. I just wanted to see."

"That's a waste," Mace said, looking back. He saw a Chuma slave take out the tray and dump the entire thing, with a clatter, into a refuse bin.

"A waste? No, you ignorant Earthman, it will all be reused. The machines need only as much material put in as you take out. They get their energy from the material as it is restructured."

"A perpetual motion machine?" Mace said dubiously. But Falana was pressing the button of another machine. What she took out was another ornate glass tray containing several bowls of prepared fruit, some kind of large boiled egg, a mug of warm drink, and nubbins of what had to be meat, crisp and fragrant. She took the tray to the nearest unoccupied table and began to eat without waiting for anyone.

Mace pushed the button on the next machine. Only he got what appeared to be a live bird, feathers and all, set on a platter surrounded by tidbits of unidentified material. He looked at it a moment, then extracted it to drop it into a bin. He went back and got a duplicate of Falana's meal and sat down across from her.

The Kurkans joined them in a few moments, each with trays of experimental breakfasts. Mace could not look at Mouthfire's tray more than once, but Longtalon's seemed to be a slice of something hamlike as thick as his wrist, and a flagon of chilled pale wine.

Breakfast was not a meal that Mace took lightly, but there were only some things he really liked. He wondered what the symbol for scrambled eggs might be.

Falana was in a very good mood, but when Mace suggested they pressure Norg to get King Naar here in a hurry, she waved her hand airily. "What is the hurry, Mace Wilde?"

"Mace."

"Yes, I said that. You think I would forget your name?"

"Perhaps you should know his number," Longtalon suggested with a small smile. "Unless it is too long a number, then you might call him by the first two or three."

"They're stalling, for some reason," Mace said, ignoring his companions.

"Prince Norg said it would take several sleeps," Falana said, delicately putting a bit of her breakfast in her mouth. "There is no hurry, Mace Wuh . . . Mace."

"What about Redpike and Liberty and the others? What about Eve and Skylance waiting outside?"

"Have them sent for. I have no objections to the Earthwoman pleasuring herself, nor the Kurkan. The land of Scarn has long been considered a neutral ground. The traders made it so." She shrugged. "I am in no hurry. After I have eaten, I think I shall ask Baron Maa to show me another of the Zull pleasure machines." Her eyes went to Mace and he turned away to hide his sudden embarrassment. He saw a tall, elegant, dark-skinned Scarn noble approaching them.

The man bowed low and apologized for interrupting their first meal. "I am Baron Kala, most noble of Kula."

"Ah, yes," Falana said with slitted eyes and an appraising look. "I have heard you spoken of."

"All kind lies, I am certain, most transcendent of Kulan." His eyes went to Mace and the others and his manner was such that Falana sighed and introduced them.

"This is an Earthman, Mace Wilde. The two Kurkans are Mouthtalon and Longfire."

The Kurkans looked amused, rather than offended, but it was to Mace that the suave, swarthy baron paid attention. "Baron Kala, Earthman Mace Wilde, Protector of the Zull Artifacts, Master of the Chuma, Viscount LoBrutto, Adviser to His Majesty, King Naar, and your friend, my dear knight."

Mace smiled back blandly. He hated people that called him "friend" on short acquaintance. "Mace Wilde, formerly of the planet Earth, and now travel guide to Princess Falana."

The abrupt and unfamiliar ritual momentarily confused the baron, but his smile returned. "Modesty is not one of the traits I have associated with Earthmen before, my dear knight."

"How many Earth people have you known?"

"A few. Curious creatures, if you do not mind me saying so. Very . . . um . . . definite in their beliefs."

"Superstitious?"

Baron Kala frowned. "I do not understand the word, my dear knight."

"Never mind. Tell me about these Earthmen, Baron."

"Oh, let us not talk about such sordid matters," Falana said, interrupting and standing up. She took Baron Kala's arm. "You are the one who *really* knows the pleasure machines, are you not?"

"They are a pastime of mine, yes, most beautiful of the flowers of Kulan."

"Princess, I'd like to talk to the baron about my fellow Earthmen, if you don't mind," Mace said.

"I do mind, but go ahead. Get it over with."

"You have one of them with you, I believe," Baron Kala said. "The angry one who brought the curses of his gods down on us." He seemed amused.

"God, singular, not gods. He is very specific on that. Yes, he sleeps still. Your Scarn wine is quite powerful . . . and quite plentiful."

"And most pleasant, too, my dear knight."

"Look, Baron, I'm not a knight. Just a soldier."

The Scarn noble looked slightly scandalized. "Sir, you are escort to Princess Falana. I have been told you are not of noble blood, certainly not Zandran blood, but you are an officer, are you not?"

"Our concept of knighthood is different on Earth. Archaic, actually."

"Archaic?" Baron Kala looked even more shocked. "How can that be? Are you savages?"

"That's something I haven't decided," Falana said archly.

"But a civilization cannot abandon the concept of knighthood, of royalty and nobility, without becoming . . . well, I do not mean to offend, my dear knight, but without becoming trivial, savage and a . . . a mob, not a governed society."

"Baron, I'm not certain I disagree with you. I am . . . or *was* . . . an officer in the United States Army, by act of Congress a gentleman. So . . . perhaps you are correct."

Baron Kala smiled. "These cultural differences are sometimes very perplexing, are they not? We must talk of your fascinating world, my dear knight." He smiled on the last word. "Your fellow Earthmen and women . . . the ones I've spoken to . . . have mostly been, well, confusing and confused. Such contradictory stories they told!"

"Are you through?" Falana said and Mace nodded. "Come, Baron, you must show me everything you know about these delightful machines."

"Everything, most precious of metals? That might take *years!*"

Falana laughed as she went off with Baron Kala. "Oh, it might? I am a fast learner, my dear baron."

Longtalon looked at Mace, who nodded. The two Kurkans left their unfinished breakfasts and followed Falana. Mace sat a moment, thinking, then got up. He went in another direction—toward the Black Tower.

The Scarn nobles looked curiously at Mace as he walked along, but no one stopped him. Both men and women smiled invitingly, and one of the women, jewels affixed to her face in an intricate pattern, bared a portion of her body invitingly. He either pretended not to see, or smiled back pleasantly, as if their invitations were misunderstood.

He went into the Black Tower and down one level. There was no one there, not even the caged Sauron. Mace looked around, but could not make sense out of the alien machinery. He understood the Zull labels clearly enough, as far as words went, but he had no idea what they meant. He left, feeling empty.

Liberty eyed the edges of the canyon nervously. The cloudship was cruising up a long winding cleft in the foothills, moving slowly, with a thin trickle of water below them. The black actress paid little attention to the aeons of time revealed by the water-cut cliffs, because they were virtually blind down in the canyon. The drasks were awake in the lower deck, snorting and shifting their weight, making the little vessel roll slightly. Barney Boone was up, awake, and outside, slumped against the control mast, looking weak and confused. Redpike stood beside Ironthroat in the mast cockpit, while Firearm paced moodily along the railing, watching the canyon walls and cradling his deadly arm.

Richter and Jardek came out of the mast-cabin and talked to Barney for a few moments, then Richter came over to Liberty. The drasks rumbled and the deck tilted slightly and Richter made a grab for her and the rail at the same time. She helped him get a grip and he smiled his thanks. "Isn't there some way of quieting those beasts down?" he asked.

Liberty shook her head. "Redpike says they get extremely sluggish and confused if they are immobilized too often. If they get much more restless he says we'll land and release them."

They stood in silence for a bit. Du and Firearm passed and the two Earth people smiled briefly, reassuringly. "Listen, Doc," Liberty said softly, "do you really think we can get out of this? Off Zandra, I mean. Back home?"

Richter glanced at Count Jardek, sitting next to Barney, then sighed. "I don't know, Miss Crockett, I—"

"Hey, Liberty, Doc."

He smiled. "Yes, of course, I'm sorry. Did I ever tell you I've seen some of your pictures? You were, um, very . . . ah . . ."

She smiled. "Thank you, Doctor Richter—that's as good a critical comment as I've ever gotten."

"There was this jungle thing. You wore, um . . ."

"Almost wore, you mean. That was *Jungle Queen,* a kind of female Tarzan, a black Sheena, right?"

He smiled and nodded. "I, uh, confess that I felt very, um, nervous going in. I mean, it wasn't the kind of picture I thought my colleagues would ever see."

Liberty made a face. "I understand. What brought you in?"

"There was that poster, you see . . ."

She grinned. "Yeah. That was some poster, wasn't it? I fought them on that. They wanted a full nude, but kind of covered, if you know what I mean. But I made it more provocative than that, didn't I? You must leave *some* mystery, right?"

Richter nodded, embarrassed. "When the lights came up, there was Coleman—he was on the Benford University faculty with me—and some of the younger faculty as well. We didn't know what to do. There wasn't a second feature to pretend we had come to see."

Liberty's smile faded. "Caught in the bawdy house by the raid, huh, Doc?"

"No, no, I . . ." He was very embarrassed. "I think it did me a lot of good. You get very isolated in academia, you know. You tend to forget most of the world and what makes it move." He cleared his throat. "Right after that I was offered the position of director at the Institute of Physical Sciences, and I took it. I don't know if it was, um, your motion picture or not. Rather, it was being *seen* there, that made me—"

"You ran?"

"Oh, no! Please don't think that! Oh, that was close!" The cloudship had passed through a narrowing of the cliff walls and they looked back. "No, you see . . . um . . . it made me think about things other than, um, just my studies, my classes, research . . . um . . ."

Liberty smiled a slow, knowing smile. "How was your love life?"

Richter almost blushed. "Well, things, um, things started changing. New adventures, new horizons, new challenges. I don't *know* that seeing your, um, jungle movie did it, Miss Crockett, um, Liberty, but . . . uh . . . it might have."

"You're welcome, Doc." They exchanged smiles and then Liberty put an arm through his. "Listen, like I was saying, are we getting out of this?"

Richter sighed and looked ahead. "I . . . I don't know. There is so much we don't know. There's a chance we can reverse the flow, but . . ."

"But don't bet on it, huh?" She slapped his arm. "Hey, Doc, don't take it so hard. It isn't your fault." She turned and looked up the stream bed. They could see a piece of the mountains ahead, much closer now.

You're stuck here, she thought. *The slim chance was not enough to hold on to. Better I should try and make it big on Zandra than spend my life dodging the black hats and performing in the sticks.*

Liberty took a deep breath and patted Richter's arm. "Thanks, Doc." She started to turn away when the black cloudship drifted out over the cliffs overhead.

There were shouts as the Zurians spotted them. At once Ironthroat brought the ship up, out of the canyon, to gain more maneuvering room. The black Zurian ship banked and a hastily aimed beam of some kind sizzled through the air and narrowly missed the control mast. It exploded a section of the cliff, showering Liberty with dirt and bits of hot rock.

Ironthroat twisted the ship around sharply, in a way that only cloudships, with their six vents spaced around the hull, could do. He passed under the Zurian ship, effectively evading the immediate danger. Firearm sent a blast up through the black ship, ripping a ragged hole in the hull.

Ironthroat braked the cloudship and reversed, letting the startled Zurian vessel fly on. It took the black-skinned warriors a few moments before they realized the fugitives were not under them. Liberty heard Captain Durak bellow a command, but already Ironthroat was rushing eastward, away from the afternoon sun.

The Zurian ship fired again and Du cried out in pain. The ray had seared the air close to her and her thick blonde braids were singed. The side of her face was red and soon blistered. But her eyes were all right, glaring back at the pursuing vessel.

Ironthroat dropped the ship suddenly, cutting southward toward the mountains, spilling his passengers who were not holding on. Liberty picked up Richter and helped him across the deck, shoving him through the hatch. She turned to help Count Jardek and Barney Boone and stopped, her eyes growing large with fear.

Count Jardek was trying to climb the tilted deck but it was Barney that had stopped Liberty. He cringed against the control mast, holding tightly to a handhold, staring back toward the black Zurian cloudship. His dark eyes seemed huge, with the round pupils somehow oddly shaped, almost vertical slits. His tanned skin was darker, the few days' growth of beard he had accumulated was longer, as was his hair. It was almost a mane. His lips parted in a snarl and his teeth seemed . . . different.

Liberty gasped. It was Dr. Jekyll and Mr. Hyde all over again, but without the benefits of the makeup department. "No," she said softly. "No!" It couldn't be; that sort of thing was total fantasy, along with talking animals and vampires. People didn't change . . . not that way, not that quickly.

Barney snarled again as a Zurian ray blast cut through the air over their head. He crouched, his fingers curling, his nails somehow longer.

Count Jardek slid suddenly into the mast as Ironthroat banked the ship in the other direction. He cried out in pain, then clawed his way up Barney's leg. But the animal trainer roared and slapped at him. The Kula count sagged against the mast and went limp. Liberty took a step, but Barney snarled again, fixing her with his strange new eyes, his claw-like hands coming up.

The cloudship tilted again and Barney fell against the thick tube of the mast and Liberty moved. Her fist lashed out, catching Barney on the hairy chin, snapping his head back brutally. He sagged, then fell forward, crashing hard into the deck as it tipped up to meet him.

Liberty scooped him up and shoved him into the mast-cabin. Then she dragged the limp Jardek in, yelling at Richter to take care of him. The scientist was staring at the strange apparition that had been Barney Boone until Liberty punched him with a stiffened finger. "Hey, Doc!"

The black actress went back on deck. Firearm was at the rear, sighting along his built-in laser. But he was not firing. Ironthroat had gotten something of a lead. They were still within the range of Durak's heavier weapons, but the sizzling ray blasts did no real damage. The air heated up, the smooth surface of the ship crinkled, but there were no cuts or explosions.

Firearm was cursing in a slow, deliberate manner, outlining Durak's ancestry and probable line of descent from various obscenities. Du was rubbing some cream into her blistered face. Redpike and Ironthroat were in the control mast, one watching the Zurians while the other kept the ship dipping in and out of every ravine and canyon, hiding behind every rock and hill.

It was a long way to the mountains, and a long time until dark.

Eve looked up at Skylance. "I want to go in. Why don't you lift the ship and stay close by? I'm afraid they might have . . . found trouble."

Skylance nodded and did not try to dissuade her. She let down the ramp and trotted off, surprising the lounging guards. The Kurkan pilot lifted the vessel almost at once.

Eve looked closely at the other two cloudships as she went by. One was operational, clean and shipshape, with a pair of half-breed Zurians guarding it, glaring sullenly at her. The other vessel seemed permanently grounded. Vines had grown over one landing leg. There was a dusty air of disuse about it. Through the ramp opening she saw debris and discarded odds and ends. The cloudship had been abandoned.

All Zandra lives on borrowed technology, she thought as she walked swiftly toward the main cavern entrance. *Why haven't they established schools to study the Zull wonders? They seem to accept the status quo, even encourage it. But that was not a unique Zandran situation*, she thought. When buttons on men's sleeves can remain, useless and expensive, for two hundred years, why did she expect the people of Zandra to be any different?

They have no history of scientific exploration, she thought as she slowed to climb the wide trail up to the cavern. *All the Zull technology was imposed from without, like giving Indians rifles. They knew how to use them, but couldn't make them and could only do rudimentary repairs. Or imposing democracy on a primitive nation that was still in feudal monarchy, before it had the desire to work "up" to that desirable state of individual freedom.*

The guards at the entrance eyed her warily, but did not stop her passage. She wore a sword and a dagger and her bow was the heaviest they had ever seen. She wore Kurkan armor, and none of the sleepy guards cared to get involved. They were there to guard against predators like the threen and to prevent any of the slaves from wandering off. They were not about to get involved in politics.

The cavern was cool. Eve felt the cool air gratefully after the sun. She saw sleeping figures among the rocks and plucked a torch from a basket and lit it to light her way. A drunken Zurian half-breed grinned at her approach but his smile faded as she looked at him.

Striding along she came quickly to the stone wall guarding the inner

Scarn. The faded murals she had seen disturbed her, but she couldn't decide just why. So much of Zandra confused and disturbed her that one more unexplained fear was easily absorbed. She saw the fires and the lounging figures. The guards were more alert here and more menacing.

"Halt!" The guard commander swaggered forth and looked her up and down insultingly. "Well, Kurkan witch, what do you want?"

"I wish to see Mace Wilde, the Earthman, and those with him."

"Oh? And do you have the fee?"

"What fee? A toll?"

The guard laughed. He was a Chuma-Zurian mixture with the less desirable attributes of both. "You come to trade, you pay a fee."

"I do not come to trade. I am with the . . . with Princess Falana."

The guard's expression changed. Sullenly he turned his back on her. "Go on," he said sharply. Eve strode on through the gate and behind her she heard a curse and a few muttered words.

Eve found the glass towers of the colorful city beautiful, yet odd, as a surreal stage set for a carnival might look. She didn't quite believe anyone actually lived in a place like that. It would be like living in a permanent circus, sleeping on a midway, settling down backstage at the Met.

She saw several people in elaborate clothing just as they discovered her. "Oh, a Kurkan!" one of the women exclaimed, breaking the group to run toward Eve, jiggling and bouncing.

"Where is Princess Falana?" Eve asked as they crowded in. They were not at all threatening, but very admiring of her hair and beauty. The woman who had first come to her smiled up at her, rubbing suggestively against the metal armor. "Command me, warrior!" she laughed. Another grabbed at Eve, saying silkily, "Tell us of your exploits! Come, we'll have wine and pleasure ourselves!"

A man crowded in close, smiling through an elaborately styled beard. "My dear knight, allow me. I am the Count Noorda, Master of the Night Games, Champion of Arga, Slavemaster of the Glassmakers. Welcome, golden Kurkan!"

"Please, I just want to find Mace Wilde. He's with Princess Falana. Do you know who I mean?"

"Oh, of course, my dear warrior," the first woman said. She was small, dark, and shapely. Her costume was minute, mostly tiny tinkling plates of colored glass on thin glass chains, strategically arranged. "I am Lady Culai, and I assist Count Noorda in the Night Games. You *will* play them tonight, won't you?" Her hand was on Eve's arm, her face expectant.

Eve felt some unease. She remembered pimps approaching her on Western Avenue, and the owner of a sleazy massage parlor who offered her a weekly "fee" to keep the other beat cops off his neck. The uneasy parallel made her nervous. These were not petty criminals but Scarn nobles. Yet the feeling persisted as she pushed her way through them.

"Kurkan flower, I am the Count of Borgani, the—"

"Excuse me, where is Princess Falana? Mace Wilde? The Kurkans?"

"Oh, they are busy," Lady Culai murmured, catching up and putting an arm through Eve's. "Why don't you come with us? We're unsealing a Zull pleasure tape that has been put away for a *generation!* Isn't that exciting? Say you'll come . . . ?"

"I want to see Falana and the Earthman," Eve said, shaking free.

"I understand it is a *wonderful* tape, my dear," Count Noorda said, pressing close. The eyes of many nobles were on her, bright and expectant. Eve had seen looks like that when guarding rock stars. "I imagine you've never experienced an *authentic* Zull tape block, have you? You Kurkans live such . . . um . . . impoverished lives, high on your mountains."

"Such *savages*," Lady Culai said with a smile.

"The copies are *so* inferior," Count Borgani said. They had gathered around her, pressing in, caressing her bare arms. They were perfumed and oiled and seemed to radiate a kind of mechanical lust. She felt like a toy fought over by children.

"It's just over here. Baron Macca will—"

"No, please! Where is the princess?" Eve turned around, then back. They were crowding close, moving her along the street. The tall glass towers, fanciful ornaments of architecture, rose over her head.

"The Kulan witch is at her *own* pleasures," Count Borgani said, his hand on her elbow. "She won't like to be disturbed. But we've been waiting *ages* for the unsealing."

"We have to do that, you know," the Lady Culai murmured. "It gets dreadfully boring having everything available *all* the time. We have nothing to look forward to."

The small but growing crowd passed into a colonnade of glass arches leading toward a brightly colored building. Swirls of colored gases seemed to be moving upward constantly, within the walls, but the smoke did not come out the top. In some way it was recycled downward, to begin again. Eve was growing more desperate. She had no intention of going into the building, yet she did not want to antagonize these lecherous people.

"Are all Kurkans as lovely as you?" Lady Culai said, stroking Eve's arm.

"I'm not a Kurkan," Eve said. "I'm from Earth."

There was an immediate pause as the Scarn nobles stared at her. "Surely not," Count Noorda said with an embarrassed smile. "We have seen people from Earth—dirty, hairy savages—"

"Real savages," Lady Culai said with disgust.

"Cursing and calling upon unseen gods." Count Noorda shook his head again. "You jest, my Kurkan jewel . . ."

"*Other* people from Earth?" Eve asked. "Are any of them here now?"

"Only this tall warrior, obviously one of the nobility, like yourself," Count Noorda said. He smiled and the others relaxed. "Tell me," he said, taking her arm again. "How many slave races do you have on Earth? How do you keep them docile? We do not have the mindsword of our cousins, the Kula, at least to that degree." He smiled again and the rest nodded, but it was a nervous agreement. "We keep our Chuma and Zurian spawn happy with the pleasure machines." He looked at the others with a sly smile. "Once these lesser minds are addicted . . ." They all laughed.

Eve was beginning to feel real fear. Up until then she had been nervous and alert, but these people did not wear real weapons—only ceremonial daggers—and had not acted at all threatening. To the contrary, they had acted most solicitous. Yet the fear had grown and was about to burst out.

She remembered the sick, hollow feeling of fear she had known. The dark alley, the knife-wielding teenager. The barricaded nut, his wife and two kids lying in pools of blood, and her going through the back door. The liquor store owner lying face down in broken glass, blood and booze making a steaming pool—and the killer with the automatic shotgun somewhere in the store. Seeing her partner, Jim Fields, his shoulder shattered by a .38, and more slugs thumping loudly into the door of the black and white. The knife appearing out of nowhere in the hand of the tall man stopped for running a red light.

That was one kind of fear: immediate, nonnegotiable survival.

But this was a different kind of fear. Eve was not even certain of what they had in mind for her, but she felt she would not be the same person afterward. Zull pleasure tapes? If they were anything like the miraculous healer, the antigravity ships, or any of the other highly advanced devices she had seen, the Zull pleasure principle would be ruthlessly efficient.

"Earthwoman, I'm sure Baron Macca will let you be the first to—"

Eve interrupted Count Noorda by ripping loose her arms from the pawing attention of the nobles. She tensed her strong Terran muscles and leaped straight up. The lesser Zandran gravity allowed her to leap to the glass arches overhead.

She clasped one and pulled herself up to balance precariously upon the slippery arch. Below, the Scarn nobles uttered exclamations of surprise, disappointment, and delight. Eve looked around. Her bow slipped from her shoulder and she thrust it back. Then with a great leap she launched herself into the air, flying right over a small glowing sculpture and into an ornamental moss bed. She rolled and came up fast as the nobles ran out of the colonnade toward her, eyes bright, hands out, and fingers spread. They wanted her.

She ran.

The Zurian cloudship kept high, out of range now, but following Redpike's ship easily as it dodged and reversed, hid and appeared. The drasks in the hold were kicking and screaming. They had fallen many times and were injured. Du and Liberty went below reluctantly and started killing the animals before they wrecked the ship. Du put a sword into the throat of one of the animals and the smell of blood frightened the others. In the narrow space Liberty was almost killed by striking hooves and the two women retreated.

Du ran up on deck and shouted to Redpike. "Can you put us down somewhere long enough to let the drasks out? They're going to wreck the hull!"

Redpike looked at the Zurian ship, cursing silently. He squinted ahead, then shouted back to Du. "Get the ramp open! We'll try there, in that canyon! We'll try to tip the ship and let them fall out into that water!"

Du waved and ran below deck. She and Liberty opened the hatch. Through it Liberty could see the river rocks moving past dangerously close. One of the drasks lost his footing and fell heavily, sliding to the hatch and wedging there, snorting and kicking.

The cloudship came to a halt and then tilted slightly. The kicking drask fell through with a scream. The other animals followed, struck by the flats of swords and urged on by yells and wordless cries. The last of the big animals was trying to keep from going out when the cloudship righted itself. The drask fell, slid back across the cargo hold, his big dangerous hooves kicking out. Liberty heard a cry from Redpike. An explosion just outside sent water spray in through the ramp entrance.

Du ran to the drask and pulled him to his feet. Liberty joined her and they shoved the frightened animal toward the exit. The drask tried to bite Liberty, but in her fright she punched him back. She tended to sometimes forget her Terran strength; the drask staggered and almost fell. With a heave the two women shoved him through the hatch. He fell, screaming, for the ship was higher, but they heard a splash.

They closed the ramp and ran up on deck. The Zurian ship was overhead, but Ironthroat kept them almost directly under the black airship, reducing their ability to fire. When the Zurian vessel swung out of sight, to gain the advantage of angle, Ironthroat reversed, gaining a small amount of distance.

With the drasks overboard—and Liberty could see them coming ashore below, shaking off the water—the cloudship was lighter and more maneuverable. The Zurian ship came over them again, but Firearm was ready. He punched two more holes in the underside of the black ship. The Zurian vessel veered away and Ironthroat streaked for cover.

They were going north now, away from the mountains. Liberty looked back. *Was she on her own now?*

The music in her head was crashing, filled with drums and trumpets, chaotic and violent.

Eve ran up to Mace in long strides, pursued by the cheerful cries of a number of Scarn nobles. Mace grabbed her. "What's going on? The ship? Zurians?"

"No!" She panted for breath, looking back. The Scarn mob slowed and stopped. Then Count Noorda, Lady Culai, and another moved closer, smiling warmly, with their smiles edged with anticipation.

"My dear and lovely flower," Count Noorda said, "you shouldn't run. We meant you no harm. Surely you—"

"What's going on?" Mace demanded.

"They . . . uh . . ." Eve hesitated. "No, it's all right. I . . . I got worried. You were gone so long. I thought . . ." She looked around, really seeing the city of the Scarn for the first time. "It's lovely . . . no, it's . . . it's . . ."

"Yeah," Mace said. He put an arm around her and turned her away from the Scarn, who sighed and drifted off reluctantly. In a few words he outlined what had happened since they had come into the caverns.

"Where is the Sauron? And this conquistador?"

Mace shrugged. "The Sauron, I don't know. Our Spanish friend is enjoying himself with some Chuma woman who . . . no, here he is."

The small brown man approached, grinning widely. "Ah, my friend, you have also found a woman!" Mace introduced them and the Spaniard grinned wolfishly.

"Ah, beautiful maiden, it is an honor! Juan Leopoldo Cristóbal y Tenorio de la Cruz at your service!" He bent to kiss her hand and Eve blinked. She had never had anyone kiss her hand before. She felt foolish . . . and excited. The follower of Cortez looked at her with burning eyes, smiling wolfishly.

"Uh, yes . . . thank you." She pulled her hand away and looked up as Falana came out of the glass tower.

The princess looked them over before she came down the glittering ramp. She stopped short, standing slightly higher and said to no one, "This king, Naar, they say he is coming. I will renew his oath of allegiance to my father and then we shall move on."

De la Cruz made his most sweeping bow, muttering in an aside to Mace, "Introduce me, Liberator, introduce me."

"Princess Falana," sighed Mace, "this is Juan de la Cruz, late of the forces of Hernando Cortez."

"Juan Leopoldo Cristóbal y Tenorio de la Cruz," the Spaniard corrected smoothly. "And you are the fabulous daughter of the most kingly of kings, the estimable Morak, Emperor of all Zandra."

Falana started a gesture but the Spaniard seized her hand and kissed it. She looked surprised, then archly pleased. "Ah, yes, the dirty one. We were not properly introduced. You have, indeed, a great many names. You must be a great warrior."

Juan de la Cruz stood straight and proud, one brow arched, but before he could speak Falana added a few words. "Or a liar." The Spaniard blinked and looked befuddled, but his moment was lost. Falana continued through the group, ignoring Eve pointedly, and taking the arm of Count Noorda.

"My dear count, kindly escort me to the meeting place."

"Of course, blossom of magnificence." Smiling, he took her away, with the rest following. De la Cruz blinked and followed, muttering to himself.

"What?" Mace demanded in a low voice.

"It is these clothes, Liberator. They are not clothing, but garments for peasants. Ah, if I had the wardrobe I was planning to buy with my Aztec gold! *Then* she would pay attention!" He whispered to Mace. "Where can one find a proper tailor here? I would cut a fine figure at court."

"You are out of luck, my seafaring friend. Even if there *was* a 'proper tailor' you wouldn't have time. We're getting out of here and you are coming with us."

The Spaniard shrugged. "Aye, Liberator. But a few yards of silk, some boots, a proper sword, a plume or two . . . ah . . . *then* these insatiable wenches would pay even more attention!"

Mace nodded wearily and they trooped between the colorful glass towers to a branching cavern. Crossing a chasm on a glass bridge they entered another passage, one smoothed by generations of feet. A wall of irregular glass blocks shut off the cavern, with entry only through a stout wooden door carved with symbolic figures.

They were given salutes by guards and ushered into a series of glass chambers, lit from the outside. Each was different, with luxurious cushions on glass furniture, and walls that looked as though they were of wet, running glass.

Norg greeted them with elaborate courtesy, surrounded by several Scarn nobles. "Our great and generous king is exhausted from his meditations, Supreme Highness, and we trust you will not tire him further."

Falana gave him an expressionless look. "Take me to him," she ordered.

They were taken into a darkened chamber with a shadowy center dais. On it rested a bed something like a hollowed egg, faintly glowing. In the bed was a very old man, his eyes closed, his chest barely rising beneath the ornate cover.

Norg spoke in a soft whisper. "He is sleeping, paragon. Perhaps tomorrow . . ."

"Wake him," Falana said.

"Majesty . . ."

"Wake him," Falana repeated. "Do not make me give you an order twice."

Norg paled and stepped back. His hands fluttered, his eyes going to the nobles just inside the chamber. Mace glanced at them, saw the concern, then stepped forward and put his fingers on the hand of the king, folded across the cover. It was cold.

Norg gave a strangled cry and the nobles gasped as Mace whipped back the embroidered cover. A machine covered the king's torso from armpits to crotch. Almost all the lights and indicators of the curving device were dark. In the center of the machine, just over the heart, was a small screen. It was lit, but a single line, wavering slightly, crossed it flatly.

Mace straightened up and looked at Falana. "He's dead. This gadget is just keeping his body going." Looking at Norg, Mace added, "As long as he seems alive you are in charge. Who becomes ruler when Naar's death is announced?"

"Majesty," Norg began, but suddenly he jerked as if struck by lightning. He staggered and fell, then lay twitching.

"Let him alone, Falana," Eve said.

Falana turned her gaze to the blonde Earthwoman but before anything more happened, Mace stepped to her side. "Easy," he said, touching her arm. Then to the nobles he said, "Who is ruler now?"

Lips were licked, eyes blinked and slid away, and fingers played nervously. Falana's voice came sharply, echoing in the glass room. "Who! Speak!"

"Uh, great fountain of beauty, it is the Princess Neola," one noble said quickly, his voice squeaking.

"Bring her here. I will crown her myself."

The nobles looked at each other, biting lips. "Ah, most excellent of monarchs, we are, um, not certain just where, um . . ." He looked for help at one of the others.

"What Lord Betron is trying to say is that, um, well, Prince Norg imprisoned the princess, um, somewhere."

"We don't know where," another noble said with a shrug.

"We never ask," a woman said.

Falana arched her eyebrows and looked down at Norg, who had stopped twitching. "Some of you take this scum to where he has put the rightful heir and exchange him for her. Clean her up and bring her to me." Without pause Falana turned to Mace. "And you, Mace Wilde, you *will* try the Green with me."

She strode off, not looking back. Mace hesitated, then shrugged and grinned. "Why not?" he said, and followed.

Eve watched him go. "Why not?" she said cynically. "Why not indeed."

The coronation of the blue-eyed blonde was swift, simple, and brief. Falana took Princess Neola's pledge of allegiance, then crowned her Queen of Scarn, by the power of Morak, Emperor of Zandra. The recitation of her new titles by one of the more pompous nobles took three full minutes, during which Falana fidgeted.

"There, that's enough," Falana said at last. To the young woman, who seemed to be still blinking at the light, she gave words of advice. "Find those who will not lie to you and those who get things done. Be loyal to Kulan . . . and try to fix those other machines."

Falana turned to Mace. "It is getting late, Mace Wilde. Let us pleasure ourselves again. This time *you* dream and *I* shall be the one watching."

With Falana's power and reputation behind him it was not long before Mace found the Sauron, slumped and sad in a tower basement. When the Earthman took the glass helmet from his reptilian head the creature came alive, blinking his hooded eyes and looking around like a sleepy dragon.

"Come with me," Mace said. "We're taking you out of here."

The Sauron tried to speak, but his voice was blurred and hoarse, a rumbling thunder in a barrel. But he followed Mace out into the light of the main cavern, his vestigial wings moving fitfully.

"But *why*, Mace Wilde?" Falana demanded. "A few more days won't hurt. We have mastered the technique of the Green, have we not?" She gave Mace a languorous look.

"Princess honey, get your bottom moving. Those Zurians are still looking. If they come here, people might get hurt. And besides, you want to see the rest of Zandra, don't you?"

"Well, yes, but . . ."

"Don't pout. Princesses don't pout."

"They do, too. Valora always pouted . . . and got her way, too!"

"*Good* princesses don't. We've got to find the others as well. God only knows where they are now."

"Are we *really* taking that disgusting Sauron with us and that obsequious little man as well?"

"He is from Earth, as I am. I haven't found any others. And if we go to the land of Saurons he can help us."

Falana sat up straight. "You are worse than my father. Always making me do things I don't want to. But we'll come back here someday, won't we?" Her face brightened. "Won't we?"

"Sure, sure, now put on all your jewelry and let's move it."

"You know, Mace Wilde, if it were not for . . . never mind." She busied herself abruptly in clothing herself with her numerous bracelets, rings, and earrings.

Mace grinned and left the sleeping chamber. There was much to do.

Juan de la Cruz whimpered and bit at his knuckles as the cloudship rose from the rocky terrace. Skylance and Mouthfire were in the control mast. Eve and Longtalon were at the aft rail, watching the cavern entrance dropping away.

At the part of the circular ship that faced the direction they were going stood Mace, Falana, and the bulky dragon-shape of the Sauron, whose reptilian eyes were glittering.

"Where to?" Skylance called out.

"What lies in that direction?" Mace asked, pointing southeast, through the misty passes.

"Astorix," Skylance called back.

"The land of robots," the Sauron rumbled, saying his first clear words in his deep, gravelly voice.

Mace pointed and the ship veered slightly, riding lightly on the late afternoon winds. Then his eyes swept the horizon once again. *Where is Redpike's ship? Richter and Jardek are aboard and I promised to find them sanctuary. And poor sick Barney.* Mace grinned at the thought of the wildly sensual Liberty Crockett. *Her I'm not too worried about. She'll always land on her feet.*

Mace looked around him. *They're dropping away. I'm losing them, one by one. Some commander I am.* He ran his eyes over the passengers. *An intelligent dragon, a sixteenth-century adventurer, an L.A. cop, three Vikings, and a headstrong princess. Great, just great. Nothing like variety.*

The Zull cloudship dipped and rose gently, reddened by the setting sun, as it cruised down the mountain valley. Juan de la Cruz crossed himself again and Mouthfire wrapped her cape around herself.

Overhead the first stars were appearing. One of them might have been the sun of Earth. But Mace Wilde didn't know which one.